Royally Dead

The Stitch in Time Mystery series by Greta McKennan

Uniformly Dead

Historically Dead

Royally Dead

Royally Dead

Greta McKennan

LYRICAL UNDERGROUND
Kensington Publishing Corp.
www.kensingtonbooks.com

LYRICAL UNDERGROUND BOOKS are published by

Kensington Publishing Corp.
119 West 40th Street
New York, NY 10018

All Kensington titles, imprints, and distributed lines are available at special quantity discounts for bulk purchases for sales promotion, premiums, fund-raising, educational, or institutional use.

Special book excerpts or customized printings can also be created to fit specific needs. For details, write or phone the office of the Kensington Sales Manager: Kensington Publishing Corp., 119 West 40th Street, New York, NY 10018. Attn. Sales Department. Phone: 1-800-221-2647.

Lyrical Underground and Lyrical Underground logo Reg. US Pat. & TM Off.

First Electronic Edition: September 2018
eISBN-13: 978-1-5161-0170-2
eISBN-10: 1-5161-0170-7

First Print Edition: September 2018
ISBN-13: 978-1-5161-0173-3
ISBN-10: 1-5161-0173-1

Printed in the United States of America

For Mike and Laura, who brought bagpipes and Highland dance into my life,

and

In memory of Anne Oliphant McKee, who I called Gran.

Acknowledgments

With thanks to Jessica Faust of Bookends Literary, and Martin Biro of Kensington Publishing, without whom Daria's story would never have been told.

Chapter 1

I'd never seen so much plaid in one place. Every booth was festooned with swaths of tartan fabric. Little girls in lace blouses and kicky plaid kilts scurried past me, searching for their dance troupes. Men and women wearing kilts and dress shirts with regimental epaulettes circled up on the edges of the field to tune their bagpipes. Even the lettering on the banner at the entrance to the event was in plaid, welcoming visitors to Laurel Springs' First Annual Highland Games.

I was lucky to get a booth at the Games. I thought it would be a great venue to showcase my historical sewing business, A Stitch in Time. I teamed up with Letty Overby, who had an antique shop on the Commons in downtown Laurel Springs. We called our booth, "Scottish Treasures, Old & New." I doubted Letty's antiques actually came from Scotland, and my handiwork was obviously made in Pennsylvania, but at least we were faithful to the theme. My handicrafts included fabric bags and placemats in a variety of tartans, an array of bow ties spilling out of a small wooden treasure chest with wrought-iron hinges, and a collection of stuffed Loch Ness monsters under a calligraphied sign that read, "Nessie." I hung a few traditional women's skirts and velvet vests along the side of the booth to highlight my skills, with the hope of taking orders for custom-made Scottish apparel. The Laurel Springs Games was early in the competition season, so I stood a good chance of drumming up some business for the rest of the summer. But even if I sold nothing but a few Nessies, I was happy to spend the day in the sunshine surrounded by the sights and sounds of eastern Pennsylvania's tribute to its Scottish heritage.

Letty's wares included an assortment of glassware and silver jewelry on a long table on the other side of the booth, piles of delicate embroidered linens, and a selection of antique dressers and side tables. She had just finished setting up and had disappeared for a cup of coffee when I got my first customer.

"You got one of these in the McCarthy tartan?" Sean McCarthy leaned on the edge of the folding table that displayed my handicrafts, to focus his camera lens on a single bow tie in the distinctive red, green, and yellow of the Royal Stewart tartan. I caught the flash of joy and wonder on his face as he turned the lens ever so slightly to bring the image into focus, working his magic with the camera. He never got tired of that moment of revelation, and I never got tired of watching him.

"Sorry, no McCarthy tartan. It's an Irish name, you know. We're pure Scots today."

He straightened up and grinned at me, his eyes crinkling up in his tanned face. "Ah, so Daria Dembrowski is pure Scottish, right?"

I couldn't help laughing. "Well, she's selling the Scottish stuff anyway, handmade in Laurel Springs, Pennsylvania." I eyed his white button-down shirt with the sleeves rolled up. "A tartan bow tie would put you in the mood while you take your pictures for the newspaper. How about the Dress MacLeod? It's the only yellow one in my book." I handed him a tie with a yellow and black pattern shot through with red and pointed to the picture in my handy *Guide to the Clans and Tartans of Scotland* booklet.

He turned it over dubiously. "Can't say I've ever worn a bow tie before."

I took it from him and slid the ribbons under his collar, brushing aside his dark blond ponytail to adjust the catch in the back. "They're better than neckties because they come pre-tied. There. Now you'll fit right in, despite your Irish name."

He peered at his reflection in the tabletop mirror next to the chest of bow ties. "I look like a walking advertisement for A Stitch in Time's Scottish line." He handed me his camera. "Go ahead, get a picture. I don't promise to wear it all day, though."

I adjusted the focus, like he'd taught me, and snapped a picture. "That'll be for advertising or for blackmail, whichever I have most need of."

He snatched the camera out of my hands. "I'm not sure how you'll manage to blackmail me with a photo from my own camera, but more power to you." He slung the camera back around his neck, knocking the bow tie askew. "Speaking of fitting in, here comes Aileen."

With her black, skin-tight leather pants and red corset embroidered with skulls in black metallic cord, Aileen might fit in at a punk bar in Scotland, but here at the Highland Games she stuck out like a bagpiper in a symphony orchestra. Which is exactly what she wanted. Lead guitarist in a metal band, the Twisted Armpits, she shared my house with my older brother Pete and me. I got the formal dining room for a fitting room for my sewing business, Aileen got the basement for her band studio, and Pete got the third-floor bedroom, where he could get away from the bustle of customers and the unholy noise of the band. Of late, Aileen's bandmate Corgi had added a bagpipe to the cacophony after joining the Laurel Springs Pipe and Drum Corps. I had always experienced bagpipes as extremely loud instruments, so it amused me to no end when Aileen described the need to mic the pipes to allow them to rise above the guitar and bass in the mix. Imagine a bagpipe getting drowned out! I could hear several bagpipes skirling, and the noise was overpowering even in the open air.

Aileen didn't seem to notice. She clomped through the growing crowd in her knee-high red patent-leather boots with the six-inch chunky heels and approached my booth.

"The bagpipe competitions are about to start. Any idea where Corgi got to?" She looked at McCarthy and said, "Whoa. You look like your thyroid has jaundice."

He straightened his bow tie and bowed as if he were James Bond on his way to a white-tie event. Affecting a thick Scottish accent, he drawled, "Even the Irish are Scottish on this day."

Aileen rolled her eyes. "Whatever. Have you seen Corgi anywhere?"

I shook my head, trying to control my laughter at McCarthy's ridiculous accent. "Is he going to compete? I thought you said he's only been playing for a few months now."

"Yeah, but he's fired up by all this competition nonsense. You wouldn't think it to look at him, but he's totally motivated by contests. He's been practicing day and night ever since he decided he wanted to compete."

She was right, I wouldn't have pictured Corgi as a competitive guy. He was a small, quiet man whose laid-back demeanor was in direct contrast to Aileen's flamboyant personality. He played bass for the Twisted Armpits, and his performances at gigs were appropriately energetic, but I'd learned it was all an act. When he wasn't helping his mom run her bed-and-breakfast, he was happy to lounge on the porch with a novel or drowse in front of the TV. He shared Pete's love of the Phillies, and the two of them could talk about double plays and relief pitchers for hours on end. But I couldn't imagine him actually playing baseball, much less participating in a bagpipe competition. This should be something to see.

I spied Letty wending her way back to our booth with two cups of coffee clutched in her hands. Tall and shapely, with masses of dark, curly hair cascading down her back, she was dressed in a clingy T-shirt that proclaimed, "Kiss a Scot," paired with a pleated plaid skirt that approximated a kilt, although it fell midthigh rather than just above the knee. She slipped back into our booth and handed me a cup. "I got you a mocha latte. I hope that's all right." Without waiting for an answer, she turned to Aileen and McCarthy with a big smile. Her eyes widened at the sight of Aileen's black leather, but her professional demeanor carried her through. "Top of the morning to you! Oh, dear, that's what we say on St. Patrick's Day, isn't it?" She flipped her long hair over her shoulder in a coquettish move and gazed at McCarthy. "I see Daria's already sold you one of her superb bow ties. Can I interest you in some antiques? Maybe a monogrammed beer stein from the 1950s, or a vintage handkerchief for a special lady?"

I laid a hand on Letty's arm, halting her before she could break out her entire line of vintage linens. "Letty, do you know Sean McCarthy from the Laurel Springs *Daily Chronicle*? He's taking photographs of the Games for the newspaper. And this is Aileen, my housemate."

Letty smiled at Aileen and turned back to McCarthy. "How about a photo of our booth for the front page?" She tidied her hair and shifted a few of her wares to the front table before throwing her arm around my waist and aiming a brilliant smile at McCarthy.

He obliged with a quick photo.

"Letty, do you mind watching the booth for a few minutes? I want to check out the bagpipe competition." I showed her my price list and slipped out before she could attempt to sell Aileen some glass candy dishes or an intricately carved cuckoo clock.

McCarthy adjusted his tie once more and waved a jaunty goodbye. "I'm off to document Pennsylvania's Scottish diaspora!"

Aileen snorted. "Whatever." She grabbed my arm and hustled me through the Scottish Marketplace toward a gazebo surrounded by various Scottish flags fluttering in the light breeze. A piper in full regalia stood in the middle of the gazebo, playing an impossibly fast tune on the bagpipes. He was dressed out in a military jacket and red and black kilt held down with a horsehide sporran slung around his waist on a silver chain. Corgi had explained to me that this small pouch was useful for carrying money or car keys, but its chief purpose, other than to keep the kilt down in a breeze, was to hold the piper's flask of whiskey.

Corgi stood in the group of bagpipers waiting their turns in the competition. I was used to seeing him in black leather and chains, so I hardly recognized him in his kilt and jacket. Although, when I looked closer, I could see that his outfit wasn't quite as natty as that of the piper who was currently playing. Corgi's blue-and-green-plaid kilt hung lower on the sides than in the back or front, and the tartan fabric looked far more lightweight than the substantial wool of a traditional kilt. His sporran was leather rather than horsehair, and he wore ordinary black dress shoes rather than the distinctive ghillie brogues with their elaborate laces twining around the ankles that the other pipers wore. He looked like what he was: a beginner. I hoped the judges wouldn't go too hard on him.

Aileen poked me in the shoulder. "He's up next. They'll grade him on his musical technique, how he holds the bagpipes, and whether or not his shoelaces are tied correctly. Bizarre way to look at music, if you ask me."

"Yeah, your idea of good music is the loudest volume possible," I teased.

She opened her mouth to retort but didn't get the chance. Someone from the crowd clapped her on the shoulder, and a man's voice called out, "Well, look who's here! Long time no see."

Aileen whirled at the touch and glared at the newcomer, a large man in his early forties wearing a muscle shirt and a solid black canvas utility kilt with spacious pouch pockets on both sides. Instead of a sporran, he wore a trio of heavy chains draped around the front of his kilt, and a thick leather belt with a brass buckle depicting an eagle in flight. His dark, wavy hair curled against his shoulders, enhancing the sensuality of his muscular physique. Wide-set eyes shaded by thick eyebrows appraised Aileen from her red leather boots to her dyed black hair held back by dozens of dragon-shaped hair clips.

"Look at you, all punked out like this. I never thought I'd see you at a Highland games."

"I never thought I'd see you again this side of hell," Aileen shot back. "Get out of my sight!" She grabbed my arm and shoved her way through the crowd to the other side of the gazebo, leaving the muscleman chuckling behind her.

I straightened my skirt and repositioned my bag on my shoulder, breathless from being dragged through the crowd. "Old friend of yours?"

Aileen glared at me. "What do you think?" She folded her arms across her chest and stared pointedly at the gazebo. "Corgi's up."

I turned my attention to the bagpiping, realizing that the better part of wisdom was to leave Aileen alone when she didn't want to discuss something. Still, I found myself looking over my shoulder. The muscleman was gone.

Corgi stepped up to the center of the gazebo and blew into his blowpipe, filling his bag with air. He punched it with his arm, starting up the drones with only a couple of squeaks. He launched into his tune, his fingers flying on the chanter, one arm pumping rhythmically on the bag. All bagpipe tunes sounded pretty much the same to me, but I could tell this one was far less complicated than that of the previous piper. I hoped the judges had different categories based on skill level, so Corgi wouldn't be competing with someone with a lot more experience than he had.

A group of young Highland dancers scurried past, led by their dance teacher, Breanna Lawton. Breanna was one of my bridal clients, engaged to a man from Philadelphia I'd never met. She was a serious woman in her midthirties who was getting married for the first time and enjoying every minute of the planning. With her glorious red hair, it was easy to imagine her at the center of the Celtic-themed ceremony she dreamed of. I hoped her groom-to-be was okay with all her plans.

I waved to Breanna and the girls, admiring their soft plaid skirts held out by the numerous petticoats they'd donned for the Scottish country dances. They were simple elastic-waist skirts anyone could whip up in an hour, but they looked sweet with the girls' ruffled white blouses and French-braided hair. The youngest dancer couldn't have been older than five, while the oldest, Gillian King, who I knew from church, was fifteen. Somehow, she managed to wear her wholesome dance outfit in an alluring manner, swaying her hips as she walked and adjusting the wide neckline to reveal more cleavage than any reasonable dress code would allow. I knew her dad had his hands full with Gillian. There was that one time she'd snuck out during a youth group retreat at the church and hadn't returned for several hours while the frantic chaperones searched the downtown streets for her. Another time, her dad had caught her hanging out with dubious company under the Waterworks Bridge that crosses the Schuylkill River in a sketchy part of town. Gillian had started dancing with the Highland dancers shortly thereafter, and tales of her escapades decreased.

I tore my eyes away from the dancers to catch the end of Corgi's performance. I half expected him to fling himself to his knees the way he did at the end of every Twisted Armpits gig, but all he did was fold up his bagpipe and stride out of the gazebo. Another eager piper took his place.

Aileen clapped him on the back. "That's showing them!"

"Very nice," I echoed. "What was that last tune you played?"

He bent over his bagpipe case, stowing the instrument. "It's called 'Rowan Tree.' I messed up a couple times there at the end—could you tell?" He wiped his forehead and slipped a small flask out of his sporran for a quick nip.

"I didn't notice anything," I said truthfully, for what it was worth.

"Yeah, well, you're just getting started, so we'll cut you some slack," Aileen said. "That bit at the beginning of 'Rowan Tree' would make a great riff in 'Midnight Hollow,' right after Pinker finishes his drum solo."

I left the two of them discussing musical composition for the Twisted Armpits and hurried back to my booth. It was probably time for me to give Letty a chance to stroll around and take in the Games.

I slipped past the small crowd milling about in front of our booth. Letty was in her element. She chattered with the customers, shook out antique linens for their inspection before folding them up again with a professional flourish, and held up delicate glassware to catch the light. She sent one elderly man off with a pair of purple glass earrings for his wife with the promise that, "They'll bring out the roses in her cheeks and the romance in her heart."

"Oh, Daria, you're back," she said. "Someone stopped by to ask about your making a dress. I didn't want to commit you, so I told her to come back in half an hour."

"Did you give her one of my cards?" I indicated the small basket holding my business cards.

She shook her head, whisking off to greet another passerby.

I shrugged it off. If the woman really wanted me to make her a dress, she'd come back, and if she didn't, then I didn't need to waste my time. I'd found that people were genuinely interested in the idea of custom-made clothing, but most weren't patient enough to wait for the finished product. Brides were the exception—most women considered that once-in-a-lifetime wedding gown to be worth the wait.

I tidied my selection of bow ties and placemats, noticing that Letty's linens had migrated onto the front of my table to overshadow my own items. I chuckled as I repositioned my Nessies. There was room for both of us here. I turned to speak to a small child looking longingly at a red plaid Nessie with a jaunty green tam o' shanter on its head.

Ultimately, his mom didn't buy the Nessie and the child had to settle for a lollipop. I waved goodbye and turned to see Letty chatting with the muscleman from earlier.

"Daria, this is Ladd Foster. He's a famous athlete in the Scottish Games circle. He throws…what was it you throw again?"

Ladd grinned, a flash of white in the stubble covering his strong chin. "I do the caber toss. It's basically a tree trunk. You heave it into the air and try to get it to flip over before it hits the ground." He struck a pose, flexing his biceps. "It's a job for the Incredible Hulk."

Letty pulled out her phone and snapped a few pictures of Ladd. "I can't wait!" She leaned on the table with her chin in both hands. "Isn't that hard to do in a kilt?"

He winked at her. "You're wondering what I'm wearing under this kilt, aren't you?"

She shrugged her shoulders. "I've heard men don't wear anything underneath, but I never knew if that was for real."

"I always go true Scot," he proclaimed. "Want to see?"

"I'd love to—another time." She straightened up, brushing back her hair. "I wouldn't want to distract the Incredible Hulk from his cabers."

"I'm all about distractions." He flashed her another toothy grin. "You'll come watch me, won't you? One o'clock on the playing fields. I'm undefeated in the caber toss."

"I'll be there." She picked out a lace-edged handkerchief from her pile of antiques. "You can wear my favor, like a jousting knight." She tucked the handkerchief into the waistband of his kilt.

I turned away, trying to hide my amusement.

I busied myself with a trio of teenage girls who exclaimed over my chest of bow ties. They spent the next twenty-five minutes rooting through all the options, trying various combinations in their hair before each one bought a tie in a different tartan. Out of the corner of my eye I saw Ladd striding away. Letty bustled about the booth, laying out some vintage jewelry to show the girls. When the teens left and the booth was quiet for a few minutes, I sat down and shook a finger at Letty. "You should be ashamed, leading him on like that."

She laughed and threw back her hair. "If he didn't notice the wedding ring on my finger, that's his problem. Can you believe that 'true Scot' line? I'll bet he uses that on all the girls."

I giggled along with her. "I don't know, what about that line about wearing your favor, like a jousting knight? That was right up there."

The next hour passed quietly enough. Letty took a stroll around the grounds while I staffed the booth. I sold a couple of Nessies and a set of antique brandy snifters for Letty and chatted with a woman whose wedding gown I had made a year ago. McCarthy stopped by to show me that he was still wearing his yellow bow tie, and then wandered off again in search of more photographs. The persistent sound of bagpipes filled the air. I closed my eyes, imagining myself on the moors of Scotland hearing the pipers marching through the mist. I could almost smell the heather, when I was snapped out of my reverie by the more familiar sound of Aileen's guitar.

Aileen and the band were setting up on the bandstand directly opposite the Marketplace. I had forgotten that the Twisted Armpits were scheduled to play a quick set over the lunch hour, while the pipers and dancers as well as the judges took a break. Amps and mics and miles of cords overflowed from the stage as the band members positioned and plugged in all their gear. Aileen stood on the platform in the midst of the chaos, a mic stand in one hand and a canvas bag bursting with cords in the other. Her guitar case lay open on the ground off the side of the stage. Open and empty.

Ladd Foster leaned on the edge of the steps leading up to the stage, strumming Aileen's guitar.

He was committing sacrilege, of course. Possibly suicide as well. No one played Aileen's guitar without permission and survived to tell the tale. I held my breath, waiting for the explosion. I didn't have to wait long.

Chapter 2

"Get your paws off my stuff," Aileen hollered, and flung her canvas bag at Ladd's head. He ducked, laughing, as it hit the ground and sent cords flying in all directions like a sackful of snakes.

She hefted a mic stand and started for him, but her bandmate Pinker grabbed her by the arm. "Hold on a sec, Aileen. He's good!" He held Aileen back, and watched in open admiration as Ladd continued to play. "He's playing that bit you wrote for 'Frankie's Fury.' He's got the chord changes down and everything."

Aileen growled and wrenched her arm free of his grasp. She picked up the mic stand again, and then slammed it back down as a crowd formed around Ladd. I cringed when I saw Gillian King front and center in the crowd, gazing at Ladd as if he were some kind of movie star. But Aileen wasn't concerned about the hero worship of a fifteen-year-old girl.

Aileen strode down the steps of the stage and snatched her guitar out of Ladd's hands. For an instant he held on, but she glared him down until he loosened his grip. She hefted the guitar over her shoulder like a baseball bat, and several people in the crowd, including Gillian, screamed. Ladd ducked again, but Aileen didn't swing. "You're not worth the price of a new guitar," she spat out. "But if you ever touch my gear again…" Leaving her threat unspecified, she swung on her heel and stomped back onto the stage. "Got any sanitizer wipes?" she demanded of Pinker.

He started to laugh, but then thought better of it. He took his shirttail and wiped down Aileen's guitar, taking extra care to go over each metal string. She stood and watched him, her back to the crowd and Ladd, her arms folded across her chest.

Her stillness scared me more than her raised guitar had. I could tell how furious she was by the intensity of her immobility. If Ladd made the slightest move toward her, she would kill him.

He must have realized that, because when I tore my eyes away from Aileen, I saw Ladd had turned away. Surrounded by the loyal crowd, he headed off in the direction of the food court with Gillian following close behind. She called out to him, and he turned to flash her a huge smile, and then the two of them walked side by side up to the funnel cakes booth. Aileen stood silent and unmoving on the stage.

I let out a sigh, surprised to find I had been holding my breath.

Letty slipped back into the booth. She held a hardcover book in her hands. "Wasn't that Aileen? She'll get herself thrown out of the Games, carrying on like that."

"God help the person who tries to throw Aileen out of anywhere," I said. "I wouldn't want to see her going up against your Incredible Hulk, though. Between the two of them, they'd probably wreck the whole place."

"Yeah, she'd better stay out of the way when he's throwing cabers around. But forget about them. Did you see who else is here?" Letty held out the book she carried. "Morris Hart! He's on a book tour and he's spending a few days in Laurel Springs, if you can believe it. Have you read his latest thriller, *Over the Sea to Skye?*"

I shook my head and took the book from her hands to skim the blurb on the back cover. "I've heard of it, of course. Everyone's reading it this summer. Something about the descendants of Scottish kings taking over Britain in the present day, right?"

She nodded. "There's a real-life treasure hunt too, to find Bonnie Prince Charlie's ring, which was lost in the seventeen hundreds. Hart is smart to set up at the Highland Games, where people have actually heard of Bonnie Prince Charlie and the Battle of Culloden." Letty pointed to the author's photo on the back of the book, showing a handsome man with an aristocratic nose and dark, glossy hair. "This picture is a few years old, but he's still got it. He could be the descendant of royalty in my book."

I laughed and handed the book back to her. "Letty, you're incorrigible."

She dropped a curtsy like a diva basking in well-earned applause, then turned to wait on a young couple with a baby asleep in a stroller.

I sat down and pulled out the basketful of bow-tie supplies I'd prepared to keep my hands busy while waiting for customers. It was a simple process of folding and pinching rectangles of tartan fabric into the shape of a bow, but it looked impressive to watch. I felt like an artist displaying her techniques for the crowd. I didn't even mind if people learned my secrets to make their own ties at home. Tartan bow ties were only a sideline for me, an excuse to be a part of this Scottish festival. They were also surprisingly popular with the teenagers. For every girl who walked away sporting a bow-tie headband, three more came to pick over my collection. It was a trend in the making.

Gillian arrived with the next wave of girls. She was dressed in her Highland costume of kilt, lace blouse, and green velvet vest, and was taking a break before dancing the Highland fling. Her friends wore denim cutoffs and sleeveless tops, and plenty of mascara and lipstick. They jostled one another and carried on an endless string of friendly abuse while two or three of them tried on bow ties.

Gillian scrabbled through the chest, spilling most of the ties onto the table. "Do you have any green ones, to match my kilt?"

I stood up to look at her kilt, a dark green and blue plaid with alternating pairs of black and white lines running both lengthwise and crosswise. I flipped through my guide booklet to show her. "You're wearing the Oliphant tartan. I made a bunch of Oliphant ones because of the connection to the university." I sifted through the bow ties and pulled out a couple for her to look at.

She held one up to her hair, tucking it into the plaits of her French braid. The contrast between the green plaid and her strawberry blond hair was beautiful. She knew it, too.

"I'll take two, in the same tartan," she said. "Can you give me a discount for two?"

I shook my head as I bagged up the bow ties. "Sorry. They go for fifteen dollars each. I don't have any bulk discounts today."

She grumbled a bit but handed over the money. As she turned away, she nudged the girl closest to her. "I'm going to give one to Ladd. We'll be matching."

"Ladd? The dude who's going to throw the tree trunk? He's as old as your dad."

Gillian pushed her. "He's nothing like my dad. He's gorgeous."

They walked away, giggling, while I sat down slowly, aghast. The last thing I wanted to see was my own matching bow ties adorning both Gillian King and Ladd Foster. The ties were hers now, and she could do whatever she wanted with them. Still, I felt like she was using me as an accomplice in her misguided attempt to chase after the man.

Letty clicked her tongue. "That Ladd does get around, doesn't he? I hope he's not planning to prove to a fifteen-year-old girl that he's going 'true Scot.'"

"Yeah, me too. He might not know she's fifteen, though. He's not very observant." I waved to her ring finger, which was literally laden down by a dazzling diamond ring paired with her thick gold wedding ring.

Letty and I didn't have to wonder long. It was only a matter of minutes before we saw Ladd hovering over a leatherworking booth, with Gillian snuggled under his powerful arm. We couldn't hear their words, but we could see him joking with the craftsman while Gillian laughed and smacked him on the chest appreciatively. He wasn't wearing the bow tie around his neck, but only because his peasant shirt was laced up to his breastbone, exposing his neck and chest hairs. With a sinking feeling in my stomach, I saw the Oliphant tartan tie twined around his right wrist, matching the bow Gillian wore in her hair.

She was no responsibility of mine, but still, I could hardly sit by and let her get into trouble with a fortysomething flirt in a kilt. They say it takes a village to raise a child, and that goes double for a teenager. I liked to think people watched out for each other in our small town, and it looked like it was my turn to do my part. Or maybe I was just minding other people's business—one of my main strengths, according to McCarthy. I jumped up and said to Letty, "I'll be back in a sec." I slipped out of the booth.

I followed the two of them as they wandered through the Marketplace toward the edge of the field, with Ladd's arm around her waist. When his hand slid down to her hip, I called out, "Gillian! Breanna is looking for you."

She turned in surprise. My heartbeats accelerated, but I resolved not to make it easy for her. "The fourteen-to-sixteen-year-old age group is about to go on. Breanna asked me to come find you. You don't want to miss your competition."

She glared at me. "I don't know what you're talking about. I don't have any dances coming up." She twined her fingers around Ladd's hand. "Come on, Ladd."

He took a good look at her. "Fourteen to sixteen?"

"Yeah, Gillian's fifteen," I chirped. "She's the best dancer in the sophomore class at high school."

Gillian tossed her head, but she didn't get the chance to respond. A slight man with balding reddish hair and black glasses grabbed her by the arm and flung her away from Ladd. She staggered and almost fell, but I caught her by the shoulders.

The newcomer doubled up both fists and squared off before the muscular athlete who was easily twice his weight. "Get your filthy hands off my daughter!"

Ladd stood staring for a moment, and then he started to laugh. He was still laughing when Ryan King's fist connected with his cheekbone. For such a small man, Ryan packed a mean punch. Ladd staggered backward, fetching up against a table filled with picnickers who jumped up and scattered in a panic. He grabbed up a folding chair and held it poised to throw.

Gillian screamed and lunged toward her father. "Daddy, stop it!" I tried to hold her back, but she broke free from my grasp and threw herself between the two men.

Ryan probably realized he wouldn't get another chance, now that his adversary knew he meant business. He took his daughter by the arm and threw me a withering glance, as if I had personally fixed up a date between Ladd and Gillian. He pointed a finger at Ladd. "You stay away from my daughter or I'll have the cops on you." He pulled her along as he turned to stride away.

Ladd lowered the chair, seeming to notice the growing crowd for the first time. Several people had their cell phones out to record the altercation. I heard the click of a camera as well. McCarthy was documenting the incident for the newspaper.

"You're the one who committed assault," Ladd hollered after Ryan. "I'd be within my rights to press charges." He pulled out his flask and unscrewed the top for a long swallow. "Nothing like a drop of single malt whiskey to dull the pain," he proclaimed to the crowd with a wink.

I chewed my lip as I watched Ryan hustle Gillian off. I hoped he wouldn't take out his anger on her. I felt compelled to follow them, to make sure she was safe.

Ryan held on to Gillian's arm until he got her behind the food tents. He pushed her up against an ice cooler and let her go. I lurked at the corner, keeping an eye on things.

Ryan pointed his finger at Gillian. "If I ever see you carrying on with someone twice your age like that again, I'll have you off to that convent before you know what happened to you."

Gillian straightened her kilt and pulled at her vest. Trails of mascara streaked down her cheeks, but she held her head high. "We're Presbyterians, Daddy."

"It's never too late to convert."

It could have been a friendly attempt at humor to defuse the situation, but I could tell Ryan wasn't interested in defusing anything or being friendly with his daughter. I doubted if he possessed anything close to a sense of humor. My heart went out to Gillian, but I didn't intervene. At least he wasn't beating her.

Ryan could have gone on berating her for a long time, but the loudspeaker interrupted him. "In two minutes at the VIP tent, we will have a presentation from the acclaimed author, Morris Hart."

"I want to hear that," Ryan said, abruptly abandoning his tirade. "Behave yourself." He turned on his heel and left.

Gillian leaned back against the cooler and put both hands over her face. I almost went to comfort her, but I was pretty sure my support wouldn't be appreciated. I backed slowly away from the food tents and began to make my way back to my booth.

As I walked past the VIP tent, I saw a crowd gathering in anticipation of the author's talk. People clutched hardcover books under their arms or eyed a sizable pile on the table next to the podium. I made out Morris Hart himself, looking a bit grayer than the photo Letty had showed me, talking with none other than Ladd Foster. The guy definitely got around. He had a red mark on his cheek but looked otherwise unscathed by his altercation over Gillian. He spoke rapidly to Hart, full of swagger and laughter. But Hart wasn't amused. He frowned with his arms crossed on his chest, clearly displeased at what he was hearing.

I wondered what that was about.

But I didn't have time to linger to find out. It was time for me to give Letty a break. She was practically dancing when I got back to the booth. "I gotta go! That rocking chair is sold, and the guy's going to come back and pick it up at three. You're almost out of red bow ties." She ducked out of the booth and ran for the ladies' room.

I tidied my wares, shifting Letty's linens back to their place to uncover a hidden trove of red bow ties. I tucked them back into the wooden chest as the thumping bass of the Twisted Armpits filled the air. Must be lunchtime.

Letty returned to the booth with her hands over her ears. "We won't get any business during lunch with that racket just across the way," she shouted.

I couldn't argue. Still, the noise wasn't as concentrated as it was in my basement, so I could actually enjoy the music here. I sent Letty off to get some lunch and watched the band.

I hadn't seen them perform on stage since Corgi had added the bagpipes. What a cool addition! Corgi had traded his military piper's coat for his customary black leather bomber jacket looped with chains, which made an imposing ensemble paired with his lightweight kilt and black army boots. He had miked the bagpipes so they could be heard clearly over the screaming guitar. He played the same tunes I'd been hearing all morning, but in the midst of the metal band they took on a whole new dimension. I was glad the assembled bagpipers got the chance to see what else their instruments could do.

McCarthy circled around the bandstand, taking pictures of Aileen and her gang. He drifted over to lean on my front table.

"Who knew these Highland Games would be so exciting? I've got photos of Aileen about to whale on Ladd Foster with her guitar, and others of Ladd about to bean Ryan King over the head with a folding chair. The man's a photog's dream!"

I laughed and accepted the sandwich he held out to me. "What, no haggis?"

He passed me a napkin. "Corgi tells me the haggis comes out at the ceilidh tomorrow evening. The Pipe and Drum Corps is going to be making it all morning. He's promised to let me document the process."

Corgi had outlined this process to me, which included mixing oatmeal with ground meat and various spices and stuffing it into a sheep's stomach for baking. I privately resolved to steer clear of the haggis at the Scottish party the following evening.

McCarthy spied Letty's copy of *Over the Sea to Skye* on the table. "You got yourself an autographed copy?"

I shook my head. "It's Letty's. I might have to, though. Everyone's raving about it."

"I read it last week. Couldn't put it down. Then I spent the next few days looking up Scottish history. I've never been big on the kings of Great Britain, but Hart made me want to know more. I'd call that a successful writer."

McCarthy had been shouting throughout this conversation, to compete with the noise from the band. A sudden lull in the music caused his voice to carry across the field. Morris Hart, who appeared to be wrapping up his question-and-answer session, turned and inclined his head toward us.

I blushed, but McCarthy was unfazed. He gave Hart a grin and a thumbs-up, then turned back to me as if nothing had happened. "I'll get you a copy, in exchange for this natty bow tie." He caressed the tie. "I've gotten loads of compliments on it. Even discounting the ones who are clearly making fun of me, I'd say you've got a winner."

"No! Somebody made fun of you?"

He laughed. "Hard to believe, isn't it?" He lifted his camera and took a few shots of me tending the booth alone. "Sounds like it's just about time for the field events."

Indeed, the Twisted Armpits were bringing their song to a crashing finale, signaling the end of lunchtime. McCarthy turned to head over to the athletic field when he was accosted by Morris Hart.

"I gather you enjoyed my book?"

McCarthy held out his hand. "Sean McCarthy, of the Laurel Springs *Daily Chronicle*." The two men shook hands. "And this is Daria Dembrowski, a seamstress with a passion for history." I smiled and shook Hart's hand as well. Up close, I could see the lines on his face. I guessed him to be in his fifties, and his trim build spoke of a passion for fitness as well as history. He gave me the barest glance, his attention still focused on McCarthy.

"I was just telling Daria that your book made me want to know more about Scottish history, a field I know very little about," McCarthy said.

Hart bowed his head. "If I can stimulate even a bit of curiosity about history through my writing, I consider I've made a useful contribution to society."

I bit back a smile. McCarthy, with his almost insatiable curiosity and boundless energy, didn't need to be the recipient of this lecture. But he merely nodded with a genuine smile. "Part of the fun for me was trying to figure out what was historical fact and what was pure invention on your part. I'm still working out some of the details."

"I never disclose my sources."

McCarthy grinned. "You must have been a journalist in another life." He held up his camera. "I'm off to cover the athletic events, but I'd like to get a book. Will you be around later?"

"I'm here all day," Hart replied. "I'll walk along with you. I always love the caber toss." The two men took off, chatting companionably, just as Letty returned to the booth.

"Oh, you got to meet Morris Hart. He's so down-to-earth for being such a famous author. I see you put out more red bow ties—good choice. Did someone purchase the bone china tea set with the lavender pattern? I hope you wrapped up each cup individually."

"Yes. I did." I figured that answered all her questions at once. "It's time for the field events. Did you want to go see Ladd Foster throw the caber?"

"Honestly, I think I'm going to pass. He thinks I'm interested in him, but after seeing him with a fifteen-year-old, I'm done." She tossed her hair over her shoulder. "Flirting is a sport to me, but you have to play by the rules. He went offside when he pursued a teenager." She chuckled at her analogy. "You go and watch, Daria. Have you ever seen anyone throw a tree trunk around for fun?"

I shook my head. "I can't even imagine it."

A crowd was gathering at the athletic field, which was delineated by a series of tall metal torches stuck into the ground every five feet or so. They weren't lit yet, but I could imagine how impressive they would look in the evening. I didn't know if I'd stay for the evening festivities, which included the awards presentation followed by another set by the Twisted Armpits. It depended on how tired I was after a day on my feet.

I found a spot on the edge of the crowd where I had a good view of the athletic field. The grass was chalked in various places, with a large circle in the middle and a number of lines along one side. A couple of officials in kilts and matching green polo shirts hovered on the sidelines. They flipped through untidy papers on the clipboards they carried. A parade approached the field, led by four bagpipers and a boy playing a snare drum, followed by a heavyset man dressed in the Kelly green polo shirt of the officials, which clashed with his kilt in the dark green Oliphant tartan. They marched in the athletes: four enormous men who were about to prove their strength. The announcer introduced himself as Herman Tisdale, and then called the name of each athlete in turn: Jamie Deakens, Tom O'Flaherty, Patrick Ames, and Ladd Foster.

The first event was the hammer throw. Each athlete would swing around the twenty-pound stone attached to the end of a stick and heave it as far as possible. I marveled at the officials, who stood without flinching in the stone's path to record its landing spot. I wouldn't want that to land on my head!

"Patrick Ames is the guy to beat today." I turned to see Corgi standing next to me, dressed in his full Highland regalia once again. "I hear he's got a blood feud going with Ladd Foster. The two of them have been fierce rivals ever since the Whidbey Island Games ten years ago."

I regarded Patrick, who was about to release the hammer. He looked like he weighed at least three hundred pounds of pure brawn. The muscles in his arms and shoulders bulged as he whirled around and flung the hammer down the field. "What happened in Whidbey Island?"

Corgi rolled his eyes. "I heard there was some serious cheating going on. How you can cheat when you're throwing sticks and stones around, I don't know. Still, Patrick accused Ladd of cheating, and Ladd said no, it was Patrick, and in the end they both got disqualified. Evidently, even after ten years, each Games is a rematch, with both guys out for revenge." He gazed out at the field. "I wouldn't want either one of those giants looking for revenge on me."

I watched as Ladd and Patrick squared up for the pole push inside the chalk circle. They each took hold of the handles on either end of a thick log about twelve feet long. At the whistle, they started pushing against the pole, trying to push the other out of the circle. It was like the opposite of a tug-of-war, with the opponents pushing toward each other, attempting to throw the other off-balance. They grunted and strained with the pole barely budging, until all of a sudden, Ladd shot out with his feet and swiped at Patrick's legs. Patrick roared and lashed out at Ladd with his own feet. The two of them started circling around, still clinging to the handles on the pole, each one trying to kick his opponent's legs while sidestepping to avoid getting kicked. It would have been laughable, watching them trying to get at each other when all they had to do was drop the pole, except for the fury on their faces. The officials hovered on the edge of the altercation, calling out for the two men to cease and desist. But the officials couldn't, or wouldn't, get close enough to stop the pole.

Finally, Ladd tripped, and on his way down, he wrenched the pole sideways and threw Patrick off-balance. The ground shook with the force of their fall. Patrick bounced up, but before he could tackle Ladd, the other two athletes stepped in. Jamie pushed on Patrick's chest to get him away from Ladd, while at the same instant, Tom wrestled Ladd's arms to his sides.

"Show some respect for the fans," Jamie growled, pointing to a terrified toddler seeking shelter in his mother's arms.

The two foes looked abashed. They didn't resist any further when Tom and Jamie led them off to the sidelines.

Herman Tisdale wiped his brow and bustled up to the microphone. "Let's give the athletes a break and have all the kids out here for the tug-of-war!"

The kids ran to line up on either end of the rope, while the officials lectured Ladd and Patrick on their conduct. It looked like they were both disqualified in the pole push event. The flame of their rivalry burned higher.

The lecture ended before the tug-of-war. Patrick sat down on the grass and massaged his calves, while Ladd wandered over toward the VIP tent and pulled out his flask for a big swallow of whiskey.

Gillian ran up to him, her bow tie askew in her hair. "I was so frightened for you! Are you okay?"

Ladd held out his arms and turned slowly in front of her. "Not a scratch on me." He slugged down another swallow and handed the flask to her. "Be a dear and hold this for me, would you? It gets in my way when I'm tossing the caber."

Gillian took the flask with a glance over her shoulder, checking to see if her father was watching, no doubt. She had just enough time to say, "I hope you win," before Ladd turned away to return to the field. He'd left a fifteen-year-old girl in charge of his flask of whiskey.

I kept a sharp eye on her. If she looked like she was going to take a nip, I planned to snatch the thing out of her hands.

She turned the flask over, running her fingers over the etching on its silver surface. She unscrewed the top. I started edging through the crowd, keeping my eye on Gillian. She lifted the flask to her nose and inhaled. Then she made a face I'm sure she didn't expect anyone else to see and screwed the top back on. She darted into the VIP tent and reappeared a moment later without the flask. She must have set it down inside for safekeeping.

Just in time. I spied Ryan on the edge of the crowd, completely absorbed in a conversation with Morris Hart. He must not have seen his daughter chatting with Ladd. It was all good. I turned my attention to the field. The caber toss was about to start.

The caber was a long, thin log, easily fifteen to twenty feet in length. Jamie Deakens, a young blond giant with a round face softened by peach fuzz, was the first to toss it. Two of the officials carried the caber to him, and then walked it to a vertical position in front of him, with the narrow end on the ground.

Jamie grasped the caber with cupped hands, about a yard above the ground. He worked his way down the caber, resting its weight on his shoulder, until he could grasp the butt of it and lift it off the ground. He staggered forward, the caber swaying slightly in its vertical position, until he gained control over it. He continued to run until he gave a huge grunt and heaved the caber into the air. It turned over, the thick end hit the ground, and the caber fell with the narrow end pointing away from the athlete. The crowd applauded.

Corgi cheered beside me. "Fantastic throw! He turned the caber on his first try. I'd say it fell at about one o'clock—pretty darn good."

I stared at him. "It's well past two. What are you talking about? The caber didn't go very far at all."

"The point isn't for it to go far. The point is for it to flip over—we say he 'turned' the caber. Not everyone can turn it. Then it's supposed to land in a straight line from where he stood when he tossed it. Twelve o'clock, if you picture the face of a clock. Jamie's was angled a bit off to the right, at one o'clock. Pretty close, if you ask me. He gets two more tries, but I'll bet he can't beat that."

Aileen walked up to stand beside me. "A bunch of overgrown guys are throwing logs around. Sheesh." She crossed her arms and watched Tom O'Flaherty throw. The caber didn't flip over. It approached the vertical, only to fall back down to the ground. The crowd sighed in disappointment.

Corgi poked her. "I'll bet you couldn't do that."

Aileen snorted. "If I thought it was important, I'd learn how. Flipping a log over endwise is not important to me." She struck a dramatic pose, her hand over her heart. "'No human thing is of serious importance.'" She bowed with a flourish. "Plato, in case you were wondering."

Corgi and I were still laughing when Ladd approached the caber to take his first turn. He saw Aileen in the crowd and flashed her a thumbs-up. She turned her back on him.

Ladd hefted the caber into his hands and staggered backward, trying to balance it before starting his run. His muscular arms shook and sweat ran down his face. The crowd gasped and parted as he staggered sideways, before finally getting it under control. I tapped Aileen's shoulder. "Not a good plan to turn your back on a caber in motion." She turned back around to watch.

Ladd ran a few steps and flung the caber into the air with a huge grunt. It had just enough momentum to flip over and land with a thump on the ground. The crowd cheered. Ladd had successfully turned the caber on his first try.

He hobbled over to the sidelines and bent over with his hands on his knees, panting for breath. He looked to be at least ten years older than any of his competitors. I watched the red slowly fade from his face and wondered if he should maybe think about retiring.

He lifted his head and scanned the crowd. Aileen crouched down behind Corgi. "See you later." She slipped through the crowd and ducked into the VIP tent, brushing past Ryan King on his way out. Ryan checked and stared at her, the way people always did at the sight of her. He dusted off his arm as if she'd sullied it with her contact, and then he returned to watching the heavy athletic events.

I turned to Corgi in confusion. "I've never seen Aileen hiding from anything before. What's the story between her and Ladd?"

He was as mystified as I was. "I've never heard her talk about him. Obviously, there's some history there. If she wants to talk about it, fine, but I'm not going to pry."

Smart guy.

It was Patrick's turn at the caber. I watched his technique to see if he was a match for Ladd. He was an immense man sporting a black goatee and an armful of Celtic tattoos. He grasped the caber with confidence and hefted it to balance against his shoulder. He ran a few steps and threw his hands up in the air, launching the caber. It flipped over and hit the ground with a resounding thud.

After the first round, three out of four of the athletes had turned the caber.

McCarthy stopped by for a quick word as Jamie stepped up to start the second round. "Given up on the bow-tie trade, have we?"

I gave a guilty start and checked the time on my phone. "I guess I should get back to the booth." The crowd roared, signaling their approval of Jamie's latest toss. "Or at least I should check in with Letty to see how things are going." I texted her, to receive the reply: "All's quiet on the Scottish front. Take your time with the hunks."

I smiled and tucked my phone into my pocket. "Sounds like everyone is gathered around to watch the show. They've probably all got their eyes on you and your camera, figuring wherever you go is the place to be."

His eyes crinkled up when he smiled at me. "And they'd be right, of course. Which begs the question—what's up with Aileen that she's skipping out on these events?"

"You'll have to ask her, if you dare."

He shrank back in mock horror. "Not I! I just thought I could quietly get the lowdown from you without having to face the beast. I'm sure you'll ferret it out of her, being the nosy seamstress that you are."

With those encouraging words, he turned back to the field in time to snap a series of photos of Tom's second toss, which just barely flipped over for a successful turn.

Ladd was up next. As he swaggered up to the line, I saw Aileen slip out of the VIP tent and stalk away. Was it possible she had remained hidden until Ladd was fully occupied with his sporting events, when she felt like she could leave? What had Ladd ever done to her to cause her to react to him this way?

Ladd's second toss went smoother than his first. He gained control over the caber straight away and tossed it high in the air. It turned smoothly and fell in a straight line from where he was standing.

"Twelve o'clock," Corgi exulted. "That was a perfect toss!"

I looked over at his competitors to see how they took his success. Jamie looked excited and Tom had a worried expression on his face, but Patrick wasn't even watching. As the announcer called his name to throw next, he emerged from the VIP tent with a scowl on his face.

Patrick practically snatched the caber from the two men who propped it up for him. He hefted it and ran a long ways down the field before launching it into the air, accompanied by a deep, powerful grunt. It flipped and fell a titch to the side, at about eleven o'clock, as far as I could tell.

Ladd called out from the sidelines, "Bonnie Patrick, you throw like a girl!" He simpered and stroked his hair, all the while laughing at the glowering brow of his adversary.

I feared we were about to witness another brawl between the two rivals. I hoped they could behave themselves, at least until the end of the caber toss. Gillian had angled her way in to stand as close to the competitors as she could get. It was a wonder to me that she chose to lavish her attention on the oldest of the four giants. I couldn't help wondering if she was deliberately trying to antagonize her father.

Patrick slapped his hands together and flexed his muscles as the crowd murmured appreciatively. He struck a few more poses for McCarthy to document and then returned to stand next to Tom.

I kept my eyes on Ladd as the judges conferred for a few minutes before the start of the third round. He had abandoned his catcalling and appeared to be patting down the pockets in his utility kilt, looking for his flask, no doubt. He turned to speak to Gillian, standing close beside him, and then he headed for the VIP tent. He almost bumped into Morris Hart, who was coming out of the tent. Hart sidestepped, keeping his eyes averted in an obvious attempt to avoid any kind of interaction with Ladd. I was surprised to see such a successful author reacting to Ladd's crude, juvenile behavior. Maybe he simply wanted nothing to do with the man.

Ladd disappeared into the VIP tent during Jamie's toss. Jamie turned the caber for the third time, proving himself to be an up-and-coming competitor to give Patrick and Ladd a run for their money. The crowd cheered for the blond giant.

Tom ran up to the caber and squatted down for a few deep knee bends accompanied by loud grunts to psych himself up. He grasped the caber, heaved it up onto his shoulder, and charged down the field to the cheers of the crowd. He launched it, stood for a moment to watch it flip over, and then ran off the field pumping his fists in the air.

"That was his best toss yet," Corgi said. "He'll still probably take fourth place, but I'd give him the most-improved trophy. Ladd's up next."

We looked around expectantly as the announcer called for Ladd to step up and take his third turn. He finally came out of the VIP tent, wiping his mouth and coughing and sputtering, as if he'd taken too big a swig and some of the whiskey had gone down the wrong pipe. Maybe he should have waited until after the event to imbibe.

He bent down to grasp the caber at knee level and stalled there for a few minutes, trying to control his coughing. He hacked and spit on the ground and then worked his cupped hands down the length of the caber to grasp the butt end. He hefted it and lurched sideways, the long pole dipping sharply toward the crowd.

"Whoa, he's not in control of the caber at all!" Corgi grasped my arm and backed up, pulling me along with him to get out of the way.

Ladd staggered in the other direction, still coughing and gasping for breath. The caber swung in a wide circle before crashing to the ground. It narrowly missed a group of young Highland dancers, who screamed and jumped out of the way. Ladd collapsed on the ground, his hands clutching his chest, his face red from coughing.

Chapter 3

Gillian screamed. I stood frozen, with Corgi's hand gripping my arm so hard it hurt. The officials ran up to Ladd, who lay unresponsive on the ground. One called out for a doctor, while parents shielded the eyes of their children. Breanna Lawton herded her Highland dance students away with an anxious glance over her shoulder. Someone started CPR, while several other people crouched down to give encouragement. McCarthy hovered on the edge of the action, snapping photos. I hoped I wouldn't see any of them on the front page of tomorrow's newspaper.

Gillian cried out again, and then clapped both hands over her mouth. Her eyes darted from side to side, as if seeking escape. I followed her gaze, wondering what she was afraid of, other than her concern for Ladd. I didn't have to look far. Her father stood across the field, glaring at her as if she were single-handedly responsible for the commotion. When I looked back toward Gillian, she was gone.

An ambulance with sirens blaring roared across the grass. People made way for the paramedics who hurried up and knelt down beside Ladd.

My phone dinged with a text from Letty. "What's going on?"

I texted back: "Ladd Foster collapsed."

She responded: "Coming."

I didn't know if she expected me to take over our booth, but I didn't budge. Like McCarthy, I wanted to be close to the action until it was over.

Letty appeared a few minutes later, clutching her cashbox in one hand. "I threw a blanket over the booth and just left it all there. I think it'll be okay." She handed me the decorative cigar box that held my proceeds. She nodded toward the urgent group on the field. "What happened to him?"

I hugged the cigar box to my chest. "Maybe a heart attack? He went into the VIP tent for a nip of whiskey, and when he came out he was coughing, like he couldn't get his breath. He went to pick up the caber to toss it, but he dropped it and fell over, clutching his chest. He's probably getting old to be exerting himself like that."

Letty craned her head to look. "Is he dead?"

The matter-of-factness of her question chilled me. "I don't know. I hope not."

On my other side, Corgi squeezed my arm. "They're loading him up."

Indeed, the paramedics had placed Ladd on a stretcher and were loading it into the back of the ambulance. They drove away with a wail of sirens.

The announcer, Herman Tisdale, took the microphone. "We regret the disturbance. Ladd Foster suffered an apparent cardiac arrest while attempting the caber toss. Thanks to the efforts of heroic bystanders, he was resuscitated and transported to the hospital. Let us honor him with a moment of silence to send our prayers and good wishes, followed by a bagpipe air." He took off his cap and bowed his head, and the people in the crowd did the same. After a few moments, the haunting sound of one bagpipe playing "Amazing Grace" filled the air.

I felt like I was at a funeral.

After the last, lingering note, the official proclaimed, "Let the Games resume!"

As Patrick stepped up for his chance at the caber, Corgi finally dropped my arm. "I better find Aileen and the rest of the band." He headed off.

I turned to Letty. "Do you want a turn to watch the athletic events? I can cover the booth."

"What, now that all the excitement is over?" But she was watching in fascination as Patrick hefted the caber and ran down the field to launch it into the air for another perfect turn. I collected Letty's cashbox and left her to enjoy the rest of the heavy events.

I found the booth just as Letty had left it. I pulled back the cloth and almost burst out laughing. She had systematically transferred all my craft items to the side table and reorganized the front table with her antique linens, jewelry, and glassware. I guess she'd earned it because I'd left her tending the booth alone for so long.

McCarthy stopped by to say he was going to collect his reporter colleague Martin Sterling and swing by the hospital to check on Ladd. "Something about his story makes me uneasy."

I frowned at him. "What do you know that I don't?"

He laughed. "How could I possibly know more than the nosiest seamstress in the state of Pennsylvania?" His grin faded. "I overheard the guy giving Ladd CPR saying he noticed a strange odor on his breath. Just curious." *Probably whiskey.* I watched thoughtfully as McCarthy walked away. To be honest, something about Ladd's collapse made me uneasy as well. He'd seemed perfectly fine before he walked into the VIP tent for a quick drink. Then he'd come out coughing and sputtering as if he were a fifteen-year-old tasting whiskey for the very first time. What was that about?

Suddenly, I wanted to know. I guess McCarthy didn't call me nosy for nothing. I threw the blanket over the tables once again, pocketed the money from my cashbox, and headed back toward the athletic field.

The competition had resumed as if nothing had happened. The caber toss was finished, and Patrick was holding two enormous swords, one in each hand, with both arms extended like wings. I supposed the point was to see how long you could hold your arms out like that while supporting the weight. Patrick's arms were starting to shake; he could only last for a few more seconds.

I didn't wait to find out. I slipped into the VIP tent, curious to see if Ladd's whiskey flask was still there. Sure enough, it lay discarded on a table. I went to pick it up, but some instinct stayed my hand. I gazed at the small stainless-steel flask for a few minutes without touching it. Its curved front was embossed with the figure of a unicorn surrounded by some words that looked like Latin—most likely a coat of arms. But I wasn't interested in Scottish clan history at the moment. I wanted to take a sniff of Ladd's flask, but I wasn't sure if I should touch the thing. I gave in to my hesitations and rummaged through my shoulder bag for a tissue pack. I pulled out a couple of tissues, using one to pick up the flask and the other to unscrew the decorative top, which was made in the shape of a Scottish thistle.

I was bringing the flask to my nose to smell the contents when Gillian entered the tent.

"What are you doing with that?" She darted to my side and snatched the flask out of my hand. Amber liquid slopped out onto my blouse.

I grabbed her arm before she could dump out the contents of the flask. "Wait!"

Gillian threw a desperate glance over her shoulder. "Let go!" She kicked me on the shins.

I bit back a cry of pain and grasped her hand with both of my own, struggling with her over the flask in a two-person parody of the tug-of-war. "Gillian, stop. Just talk to me for a minute."

"I haven't got a minute." Her shoulders slumped. "My dad's gonna come looking for me any second now. If he catches me here, I'm in big trouble, and it will be all your fault."

"I'll cover for you. Tell me why you came back for Ladd Foster's flask." I bent back her thumb and slipped the flask out of her fingers. "Quick, before somebody comes in here."

"Ow!" She massaged her hand, glaring at me. "You hurt me."

"Yeah, well, you kicked me hard enough to cause a bruise, so I guess we're even." I waved to my shin, where we could both see the bruise coming up. "What's in this flask?"

She folded her arms over her chest, the picture of a sullen teen. "Whiskey?"

I took a quick sniff, and nearly gagged. "It smells horrible." I held it under her nose. "Is this what it smelled like when Ladd handed the flask to you for safekeeping?"

She recoiled from the smell and fought to maintain her defiant pose. "How should I know?"

"Gillian, I saw Ladd hand you his flask before the caber toss so it wouldn't be in his way. I watched you take a sniff and make a face. Then you came in here, and when you came out again, you didn't have the flask with you. That's how I knew it was here."

"What are you, the flask police?"

I rolled my eyes. "No, I'm the teenage-girl police. I don't allow middle-aged men to prey on teenage girls. Who cares? All I want to know is, does this smell the same as it did before, or is there something in here that wasn't before?"

She stared me down for a full minute, and then she dropped her gaze. "It smells different. Nastier."

"Did you put anything in it?"

Her head snapped up again. "No! I brought it in here and put it down and came right out. I didn't want my dad to catch me with it."

I risked another sniff. I could make out the tangy smell of whiskey, but it was nearly drowned out by an overpowering smell that reminded me of gasoline—an oily, fuel kind of smell. I screwed the top back on and laid the flask down on the table.

Gillian twisted her hands together. "You think somebody put something in his flask, some kind of poison, and that's why he fell over?"

She'd put her finger on the nameless fears I was only beginning to sort out. I nodded. Before I could say anything, she lashed out at me.

"You can't pin this on me! Just because I touched it doesn't mean I poisoned it. Loads of people could have done this!"

I gripped her by the shoulders. "Gillian, I'm not the police! I'm a seamstress, okay? I'm just minding other people's business right now. But you cared about Ladd Foster, at least for a little while, so maybe you could help me figure out what happened to him."

She shook me off.

Out on the field, the announcer called out, "Our final event is the Atlas Stones. Jamie Deakens, step right up."

Gillian opened her mouth to speak when Patrick Ames walked into the tent.

I patted Gillian on the shoulder. "There. Your vest should be fine for your next dance."

She looked at me in confusion, so I went on, "It's almost three-thirty. Breanna's probably wondering where you are." I took her arm and turned her to the exit. "I'll walk along with you."

Patrick merely nodded at us as we walked out, then he turned back to the water cooler.

Gillian kept looking sideways at me as I walked her out of the tent.

"I told you I'd cover for you," I said. I led her away from the crowd.

She pulled her arm free. "Are you going to call the police?"

I nodded.

"You can't call the police! My fingerprints are on that flask. They're going to think I did it."

"Gillian, I have to call the police. If someone poisoned his whiskey, they were trying to kill him. That's something the police need to know."

She stopped and faced me. "Just leave me out of it, okay? I don't want to get in trouble. Whenever I have anything to do with the cops, they always twist things around so it looks like I'm a juvenile delinquent. They'd love to pin a poisoning on me." She looked pointedly at my blouse. "You might want to watch out yourself. You're wearing that poisoned whiskey right now. Your fingerprints aren't on the flask because you held it with a tissue. How are you going to explain that when the cops start asking you questions?"

How indeed? She had a point there. I couldn't go around wearing the blouse, which I now realized smelled awful and had a visible stain. But if I took it off and hid it, and someone found out, it would look like I had something to hide. If I confessed I had snooped in the VIP tent and spilled some of the poisoned whiskey but didn't mention Gillian's presence, I could get caught in inconsistencies later on. In the worst-case scenario, the police would think I was the poisoner. I had found myself in the position of discovering a dead body or two in my time. I inwardly cursed myself for ending up in this position through my curiosity.

McCarthy had once told me that unless there was a good reason to lie, it was always better to tell the truth. Maybe the best thing for me to do would be to go back to the VIP tent, pick up the flask so my fingerprints were on it, and then call the police and tell them the whole story. *Sorry, Gillian.*

It was only fair to warn her. "I'm going to call the police now. They'll probably want to talk to you."

She tossed her head. "I have to dance." She ducked through the crowd and disappeared.

I didn't bother going after her. I figured it wouldn't be too hard for the police to catch up with her, so I headed back toward the VIP tent. I needed to put my prints on Ladd's flask and then call the police.

The crowd around the athletic field gasped as I walked up, their eyes all fixed on Patrick Ames. He was straining to lift a huge boulder to drop onto an upended barrel. I paused for a moment to watch, thinking he should have been dressed in animal skins for this caveman event. He gave a huge grunt and dropped the boulder onto the barrel, which tipped but didn't overturn. The crowd roared.

Someone prodded my shoulder from behind. I turned to see Letty standing with her hands on her hips. "Can't keep your eyes off the hunks, can you? Is anyone minding the booth?"

I let a look of embarrassment show on my face. "You caught me. I'll get right back to the booth, Letty. I promise."

She laughed. "I can't blame you. That blond one could pass for a god in my book." She waved an arm at my blouse. "You should do something about your shirt, there. What did you do, spill some coffee on it or something? Coffee will stain like anything, you know."

"I know. I'd better go change." I hastened off before she could say anything else. I dodged through the crowd so she wouldn't see where I was going and made for the VIP tent. I slipped inside to grab Ladd's flask.

It was gone.

Chapter 4

I stared at the table in disbelief. I scanned the entire tent, but the flask was nowhere to be seen. Just a few minutes ago, evidence of a poisoning lay in plain sight, and now it was gone. Someone had taken it. It could have been someone trying to be helpful, dropping it off at the lost-and-found or something. Or it could have been an attempted murderer, come back to remove traces of his crime. That thought chilled me to the bone.

The tent was empty. I stood at a loss, not sure what to do next. I had planned to call the police and tell them that Ladd's flask had been tampered with, but I could no longer do that. As Gillian had pointed out, I was wearing traces of the poison on my blouse. Now, with the flask missing, that might be the only clue as to the nature of the poison. Unless…maybe the poison was still here, in the VIP tent, waiting for someone to discover it. A nosy someone…

I threw a glance over my shoulder and started searching the tent. There was a small folding table that held a water cooler and piles of paper cups, with a full trash can by its side. I considered the possibility that Ladd's flask was in the trash and resolved to check through it once I'd finished my search. The podium Hart had used was pushed into a corner. There were two long folding tables set up in the middle of the tent, with piles of rosters and other papers next to a first aid kit and a variety of ribbons and trophies. Numerous cardboard boxes and plastic totes were stashed underneath.

With another glance over my shoulder, I knelt down and checked out the boxes, which all appeared to be filled with copies of *Over the Sea to Skye*. No flask there. I pulled out the first plastic tote, using my skirt to touch its plastic side. I slipped off the top and peered inside. The tote contained a conglomeration of clips, ropes, plastic flowers and greenery, and triangular pieces of nylon in all colors. The second tote was empty except for a scattering of sticky notes in the bottom, and the third one held several bottles of torch fuel. I remembered the torches stuck in the ground surrounding the athletic field, waiting for darkness, when they would be illuminated. I closed my eyes for an instant and then pulled out a tissue from my shoulder bag and began picking up the bottles, hefting them to find out if one had been previously opened.

Three bottles were unopened, but the fourth felt lighter, and the seal around the neck was broken. My heart beat faster as I unscrewed the top and brought the bottle up to my nose for a sniff. I gagged on the overpowering smell of fuel. It was the same smell I had picked up in Ladd's whiskey. My hands shook slightly as I screwed the top back on. I'd found my poison.

I jumped as my phone dinged. I slipped the bottle back into the tote, which I pushed back under the table. I checked my phone, to see a text from McCarthy. It read: "Bad news. Ladd Foster died at the hospital. Call me."

I heaved a sigh, trying to release the tension building up inside me. I had one more thing to check before I could leave the VIP tent. Wishing desperately for plastic gloves, I tipped out the trash can on the ground and sifted through the mess, looking for Ladd's flask. It wasn't there.

I shoveled the trash back into the trash can and pushed it into its spot by the water cooler. I checked around to be sure I'd left everything the way I found it and then snuck out of the tent and sought a relatively private spot behind the bank of portable toilets. The rank smell kept people from hanging out back there. I called McCarthy, but his phone went to voice mail.

I tucked my phone back into my shoulder bag and set off in search of a lost-and-found, on the off chance that someone had simply tidied up the tent with no malicious intent.

I wandered around the park for the next few minutes until I finally found someone at the admissions table to pull out a cardboard box for me to look in. There were a variety of items, including a couple of water bottles, a well-worn teddy bear, and even one of my tartan bow ties, but no flask. I thanked the woman and turned away.

The police had arrived.

Two police cars drove into the parking lot and four officers stepped out. My stomach sank as I watched them stride up to the admissions table and speak to the woman who had helped me. I dreaded what the next few minutes could hold for me. I could either become a star witness in a crime or the main suspect, through no fault of my own other than my unfortunate habit of sticking my nose into other people's business.

I squared my shoulders. *Might as well get it over with.* I'd rather talk to them here than disrupt the business at my booth under Letty's watchful eye. I walked up to the officers.

"I'm Daria Dembrowski. You're looking into Ladd Foster's death, right?" Two officers stopped, while the other two continued into the park. I had met one of them before, Maureen Franklin, a brisk young officer with dark hair and snapping black eyes that missed nothing. She frowned at me. "News travels fast." She pulled out a notebook and jotted down my name. "How did you know he'd died?"

"Sean McCarthy texted me. He's a friend of mine. He was at the hospital with Ladd." I gulped and went on. "I have some information for you. Ladd's flask of whiskey was poisoned."

Officer Franklin and her partner, a weary-looking man whose name tag identified him as Butler, both stared at me.

I took a deep breath. "I had my eye on Ladd's flask because he had given it to a teenage girl and I didn't want her to take a drink." I told them how the flask had ended up in the VIP tent and how I'd discovered it after Ladd collapsed. "Gillian came in and grabbed the flask and some of the whiskey got spilled on me." I indicated the stain on my blouse. "It smelled terrible, kind of like gasoline or something." The two officers exchanged a glance, and then Officer Franklin leaned in and sniffed at my blouse. If she came to any conclusions from the smell alone, she didn't let on. I bit my tongue, resolving not to mention the torch fuel, because the officers would surely find it when they searched the VIP tent. I didn't want to display too much knowledge about the crime for fear of standing out as the prime suspect.

"Do you have the flask now?" Officer Franklin asked.

"No, we left it in the tent when someone else came in, and when I went back it was gone."

"Who else came in?"

I thought back. "Patrick Ames, one of the other athletes. He was getting a drink of water."

Officer Franklin noted that down. "Come show us this VIP tent."

"Okay." I hesitated. "I've got a booth here, along with a friend. Can I let her know I'll be a while?"

She nodded, and I texted Letty: "I'm talking with police about Ladd. Don't know when I'll get back to booth." I pressed Send and looked up to see both officers looking at my phone screen. I quickly switched it off, wondering if they had learned anything from my previous exchanges with Letty.

I led the officers to the tent and showed them where I had first seen the flask, where I had been standing when Gillian and I struggled over control of it, and where we had placed it on the table when we left the tent. Officer Butler searched the ground but didn't find any trace of either poison or whiskey there. All the spilled liquid had ended up on me.

Officer Franklin poked around the tent and then started pulling the boxes and totes out from under the table. I watched her, willing her to notice the torch fuel and spare me from having to confess I'd snooped there as well.

"Butler, take a look at this." Officer Franklin picked up one of the bottles and held it out to her partner. I closed my eyes in relief and then popped them open again in case either of them was watching me. Lucky for me, they were both bending over the bottle, smelling the torch fuel.

Officer Franklin poured a bit of the fuel into a paper cup and held it out to me. "Is this what you smelled in Foster's flask?"

I took a whiff of the amber liquid, which looked a lot like whiskey, or even apple juice. I nodded. "I think so. It wasn't exactly like this, though."

Officer Franklin sniffed at my blouse again and compared it to the cup in her hand. "I can smell whiskey on you as well. Whoever did this added torch fuel to the existing whiskey." She set the cup down on the table to make a few notes in her notebook. "We're going to need your blouse for evidence. Do you have something else you can wear?"

"I can probably find something at my booth."

"I'll come with you." Officer Franklin started to usher me out of the tent when one of the little Highland dancers, no more than seven years old, entered the tent. She gave me a shy smile, walked over to the table, and picked up the cup of torch fuel. She raised it to her lips.

"Stop!" I yelled. "Don't drink that!"

Officer Franklin spun around, calling out as well. But the two of us were across the tent, too far away to reach her in time.

Officer Butler moved with a speed I wouldn't have guessed he could achieve. He snatched the cup out of the child's hand and held it out of reach. "That's not apple juice," he gasped. "It's yucky."

The little girl gaped at him, looking like she might burst into tears. I pushed my way past Officer Franklin and poured a cup of water for the child. "It's okay, honey. We just had some fuel for the big torches in that cup. We didn't want you to drink it." I handed her the water. "Did you just finish your dance?"

She nodded, her wide eyes flitting from one officer to the other. She didn't resist when I turned her toward the entrance. "Miss Breanna is probably wondering where you went." I propelled her out of the tent.

Officer Butler still held the cup aloft, his face returning to its customary ruddy complexion. Officer Franklin took it out of his fingers and poured its contents back into the torch fuel bottle. Her fingers shook the tiniest bit as she crumpled up the cup and shoved it down into the trash. "That was on me," she said. "I never should have left it sitting out on the table like that. Good save, Butler."

He dusted his hands on his thighs. "I've got three grandkids at home who get into everything. I've learned to be quick."

Officer Franklin turned back to me with a return of her brisk manner. "Let's get you something to wear."

People stared at me walking back to my booth escorted by a police officer. I noticed one man taking a picture and groaned inwardly. I hoped I wouldn't end up on social media as the presumed poisoner. That would be almost as bad as actually getting arrested for the crime.

Letty was back at the booth when we arrived. She took the sight of the police officer in stride. While she refrained from attempting to sell Officer Franklin a piece of antique jewelry, she didn't flinch when I asked her if she had a blouse I could borrow. She looked me over and then pulled out a couple of checkered blouses that looked like they came from the 1940s. Both clashed with my skirt, but I knew Officer Franklin wasn't concerned with any fashion statement I might make. I chose the green one. "I'll take this over to the toilet and change real quick," I said.

Officer Franklin picked up the blanket I'd used to cover the merchandise and stretched it out with both hands for a screen. "Just slip that off right here and I'll be on my way."

I complied, realizing I had no other choice. *Did she think I was going to run off with the incriminating evidence after all that?* I buttoned myself up and handed her the soiled blouse. "I guess I don't need that back. There's probably no way to get that stain out."

She snagged one of our plastic bags to put the blouse in. "I'll be in touch if we have any further questions."

Letty watched her stride away and then turned to pepper me with questions.

"What did the cops ask you? Do they think Ladd was the victim of foul play? Did you tell them how he was flirting with that fifteen-year-old dancer?"

I waited until she paused for a breath and then said, "Ladd died at the hospital. His whiskey flask was poisoned."

She stared at me in silence for a full minute, which must have been a record for her. The silence was interrupted by the sound of my phone ringing. I snatched it up. It was McCarthy.

"Sorry I didn't answer before," he said. "The police were questioning me about Ladd Foster's collapse. He died shortly after he arrived here. It was cardiac arrest caused by pulmonary injury, not by exertion. He never regained consciousness. The ER doc thinks he drank something that got into his lungs."

"It was torch oil, in his flask." I could hear McCarthy draw in his breath sharply. I told him about how I'd checked out Ladd's flask and about its subsequent disappearance.

He let out a low whistle. "Kudos to the nosy seamstress for investigating a crime that hadn't even been identified as a crime yet. Where did the flask go?"

I groaned. "I don't know. I checked the lost-and-found, but it wasn't there. I'm guessing the murderer snuck back in to remove the evidence. Which means he's still hanging around the Games." I glanced over my shoulder, but no murderer lurked behind the booth. "Did you learn anything from the police?"

"The cops were asking questions, not offering information. They spent a good half hour interviewing Sterling and me as eyewitnesses, even though Sterling was miles away mowing his grass when Ladd collapsed. What about you? Did the police finger you as the number one suspect?"

"Ha, ha, very funny."

I heard a car honking in the background, and McCarthy swore under his breath.

"What was that? Are you driving right now?"

"Yeah. I'm on my way back to the Games."

"I'm hanging up! Come to my booth when you get here." I disconnected before he could reply. I tried never to talk to people when they were driving. I didn't want to hear a car crash and know it was all my fault for distracting the driver.

I generally considered myself a strong, independent woman, except for that one area of my life where I was hampered by an illogical fear that I could not overcome: I had a phobia about driving. I had learned how to drive enough to get my license when I was a teenager, but every time I got behind the wheel, my heart would race and my hands would start to shake until I was virtually paralyzed by fear. I would feel completely out of control, which isn't the way a responsible driver should feel. I didn't own a car and never drove if I didn't have to. I resolved that one of these days

I would seek treatment for my phobia, but in the meantime, both Aileen and my brother Pete helped me out with rides as a condition of living in my house. I figured we all came out on top in the end.

"Was that your photographer friend?"

I realized Letty had been listening to our entire conversation and now knew as much about Ladd's death as McCarthy and I combined. Talk about nosy!

We didn't get a chance to hash over the details, however. The loudspeaker announced the end of the musical competitions and athletic events and highlighted the closing of the Scottish Marketplace in time for the awards ceremony in the next half hour. Hordes of pipers, dancers, and spectators flocked to browse through the booths one last time. Letty and I had our hands full.

McCarthy stopped by while I was waiting on a woman who wanted to order a child's dress. He stood grinning behind her as she thrust a page torn out of a fashion magazine into my hands. "I want you to make a dress for my daughter Pearl. She's got her very first piano recital next Saturday. She's doing a Celtic piece, so I want her to wear a tartan dress. Like this."

It was a picture of a curvy model wearing an off-the-shoulder gown with an enormous bow to one side of the tightly fitting skirt. Nothing about the gown was age-appropriate for a child.

The best part about being my own boss was that I could turn down any project I didn't want to undertake. I summoned up my best smile, trying to ignore McCarthy's facial contortions behind the woman. "I'm sorry, I wouldn't have enough time to complete the dress in one week." I handed the picture back to her with as sincere a look of apology as I could muster. "I'm sure you can find a lovely dress for Pearl in one of the shops on the Commons."

The woman grumbled, "I would have expected better customer service here!" and turned away, almost bumping into McCarthy as she stormed off.

"Customer service is dead," McCarthy droned.

I rolled my eyes and turned to a group of young girls sifting through my bow ties one more time. "Sean, I can't talk right now. Letty and I need to pack everything up here."

Letty leaned her elbows on the front table and batted her eyelashes at McCarthy. "Everything is half off for the next fifteen minutes. See anything here you can't live without?"

He laughed. "Maybe one thing, but it'll have to wait for now."

As he turned to go, Letty called after him, "What is it? I can hold it for you!"

Chapter 5

I sold more in the next fifteen minutes than I had all afternoon. At the end, I had seven stuffed Nessies left over, a pile of table linens, and one lone bow tie in the Oliphant tartan. I clipped it into my hair and piled the rest of the stuff into boxes. At the stroke of five, Pete arrived to pick me up.

People would often tell me that Pete and I could be twins, but I didn't think so. For one thing, he was two years older than me, and for another, he was six feet tall. I liked to say I was tall for my size at five-foot-three. Sure, we had the same thick brown hair, which he wore long over his ears and I wore down to the middle of my back. We also had the same nose, until he broke his when he got into trouble in Hollywood.

"Hey, Daria. What's going on? There were a bunch of cops at the entrance when I got here. They took down my name before they would even let me in. I had to resist the overwhelming urge to blurt out, 'I didn't do anything!'"

I chuckled and handed him a box. Poor Pete! He'd paid his debt to society for doing drugs, but he sometimes felt like the police were keeping an eye on him.

"One of the athletes collapsed and later died at the hospital. It turns out he was poisoned." I filled him in on the details as we loaded my boxes into his truck. "They probably just want your name so they know you weren't here when it happened."

"So, this guy was murdered, then? What is it with this town lately? Seems like there's nothing but murders anymore."

I shook my head. I loved Laurel Springs with all my heart, but I had to agree. Even one or two murders were shocking in our serene little town.

This latest one seemed especially personal because the victim had collapsed in front of half the town.

Pete tossed the last box into his truck. "What's up with Aileen?"

I followed his gaze to see Aileen surrounded by police officers. "She had an altercation with Ladd before the athletic events. Oh, dear, I hope the cops don't think she poisoned him." I hurried across the lot to Aileen, with Pete close behind me.

Aileen glared at the police officers surrounding her. With her nearly six-foot height augmented by six-inch boot heels, she towered over more than half of them. No police officer was about to intimidate Aileen!

"I'm going to ask you one more time," a large officer with black stubble covering his head said. "What is your relationship to Ladd Foster?"

Another officer cut in before Aileen could speak, if she was even going to. "You were seen threatening Mr. Foster with your instrument. Numerous eyewitnesses claim you appeared to know him. What was the nature of your relationship?"

"I knew him a long time ago," Aileen growled. "I've got no use for him." She folded her arms on her chest. "Are we done here?"

The large officer glared right back at her. "Are you aware that the victim has died? We're investigating a suspected murder here. I would advise you to cooperate with our questions."

Aileen couldn't hide the flicker of surprise in her eyes at his words. I glanced at Pete, to see that he had his phone out and was filming this entire exchange.

"What are you doing?" I whispered to him.

"I'm acting as a witness," he said in a loud voice, drawing the attention of a couple of the officers. "I'm making a video record, in case things get out of hand."

"What, police brutality?" I whispered back, aghast. "This is Laurel Springs, not Chicago or New York!"

"Relax," the large officer said to Pete and me in a calmer tone than he'd yet used. He surveyed the growing crowd of onlookers. "Nothing is going to happen here." He turned back to Aileen. "You can give a statement now or you can come down to the station with us for formal questioning." He forced a shrug, as if he really didn't care. "Your choice, now."

"Fine," Aileen shot back at him. "I'll talk to you at the station. But I have a gig here first, so you'll have to wait." She hefted her guitar case and turned aside to find her way blocked by yet another police officer.

"We'd like you to come with us now," the officer said, his hands hovering perilously close to his firearm.

Aileen bared her teeth like a wild animal about to spring. She started to swing her guitar case forward.

Pete shoved his phone into my hands and barged into the circle of cops holding Aileen at bay. He laid a hand on her arm, halting the upward motion of her guitar case. "I'll come with you, Aileen."

"Stay out of this, Moron," she snapped at him. "This has nothing to do with you."

He wrapped his hand around hers, gripping the guitar case handle. "You know how much I love a good chat down at the police station." His light tone couldn't mask the anxiety in his voice.

She locked eyes with him for a full minute while the crowd of police officers and onlookers all held their breath. Finally, she rolled her eyes with an exasperated grunt. "Fine!" She glared at the police. "I'll 'come quietly.' Satisfied?" She pushed Pete on the chest. "You don't have to come, Moron."

"No. But I want to." He held out his hand, and I pressed his phone into it with shaking fingers. He kept his other hand twined around Aileen's.

"Tell Corgi and Pinker they might have to go on without me," Aileen called out to me. "Frigging overbearing cops," she muttered under her breath. She suffered herself to be led off by the police officers, her right hand still covered by Pete's.

I heaved a sigh of relief and turned to find McCarthy and his camera standing next to me. Apparently, he was acting as a witness as well.

"You gotta hand it to Pete, being willing to confront the beast like that," he said.

"Or maybe he's just living up to Aileen's nickname for him."

He chuckled. "What, 'Moron?' Better him than me, that's all I can say. I thought she was going to take a swing at that cop and we'd all have to pile in to hold her back."

I shot him a sharp glance. He looked like he meant it. Good old McCarthy!

"Well, that danger is averted for the moment," I said. "This isn't going to end up on the front page of the *Chronicle*, is it?"

McCarthy held out his camera to me while rapidly scrolling through the photos. "I've taken hundreds of pictures of this entire event. I'm guessing one or two of them is more likely than Aileen to end up on the front page." He paused on one of Letty and me posing in our booth. "This one, perhaps?"

I laughed and pushed the camera away. "Looks like it's time for the awards ceremony."

I found a spot on the edge of the crowd where I had a good view of the podium. McCarthy prowled throughout the crowd, taking more photos.

The announcer, Herman Tisdale, held a clipboard stacked up with a thick sheaf of papers in one hand and a microphone in the other. He looked like the strain of the day was starting to get to him. His dark green kilt had shifted to sag below his belly, and his Glengarry cap was slightly askew, giving him an overall look of disarray more than distinction. But the crowd was silent, with the pipers, dancers, and athletes anxiously awaiting their results.

"We'll begin with the primary dancers for their rendition of the pas de basques and highcuts." Tisdale began droning off the names of young dancers, who squealed in delight or hid their faces in their mothers' skirts. He began to talk about turnout and elevation as he announced the results of the older girls' dances. I could see we were in for the long haul here. I wandered through the crowd until I saw Corgi lounging on the outskirts, taking a quick nip from his flask. He'd returned to his proper Highland attire, and his bloodshot eyes indicated that he'd had more than one or two goes at the flask.

"Still here until the bitter end, are we?" he said.

I nodded, wondering if he had witnessed Aileen being taken off by the cops. "I hope it's not a bitter end for you, Corgi."

He shrugged. "I'm not getting any awards today. I made a few mistakes in my music, so I got graded down on that. But the judges came down really hard on my appearance. They almost didn't let me compete at all because I didn't have the right kind of shoes." He stuck out his foot, clad with a perfectly ordinary black dress shoe. "You're supposed to wear those ghillie brogues that lace up your ankles. I'd look like a fool wearing shoes like that around town." He plucked at his kilt. "Then they said my kilt was a cheap knockoff and if I wanted to take myself seriously in the piping world I needed to get a real kilt. They handed out brochures for custom-made kilts from Scotland." He pulled a crumpled-up brochure out of his sporran and handed it to me. "Great idea, but they take six-to-ten weeks to arrive. My next competition is in two weeks. Where am I going to get a quality kilt in that amount of time?"

I scanned the brochure, which touted hundreds of tartans for their custom-made kilts. The design looked pretty straightforward, and I liked to think I was always up for a challenge. How hard could it be to sew a kilt?

I handed back the brochure and followed it up with one of my business cards. "I'll bet you could get a custom-made kilt in Laurel Springs if you knew where to look."

He read the card and raised his eyes to mine. "Seriously? You make kilts?"

I nodded. "It's a new sideline for me. You could be my very first kilt customer."

He laughed and offered me his flask, which I politely declined. "Could you get it done in two weeks?"

"I'll have to order the fabric. There's no one in Philly who sells authentic tartan wool for kilts. But if I can get next day shipping, I'm sure I can get the kilt finished in time for your next competition." I pulled out my phone and called up a Scottish goods website. "Want to go for it?"

He took another swig from his flask and bent over my phone. "Right now?"

"Clock's ticking." I started scrolling through different tartans. "What clan do you want to represent?"

"You can't just choose a clan. You have to be related somehow, or else you're stuck with the tartans that don't belong to a particular clan. But my grandmother's maiden name was Guthrie. My claim to fame is that she was distantly related to Woody Guthrie." He grinned at me. "That's why I started out my musical career on the harmonica when I was five years old. I sometimes wonder what Woody would think of the Twisted Armpits. Anyway, I get the Guthrie tartan."

He indicated his lightweight kilt, which was a blue and green plaid on a field of black, shot through with reddish orange stripes. "This really is the Ancient Guthrie tartan, even if it's made of polyester instead of bona fide Scottish wool."

I scrutinized his kilt. "That's not straight polyester. It's probably a lightweight wool/polyester blend that's kind of loosely woven, so it has a tendency to sag. I'll look for a good quality wool that will hold its shape."

I pulled up the Ancient Guthrie tartan and was about to place the order when I realized I needed to do a little more research on kilt construction before I could go forward. I looked up at Corgi. "Are you committed to this? I'll need to figure out how much fabric I need, and then I can get back to you with an estimate."

"Yeah, I'm all in. Whatever it takes to get me suited up for the Ligonier Highland Games in two weeks."

As he took another swig from his flask, it occurred to me that I should review his order when he was completely sober. Custom-made clothing could be a considerable investment for me if a customer backed out of a project without paying the full amount. I pocketed my phone. "I'll work up an estimate and get back to you tomorrow morning, and you can say, 'go or no go' at that time. Okay?"

"Sounds good. I'll be at the Catholic church tomorrow afternoon working on the haggis for the ceilidh in the evening. You can catch me there."

He turned his attention back to Herman Tisdale, who was detailing the awards for the athletic events. As predicted, Patrick Ames came in first place overall, with Jamie Deakens running a close second and Tom O'Flaherty coming in a respectable third. Tisdale made no mention of Ladd Foster's participation in the event.

Pinker jostled my arm and rapped Corgi on the shoulder. "We gotta set up, dude. We go on in half an hour. Where's Aileen?"

Corgi looked around, as if he'd just that moment misplaced her.

I hated to be the one to have to tell them. "Aileen went down to the police station to talk to the cops about Ladd Foster. She said to tell you that you might have to go on without her."

Pinker swore loudly. It was a good thing Aileen didn't hear what he said about her or she might not have gone on even if she were available.

Corgi blinked at me. "Did they arrest her? I can't picture her going to the police station any other way."

"Not exactly, but it was a close thing. Pete went along to make sure everyone behaves."

Pinker snorted, a habit he'd evidently picked up from Aileen. "More power to him. She's not going to hear the end of this in a hurry. I just hope nobody notices she's gone—that'll learn her!" He stalked off.

"Is there anything I can do to help?" I was pretty sure the answer was no, but it seemed like the right thing to say.

"You don't play lead guitar, by any chance?"

I had to laugh at the wistful note in Corgi's voice, even as I dashed his hopes. "Maybe one of the other guys can pick it up."

The other two band members, Raldo and Tim, looked dismayed when Corgi explained they'd have to go on without Aileen. I left them fussing among their gear, trying to figure out what songs to play without their lead guitar and vocalist.

I wandered back to the awards ceremony in time to catch the final announcement about the Twisted Armpits wrapping up the event. Herman Tisdale looked exhausted, as if the last thing he wanted was to hang around listening to a metal band, even if it did have a bagpipe in it.

The Twisted Armpits kicked in just as the crowd started to break up. The band appeared to be compensating for the lack of Aileen by cranking up the volume to astronomical levels. Half of the people in the crowd whooped and stampeded to the bandstand, and the other half threw their hands over their ears and ran for the exit. I slipped off to the edge of the crowd, undecided as to which group to join. That's when I realized that Pete hadn't yet returned from the police station. He was my ride home, with all my wares tucked into his truck. I was pretty tired from a day on my feet, compounded by the strain of a murder. I didn't know if I had the energy for a dance party with the Twisted Armpits, but the alternative was a long wait for the bus, which might require more patience than I could summon up at the moment. I closed my eyes and took a deep, cleansing breath, trying to decide which would win out, energy or patience.

I was still contemplating when I heard the click of a camera. "Looks like you've mastered the art of sleeping standing up."

My eyes flew open to catch McCarthy in the act of taking a picture of me. "That one won't be on the front page of the newspaper either, right?" I said.

He squinted at the image on his camera screen. "I can see the caption now, 'Peace in the eye of the storm,' or maybe 'Scottish Sleeping Beauty.'"

I laughed. "More like, 'Too tired to dance with the metalheads.'"

"Is that a hint? I was just coming to see if you were waiting for someone to ask you to dance." He waved an arm at the small crowd gyrating in front of the bandstand.

I loved dancing with McCarthy, who threw himself into the activity with such gusto that he always made me feel like I could fly. But right now I felt more like flopping than flying. "Maybe we should save this dance for the ceilidh tomorrow night."

McCarthy nodded, his attention focused on the band. "Aileen hasn't come back from the police station yet?"

"Nope." I found myself twisting my hands in my skirt and smoothed the flowing fabric quickly. "I hope they don't pick her as their prime suspect."

"God help them if they do." He tore his eyes away from the band. "Does that mean you're stranded?"

"Yeah. I was going to go home with Pete, but he hasn't come back yet either. I'm taking that as a good sign—if anyone can keep the lid on Aileen, it's Pete." I leaned over and knocked on a wooden fence post beside me. "Knock on wood."

McCarthy snapped a few pictures of the Twisted Armpits, who were clearly struggling without the guiding influence of Aileen. Another good reason to pass on the dancing.

"Want me to spin you home, then?" he said. "I've got all the photos I need."

"Yes, please." I flung my bag over one shoulder and followed him to the exit. We ran into a slight delay as several police officers checked out each person who was leaving the park. They took our names and consulted a list they were compiling of everyone who had been at the event. Luckily, both McCarthy and I had been questioned already, so we were free to leave.

We hopped into McCarthy's bright yellow Mustang and he peeled out of the parking lot. I double-checked my seat belt and leaned my head back on the headrest. "It's been a long day."

"Murder to the tune of bagpipes, with a chest of tartan bow ties on the side." He straightened the yellow bow tie he still wore. "I made it through the entire day with this one." He flung an arm over the seat to rummage in the backseat. He pulled out a white paper bag and handed it to me. "I got you that signed copy of *Over the Sea to Skye*, like I said I would. If you're really tired, don't start it tonight. It'll keep you up to the wee hours."

"Thanks." I pulled the book out of the bag and flipped it open to admire the autograph on the title page. Morris Hart had signed his name with a flourish worthy of the bestselling author he was. "I know I won't be able to sleep until Pete and Aileen get home. This will be just the thing to pass the time."

McCarthy dropped me off at the curb with a kiss and a cheery wave goodbye. He waited until I walked up the porch steps and unlocked the door before zooming off down the street. I watched his Mustang disappear around the corner and then went inside and locked the door behind me.

My house seemed so quiet after the persistent noise of the skirling bagpipes and blaring guitars I'd been hearing all day. I dropped onto the window bench beside the front door and soaked in the peaceful silence. The high-ceilinged rooms of my nineteenth-century house exuded a bit of the grace and charm of a bygone era. I tried to encourage that illusion with the comfortable furnishings in the more public areas of the first floor, with an antique dresser here or a working spinning wheel there. A classy silhouette of my muse, Betsy Ross, hung on the wall in my fitting room, which would have been the formal dining room if Pete, Aileen, and I had felt the need for such an extravagance. For the three of us, the stenciled white table in the homey kitchen was all we needed.

My orange cat, Mohair, pulled me out of my reverie with her plaintive meows. She stropped against my ankles to convince me that I had abandoned her for all time, instead of just the one day. I scooped her up and carried her into the kitchen, where I filled her bowls and then settled down with some peanut butter crackers and orange slices for a light supper. Too tired to think about either sewing or murder, I put all thoughts of Aileen out of my head, pulled out my new autographed thriller, and started in on page one.

I was soon immersed in the palace intrigue that filled the opening pages of *Over the Sea to Skye*. The novel opened with a dramatization of the true events surrounding the overthrow of James II of England, aka James VII of Scotland, who was deposed in the Glorious Revolution of 1688 and fled to France. His grandson, Charles Edward Stuart, better known as Bonnie Prince Charlie, gathered the Scottish clans in the Jacobite Rising of 1745 and challenged King George II of Great Britain for the throne. I had just gotten to their crushing defeat at the Battle of Culloden, which dashed Bonnie Prince Charlie's chances of restoring the Stuart line to the throne, when I heard the front door closing.

It was Pete. He was alone. He dragged into the kitchen and dropped into a chair at the table. He ran both hands through his long brown hair and then looked at me. "They're holding Aileen at the jail. I tried to post bail, but they wouldn't let me."

I filled a glass at the sink and plunked it down on the table in front of him. "What are they holding her for? You stopped her from swinging her guitar at the cops. She went quietly in the end."

He sighed and reached for the glass of water. "Yeah, she went quietly, all right. She completely clammed up at the station when they started asking about her relationship with Ladd. Wouldn't say a single word. When the officer told her she'd be arrested if she didn't start talking, she started quoting Ecclesiastes: 'For everything there is a season.' Who would have guessed that she knew the whole passage? I would have busted out laughing if it weren't for the seriousness of the issue. After fifteen minutes or so of '...a time to keep silence, and a time to speak,' the officer got fed up and told her she was being detained on suspicion of murder."

I sat down next to him at the table. "What's gotten into her?"

"I dunno, she feels like her privacy is being violated or something? She's choosing to go to jail rather than talk about this Ladd Foster dude. What's up with that?"

What indeed? I filled Pete in on Aileen's reaction to seeing Ladd at the Highland Games. "She obviously has some history with him. I thought she was going to kill him with her bare hands when he was playing her guitar."

"Well, anyone fool enough to touch Aileen's gear without permission deserves what he's got coming to him." The short-lived grin faded from his face. "You don't think she really did kill him, do you?"

I didn't even want to go there. "What do the police think? That's what matters."

Pete got up to place his glass in the sink. He turned back to face me. "Since when does the opinion of the Laurel Springs Police Department make the slightest bit of difference to you? If you think she's innocent, you'll move heaven and earth in your quest for proof. Right?"

I could have laughed at the plaintive note in his final word, but this wasn't a laughing matter. Pete obviously wanted Aileen to be proven innocent, and he was counting on me to do it. I hoped I could live up to his faith in me.

Chapter 6

I woke up the next morning with my mind filled with the confusing images of a murdered caber tosser mixed up with the grandson of a deposed king raising an army to fight to regain the throne he himself had never held. McCarthy was right; I shouldn't have started reading *Over the Sea to Skye* if I didn't want to be up all night. But Hart's prose was so riveting, I couldn't stop until I'd finished the section on historical background in the novel.

I refrained from diving into the contemporary part that opened with the introduction of Stu Rohan, an architect in Eastern Pennsylvania. I couldn't spend my day curled up with the hottest thriller of the summer. In addition to establishing the innocence of my housemate, I had a kilt to construct.

I settled down with a cup of tea and my computer to research Scottish kilts. All I really knew was that they had to be constructed a certain way for the plaid pattern of the tartan to come out right across the pleats in the back of the kilt. For the next half hour, I took note of the difference between casual and formal kilts and considered the merits of a five-yard versus an eight-yard kilt. I decided Corgi wanted to look professional, so I opted to go with a heavyweight eight-yard kilt. I could only find sketchy instructions online to describe making the kilt, so I just had to guess that I would be buying four yards of sixty-inch-wide tartan fabric and cutting it lengthwise to come up with the requisite eight yards. Then I would need cotton duck cloth to make the lining, and some leather strips for the straps. I could get those items locally, but I would need to order the tartan fabric. I worked up an estimate for Corgi and then called him to arrange a meeting to get his measurements. Unfortunately, I woke him up. I would have guessed that ten o'clock on a Sunday morning was fair game, but evidently not. Like Aileen, he tended to sleep until all hours. He mumbled the suggestion that I meet him at the Catholic church at one-thirty, where he would be making the haggis for the ceilidh later in the evening.

I chafed at the delay, because I wanted to get the tartan fabric ordered as soon as possible. Corgi was the one who wanted me to make the kilt on a tight timeline. He must think of me as a miracle worker or something.

I thumbed through my planner, wondering how to best use my time this morning. I was too late to go to church. I didn't always make it to Sunday services at First Presbyterian Church, even if it was only a few blocks away from my downtown neighborhood. I was more of a casual believer than a committed convert. If I had realized Corgi wouldn't be available until afternoon, I might have made an extra effort to go to church, if for no other reason than to keep tabs on Gillian and her father. He fell into the "committed" category, so I knew they would be in worship.

Pete was out, off to work on the set of *Amish Christmas*, a movie filming outside of town. Movie producers didn't have any qualms about working on a Sunday. They were keeping him busy in his job as camera operator.

I saw a note in my planner about Breanna's next fitting tomorrow. Her Scottish-themed wedding was coming up in a week and a half. I had her gown mostly finished and ready for a full fitting. She and I had designed a simple, long-sleeved satin gown with a low, off-the-shoulder neckline and a fitted princess-seamed bodice that flared out to a sweeping skirt with a full-length train. Instead of lace or beading, she had chosen a tartan sash to wear over the shoulder, along with a lovely headpiece comprised of tiny tartan bows and a stunning sprig of heather. She dearly desired her groom to wear a dress kilt with an appropriate evening jacket, but to date she hadn't gotten him to agree. I had suggested I could make him a tartan cummerbund and bow tie to match her sash, but she hadn't given me the go-ahead for that yet. She was still holding out hope for the full Highland dress. I hoped she didn't think I was going to make her fiancé a kilt at the last minute! I had my hands full to bursting with Corgi's kilt.

I decided to use my time to fringe Breanna's sash. Rather than a tidy hem around the edges and along the ends, she wanted a raveled edge a good inch deep. This involved pulling out thread after thread of the woven cloth all along the three-yard length of the sash. It was a mindless task, although I did have to keep an eye on the pattern so I didn't destroy the sett, or sequence of threads making up the tartan, by pulling out too many threads. Still, it gave me ample time to think.

Unfortunately, the only thing I could think about was Ladd Foster's spectacular collapse. Honestly, it was a wonder that no one else had gotten hurt. I shuddered at the thought of that mammoth caber swinging through the air. It could have landed on an innocent spectator, even a small child. I wondered if the murderer had thought of that possibility, or if he even cared.

So, what did I know about this murderer? If I assumed it wasn't Aileen, I needed to consider who else might have wanted Ladd dead. I supposed I was making a big assumption about Aileen's innocence. She did have an altercation with Ladd that could have turned ugly at the drop of a guitar pick. I even thought she looked enraged enough to kill him. Did she in fact do that sometime later, by slipping torch fuel into his flask of whiskey? It was hard to imagine. I could far more easily picture her slamming her guitar over his head.

I pushed aside that disturbing image and concentrated on my fringe. Breanna would look lovely on her wedding day. She'd asked her Highland dancers to perform a lilt during the service. Privately, I questioned the wisdom of this idea. The lilt was such a lovely dance and the Highland dancers were so adorable, they posed the very real risk of outshining the bride. I knew Breanna was looking for the perfect wedding of her dreams, and I hoped she wouldn't feel upstaged by her students.

I thought about Gillian, the oldest of the Highland dancers. Could she have been the one who poured that torch fuel into Ladd's flask? Even though she'd had it in her possession, I didn't think she was a viable suspect. She had seemed genuinely upset about his death, and she didn't seem to know about the poison when the two of us had struggled over the flask.

Maybe I should focus on the flask itself. Gillian had left it on a table in the VIP tent, where it sat until Ladd went in and took a swig. He'd left it there on his way out of the tent, and it stayed there until Gillian and I found it and then subsequently left it when Patrick Ames came in. After that, it disappeared.

Gillian had said the whiskey smelled different from the time when she'd sniffed it right after Ladd handed her the flask to the moment when she and I smelled it after he collapsed. I think it was fair to surmise that the torch fuel was added to the whiskey between the time that Gillian stashed the flask and the time when Ladd went in to take a drink.

So who had been in the VIP tent during that time? I thought back to the field events yesterday. I had been standing with Corgi, watching the four massive men take their turns at the various events. We had both been surprised by Aileen's reaction to seeing Ladd. She had gone into the VIP tent to hide—and bumped into Ryan King on his way out. So both Aileen and Ryan had had access to the flask. Then Patrick Ames had missed Ladd's perfect toss because he was in the VIP tent at the time. He had also come in and interrupted Gillian and me when we were trying to make sense of the smelly flask. We had skedaddled, and when I went back the flask was gone. Patrick was the most logical person to have taken it. I resolved to look closely into his rivalry with Ladd.

Then Ladd had ducked into the tent for a quick drink—and he had bumped into Morris Hart, the author, on the way in. Hart had pointedly ignored Ladd, as if he wanted nothing to do with the boisterous athlete. It seemed ludicrous to imagine a bestselling author poisoning one of his fans, but I had to admit Hart did have the opportunity to tamper with the flask. Plus, he had had a conversation with Ladd before the caber toss in which it looked like Hart wasn't pleased with what Ladd was saying. I wondered if that was a casual conversation between two people who'd just met or if they had some kind of deeper relationship.

I racked my brain, but I couldn't remember seeing anyone else go into the VIP tent between the time Gillian dropped off the flask and when Ladd went in for his fateful drink. Unless there was someone in the tent the whole time that I'd never seen, there were only four people who could have poisoned Ladd's flask: Aileen, Ryan King, Patrick Ames, and Morris Hart. I had my list of suspects.

I also had a cramp in my hand from pulling threads for the past hour and a half. I still had a couple of yards to go, but I bundled up the sash and stood up to stretch and shake out my hands. I had time for a leisurely lunch before meeting Corgi at the church at one-thirty.

I thought about texting McCarthy to see if he wanted to go out to lunch with me, but then my eye fell on my new copy of *Over the Sea to Skye*. I made a quick peanut butter sandwich and took it and the novel out to the porch. I curled up on the porch swing and immersed myself in the tale of Stu Rohan, the Pennsylvania architect whose journey began with an unexpected message that accompanied the results from a DNA kit he'd received as a Christmas gift. I was up to the part where he was about to meet the message writer in a dark parking garage on the south side of Philadelphia when my phone dinged. It was a text from Pete: "I get off at 5:30 today. Going over to the jail to see Aileen. Want to come?"

I checked the time—I needed to head over to the Catholic church to meet with Corgi. I texted Pete back: "Sure," and reluctantly tore myself away from the novel.

St. Martin's Catholic Church was one of the half-dozen historic churches spread out along Church Street, just a few blocks away from my house. The congregation had just celebrated their three-hundred-year anniversary with much pomp and circumstance. The church building wasn't quite that old; it was the third structure on that site since its founding. Still, the present building dated from the mid-eighteen hundreds, requiring constant and expensive upkeep. Its wooden belfry needed shoring up, and the rose window in the front of the sanctuary leaked around the lead seals holding the delicate stained-glass pieces together. Luckily, today wasn't a rainy day.

The cold stone sanctuary was deserted when I entered, but the sound of voices carried up the stairs from the basement. I clattered down the stairs and collided with McCarthy on the landing. His camera, which dangled from a cord around his neck, banged sharply against the railing.

"Whoa, not so fast!" He caught me before I could careen into the opposite wall. "Can't wait to get to that half-baked haggis, can you?"

"Sorry." I indicated his camera, which he was carefully examining. "I thought you were going to take pictures of the whole haggis-making process."

He released the camera, satisfied it was undamaged. "I did get a bunch. But there's a student photography exhibit opening at the Tremington tomorrow afternoon, so I'm off to cover the setup for that."

I had first encountered McCarthy at the Tremington Museum, when he was photographing an exhibit of Civil War artifacts and I was making uniforms for a group of Civil War reenactors. I hoped this new exhibit wouldn't cause as much trouble as that one had.

"I'll see you at the ceilidh tonight, right?" I said.

He grinned and fired off a series of shots of me in the stairwell. Who knows what he wanted with those? "Sure. I need to get some shots of the finished product, and of the expressions of the people who try it. I can't wait!" He blew me a kiss as he bounded up the next flight of stairs on to his next gig. Always busy; that was McCarthy.

I continued down the stairs, breathing in the sweet and savory aromas that led me to the kitchen.

I found Corgi at work in the kitchen, his arms up to his elbows churning through a large pan that appeared to be filled with some kind of porridge. Another man shook on a liberal amount of spices from an oversize spice jar. Corgi saw me come in and waved before he thought, spewing oatmeal about like drops of water off a dog's back. His companion swore as he swiped at his glasses, speckled now with the thick mixture. Corgi hastened to apologize, and the man trudged off to wash up.

"What's in the pan?" I asked, leaning over Corgi's shoulder. On closer inspection, it appeared to be a mixture of oatmeal, water, and seasoned ground beef, a bit like the meatloaf my mother used to make of a Saturday evening. I looked around for the ketchup bottle, but apparently Scots didn't use ketchup.

"Haggis, of course." Corgi scratched his forehead with a slimy gloved finger before diving into the pan once again. He was dressed in an oversize apron with a shocking-pink image of Kokopelli emblazoned across the front. His light brown hair was streaked with bits of oatmeal and his apron sported liberal chunks of the stuff as well. "Everyone groans about how nasty haggis is," he went on, "but it's nothing more than Scottish sausage. Robbie Burns calls it the 'chieftan o' the puddin-race,' but it's just oatmeal, ground beef, and organ meat cooked in a sheep's stomach. How's that different from the link sausages you get at the grocery store?"

I bit back a smile at his comfortable use of the poet's nickname. "You lost me at the sheep's stomach. Where do you even get one of those?"

Corgi waved at a tray sitting on the counter, which contained a number of gray, leathery-looking lumps. I tried not to think of them as "lumps of flesh," but honestly, that was what they were. "We had to improvise. Percy's Meats and Stuff was fresh out of stomachs of any description, so we went with some deer stomachs Ryan saved from last year's hunting season. It's a good thing we're only inviting friends and relations, because you can't serve the public game you hunted, evidently. Five deer stomachs should do the job."

I tore my gaze away from the stomachs and pulled out my estimate pad. "I've done some research on kilt-making and worked up an estimate for you." I shot him a sharp glance, looking for signs of whiskey imbibing even at this early hour. Apart from his customary scatterbrained demeanor, he looked quite sober to me. I held out the pad so he could see it. "Have a look at this and then let me know if you're ready to proceed."

Corgi wiped his hands on his apron and reached for the pad, but I pulled it away.

"I'll hold it, so it doesn't get messy." I pointed out the costs for fabric, expedited shipping, and labor. "The whole thing will cost you eight hundred fifty dollars. Honestly, you could get a made-to-order kilt from Scotland for less than that. Are you sure you want to go through with this?"

He looked up from the pad. "I can't get a made-to-order kilt from Scotland in time for the Ligonier Highland Games in two weeks. I figure I'm paying for speed as much as anything. You're not backing out on me, are you?"

"Not at all. This will be a fabulous challenge for me. I just wanted to make sure you were okay with the cost."

He waved his hand dismissively, scattering more flecks of haggis. "Cost, schmost. With a little more practice and a proper kilt, I can start playing the funeral circuit. Half a dozen renditions of 'Amazing Grace' and I've paid for the whole thing."

"Okay." I held a pen out to him. "I just need you to sign here, and I'll need half for the deposit. I'll order the fabric right away." I wiped the pen on the hem of his apron after he signed, and then I scrolled through the fabric website on my phone. "This is the tartan fabric I'm ordering. I'm choosing the heavyweight wool and making you an eight-yard kilt, so it will turn out to be a lot nicer than the one you've got now."

"Practically a first down," Corgi said with a chuckle.

It took me a minute to realize he was making a football reference. I was just glad he wasn't freaked out by the cost in the sober light of day. "I'll also need to take your measurements before I can get started sewing."

He held out both arms, as if I were going to break out the measuring tape in the middle of the kitchen.

"I can wait until you get the haggis into the oven, then take your measurements." I edged out of the kitchen before he could object.

"Hey, Daria!" Corgi called after me. "What's the story with Aileen?"

I turned back around. "The police are holding her on suspicion of murder. Pete says she refused to tell them about her history with Ladd Foster, so they think she might be guilty. Or else they're just making her sweat—as if that would work with Aileen. I haven't heard anything from her yet today. Pete and I are going to stop by the jail later this afternoon."

He nodded. "Our gig was a disaster last night. Aileen's the only one in the band who sings, so we couldn't do any songs with vocals. Then we forgot about her guitar solo in 'Rage the Stage,' so there was a huge hole in the middle of that tune. We're supposed to play at the ceilidh tonight. I sure hope she gets out by then."

"Me too."

Corgi's fellow chef rejoined him at this point, so I slipped out of the kitchen. I wandered into the sanctuary and slid into a back pew so I could go ahead and place my fabric order while waiting to take Corgi's measurements.

My quiet moment didn't last long. Breanna and her Scottish dancers trooped into the sanctuary to practice. The dozen or so girls chattered as they took off their sneakers and changed into their dance shoes while Breanna cued up the music on her boom box. Gillian slumped on a front pew, sulking. I didn't envy Breanna her job of motivating Gillian.

Breanna called the girls together at the front of the sanctuary and brought out the swords for the sword dance. This was my favorite dance. Each girl drew a sword out of its sheath and laid them on the floor in the shape of a cross. The point was to dance in each of the four quadrants formed by the crossed blades without touching sheath or sword. Breanna had told me that the dance originated as a battle celebration, when the victor would dance over the swords of his fallen enemies. Hardly a dance for sweet young girls, but it was a crowd-pleaser nonetheless. As the girls danced faster and faster, their feet falling ever closer to the center of the cross, the audience invariably cheered. I felt like cheering now as I watched them practice.

I lingered in the back pew, scrolling through online fabric vendors until I found the one I wanted. I placed the order for four yards of heavyweight wool in the Ancient Guthrie tartan. The blue and green plaid on a field of black with the reddish orange stripes looked just like Corgi's lightweight kilt. I hoped my creation would be an improvement for him.

Gillian stumbled against her sword, kicking the blade out of alignment. She yelped in pain. "I stubbed my toe, Breanna. I'm going to sit down for a few minutes."

Ignoring Breanna's frown, she limped to the back of the church and flung herself down in the pew in front of me. She leaned back until her head lolled on the back and looked upside down at me. "Why are you spying on me? Quit following me around!"

"I'm not following you. I'm waiting for my client, who happens to be making haggis in the kitchen right now."

She popped upright and turned around to stare at me. "Your client? What are you, some kind of private eye or something? You can't make me tell you anything. Show me your badge!"

I held out my measuring tape. "I'm a seamstress. You bought a couple of my bow ties yesterday, remember?" I usually didn't go into details of my clients' needs in their absence, but I didn't feel like it was a breach of confidentiality for me to say, "Do you know Corgi? He needs a new kilt for some more Highland competitions this summer."

Gillian continued to stare at me without saying a word, so I pressed her. "What can you tell me about Ladd Foster's death that I don't already know?"

She flinched at his name. "If you know so much, you don't need me."

I turned back to my phone, feigning indifference. "Okay. But maybe *you'd* like to hear what *I* know."

"What do you know?" It slipped out before she could stop herself. For all her tough-gal persona, I could tell Gillian was worrying about Ladd's death.

"I know Ladd did die from poison in his flask. It was torch oil, for the big torches they lighted in the evening." I watched her closely.

Her face flushed. "I told you, it wasn't me! Anyone could have put poison in that flask. It had nothing to do with me. Just because I put the flask down on that table doesn't mean it's my fault it got poisoned. You can't put the blame on me!" Tears filled her eyes, threatening her heavy mascara. She blinked them away angrily.

I took a deep breath, calling to mind the intensity of emotions that had blindsided me at the age of fifteen. At that age, the world was black and white, with no room for any shades of gray. Love, hate, passion, fear, sense of responsibility—they all jostled for prominence in the brain of a teenager. In Gillian's case, it looked like guilt was winning out.

"Gillian, you know it's not your fault Ladd was poisoned. You didn't do it, and you didn't cause anyone else to either."

The tears spilled down her cheeks. "He asked me to hold his flask. If I had just held it, this whole thing would never have happened. He'd still be alive and the police wouldn't have anything to do with me or my dad. I should've just held on to his stupid flask!" She hid her face in her hands.

I wanted to put my hand on her shoulder, but I knew she would pull away. I settled for leaning in close. "Gillian. Somebody wanted to kill Ladd. If they didn't get their hands on his flask, they would have found another way to do it. They could have stabbed him or shot him or strangled him or hit him over the head with the caber, assuming they could lift it." She looked up at me, unsure whether to sob or chuckle. I looked her in the eye. "You putting his flask down did *not* lead to his death. It is *not* your fault."

"What if somebody killed him because of me?" she whispered. All her bluster was gone. "What if they wanted to keep him away from me permanently?"

It was my turn to stare. Luckily, she didn't notice because her eyes were averted. I took another deep breath and said softly, "Your dad? You're afraid your dad killed Ladd Foster?"

Her nod was imperceptible. She fiddled with the ragged ends of the friendship bracelet encircling her wrist. She wasn't offering any bit of this without a supreme effort on my part. I knew I had to go slowly or she would clam up completely.

I glanced up at Breanna, who was still immersed in instruction for the sword dance. We probably didn't have much time before she would be expecting Gillian to join the dancers again.

"I saw how upset your dad was to see you with Ladd. You think he was mad enough to kill him?"

"I don't know." It came out in a whisper. "I guess you saw him punch Ladd in the face. He usually only gets one good punch because he's so puny that the other guy will clobber him. But Dad's got a really bad temper, and he hates it when I go out with anyone." Her voice trailed off as she concentrated on untying her bracelet.

"Does he ever hit you?" I said it quietly, but I could have shouted it from the rooftops by her reaction. She flounced away from me and huddled at the end of her pew, unwilling either to talk to me or go back to her dancing rehearsal.

I took another deep breath, thinking I should adopt a spiritual breathing practice or something. Then I scooted along my pew until I was close behind her. "I'm sorry. That was out of line. It has nothing to do with Ladd." When she didn't move, I racked my brain to try to figure out what to say next. "Has he fought with other guys you've been interested in?"

She kept her face hidden from me. "Yeah, sure. All of them. He broke this one guy's nose when we got home late from a party. Another time he pushed a guy down the porch steps when he was in the middle of kissing me goodnight." She raised her eyes for an instant. "I don't get very many second dates, if you can believe it."

"I can imagine." My own father was pretty controlling throughout my childhood and teen years. I didn't give him as much trouble as Gillian gave her dad, but I still remembered the dictatorial rules he imposed on any chance I had for boyfriends. I'd often wondered if my strained relationship with my father set the stage for my own disastrous choices in men, which left me abandoned by a faithless fiancé who ran off with our joint bank account while I naively sewed my wedding dress.

I pushed aside the bitter memories. It didn't feel like the right time to share my own experiences with Gillian. Instead, I said, "But he's never killed anyone, right?"

I assumed the answer would be no, so I was surprised by Gillian's reaction. She hunched over her bent knees, hiding her head in her arms. She pressed her hands over her ears, whether to block out my questions, the Scottish music, or the entire world, I didn't know.

"Leave me alone," she snarled. "You ask too many questions for a dumb seamstress!" She flounced out of her seat and stormed back to the line of dancers, leaving me staring in astonishment.

I barely had time to wipe the shock off my face before Corgi dropped into the pew beside me. He leaned back and flung his arms across the back of the pew, dripping bits of meat and oats onto the seat cushions. "It's a hundred degrees in that kitchen."

I shook my head to clear it of the tension of my conversation with Gillian and reached for my measuring tape. "Did you get the haggis into the oven, then?"

He nodded with a grimace. "After shoveling that disgusting mixture into those foul stomachs, I've got no desire to eat any of it." He flashed me a sheepish grin. "Hey, don't listen to me. You should try it for yourself. You're coming tonight, right?" He stood up and stretched out his arms.

"Let's find a private spot to do this." I led Corgi to an empty Sunday school room, where he stretched out his arms for the third time. I passed the tape around his waist and hips, trying to avoid the splotches of haggis staining his apron. I noted down the measurements in the small notebook I always carried in my shoulder bag. "I wouldn't miss it for the world." I asked him to kneel and measured the distance from his waist to the floor. "Your kilt should break right across the kneecap." I folded up the tape measure. "Great. I can get started as soon as the fabric arrives."

"Cool. I'd better get back to the kitchen. We're making the Atholl Brose next."

I stowed my notebook and tape measure back in my shoulder bag. "What's Atholl Brose?"

"It's a traditional Scottish drink made by soaking oats in water and then squeezing the liquid out through cheesecloth and mixing in honey and whiskey. We'll use it to toast the haggis." He started to wander off and then turned back around to face me. "Say hi to Aileen for me when you go to the jail. Tell her we need her at the ceilidh tonight."

"Okay," I said to his retreating back. I wasn't sure what good it would do telling Aileen that she needed to show up at the ceilidh when she was being held by the police. But I could pass along the message.

I returned to the sanctuary and stood watching the Highland dancers for a couple more minutes while I tried to sort out my thoughts. I saw no reason to suspect Gillian of putting poison into Ladd's flask, even though she did have the opportunity because he'd entrusted it to her. She was rebellious and hard to reach, but her powerful emotions rode close to the surface for an astute observer to see. She felt guilty that she had provided the opportunity for a murderer to act. Further, she feared that murderer could be her father.

I made my way out of the sanctuary and into the afternoon sunshine. It was too bad McCarthy had to hustle off to that museum exhibit. I would have liked to walk and talk things over with him, just to get it all straight in my mind. I strolled along the cracked downtown sidewalk, enjoying the sight of children playing in their front yards like I'd seen so many times before. The peace of the moment enveloped me. I couldn't believe I had to think about who might have committed a murder.

Although I didn't consider Gillian to be a suspect, it looked like I should take a closer look at her dad. He had punched Ladd to keep him away from his daughter. I couldn't blame him for that—I would have punched Ladd too if Gillian was my child. But Gillian's tale of his violence toward her dates gave me pause. If he'd break the nose of a teenager—I was assuming her dates were her own age, which might not be true, come to think of it—how much more might he react to a middle-aged man who had no business cavorting with a teenager? It didn't stretch the imagination too much to picture Ryan as a righteous vigilante, ridding the world of this threat to his daughter's virtue. In other words, a murderer.

I shook off the thought with a shudder. I shouldn't let my imagination run away with me. I focused on the work ahead of me, making a Scottish kilt. Maybe it was time for me to do some more research. And I knew just where to start.

Chapter 7

I sent a quick text to McCarthy, to see if he was still at the museum. He had already moved on to the firefighters' picnic. I caught the bus to the Tremington Museum, which was located on the hill in the Highlands, adjacent to Oliphant University. It was housed in the eighteenth-century mansion of Judge Walter Tremington, one of the founders of our town. He and his wife, Margaret Oliphant Tremington, had owned the entire hilltop before they gifted the land for what would become Oliphant University. I remember learning about the Judge and his young wife in elementary school, when the class focused on local and state history. I always liked the part about Margaret Oliphant emigrating from Scotland as a teenager and falling in love with the judge in the wilds of eastern Pennsylvania. By the time of the Revolutionary War, they'd established a solid little township and broken ground for the university that would bear her name.

The Tremington Museum contained a wealth of articles from the Judge and Margaret's household, both in the upstairs local history exhibit that had been there since I was a child and in the gloriously chaotic basement that held random historical artifacts in a vast series of shelves and display areas organized with no rhyme or reason whatsoever. Visitors could wander through the partitions, taking in a wooden churn from 1855 and a pair of Victorian opera gloves sitting next to a letter from the Apollo 11 astronauts to the mayor of Laurel Springs. This lackadaisical approach to historical preservation irked some of the city assembly members, but I loved it. I could visit the basement every day for a month and make a new discovery each time. Today, I hoped to see something I'd seen before: a vintage Scottish kilt that had come to America with Margaret Oliphant. I didn't really think it would help me much in terms of crafting Corgi's kilt, but I wanted to ground myself in the history of such a unique, traditional garment.

I couldn't remember if I'd seen the kilt upstairs or in the basement. There was only one way to find out. I headed straight for the permanent exhibit upstairs, where the local history was laid out methodically in a series of chronological displays. It took only a matter of minutes to determine that the kilt wasn't among the items of clothing on display upstairs. I resisted the impulse to linger over Margaret's ball gowns and silk nightgowns and made my way down to the basement.

The basement was quiet, with only a few visitors roaming through the rows of artifacts. I felt like I was on a mission, only interested in one particular item, but it still took me almost forty minutes to find it. I kept pausing to look at something else along the way. I remembered my mother talking about looking up words in the dictionary in much the same way. She would turn the pages to find her word, but her eyes would be distracted by all the other fascinating words on the pages, and it would take her ten minutes to land on the word she was looking for. I'd never had that experience; the online dictionary takes you directly to the word you want. Sometimes I wished for the slower, more circuitous olden days. Finding something in the Tremington basement was certainly circuitous!

Finally, I stumbled upon the kilt I was looking for. It was hanging on a wire skirt hanger in the midst of a jumble of items, including a tattered Bible opened to the first chapter of Exodus, an ornate silver ring with a big red stone, and a sword with a long, fringed tassel on the hilt and a chip out of the blade. The kilt was made in the Oliphant tartan, which looked identical to the fabric I had used for my bow ties for the Highland Games. It was flat in the front and presumably pleated across the back, although I couldn't examine that part because of the way it was hanging. I longed to lift up the hanger so I could see the back of the kilt, but one didn't do such things in a museum, even one as informal as the Tremington. I settled for taking a series of photographs of the kilt from as many angles as I could. I even leaned in close to smell it. It smelled like musty wool, with overtones of mothballs. Not a bad smell.

"Getting the full effect, are we?"

I straightened up with a start and turned to face a woman about my own age, dressed in faded bib overalls covering a soccer jersey. Her wispy hair was loose about her face and her tawny eyes seemed to take in everything. An official museum badge dangled from a lanyard around her neck, and she held a feather duster, of all things, in one hand. She brushed her oversize headphones away from her ears and regarded me calmly, waiting for an explanation, no doubt.

I gave her a big smile, trying to channel McCarthy. "Yes! I'm making a kilt for a client, so I came to get as much information as I could from observing this historic kilt. I'm a seamstress. My name's Daria Dembrowski." I rummaged through my shoulder bag and produced one of my business cards, which promoted my business, A Stitch in Time. "I was just wishing I could get a look at the back of the kilt, to see the stitching on the pleats."

The young woman read my business card, then turned it over to check the other side before handing it back to me. "No worries." She slipped on a latex glove and plucked the hanger off the wall and held it out at arm's length so I could see the kilt in its entirety. "I'm Julie Lombard. I'm an intern here at the museum." She lifted the overlay of the kilt so I could see the inner construction. She made no objection when I took photo after photo. When I was finished, she simply hung the kilt back up and peeled off the glove.

"Thanks, that was awesome," I said. "How long have you been interning at the museum?"

"I've been here for a couple of months. I'm a grad student at St. Andrews University in North Carolina. I'm doing a project on the Oliphant collection." She indicated the kilt and surrounding objects. "You got a good look at how it was made. Want to know who wore it and when?"

"Absolutely!" I didn't really have a ton of time because I needed to meet Pete to go visit Aileen in jail, but Julie's offer was tantalizing. "What can you tell me about the history of this kilt?"

"It belonged to Margaret Oliphant Tremington's father, Jock Oliphant. His real name was Jacob, but his clansmen called him Jock. He was the leader of the Clan Oliphant in Gask, Scotland, and led his clansmen in the Forty-Five. He …" She paused at the blank look on my face. "You know, the Forty-Five. The Rising of the Clans. The Jacobite rising of 1745, led by Bonnie Prince Charlie, in his quest to regain the British throne. They call it the Forty-Five to distinguish it from the Fifteen, when the clans attempted to retake the throne for Charles's father, James Stuart, in 1715. They called James the Old Pretender, and Charlie was the Young Pretender. The Fifteen failed, and then the clans rose again in the Forty-Five."

"Kind of like World War I and World War II?" I said, fascinated by this history lesson.

She smiled, as if I were a child just about to finally understand. "Kind of…but actually, not at all like that. Anyway, the Oliphant clan was one of Charlie's most steadfast allies, so they fought with him at Culloden on April

16, 1746. Legend has it that Jock wore this very kilt on the battlefield." She slipped the glove back onto her hand and lifted the front flap. "You can see a tear right here, which might have been made by a thrusting bayonet." I looked at the frayed little tear. It was small, so the bayonet thrust must not have been significant.

"When Bonnie Prince Charlie was defeated at Culloden," Julie went on, "the clan chieftains had to flee Scotland just like he did. Charlie returned to France, but Jock and his family went to America. That's how Margaret Oliphant came to Laurel Springs. She was heartbroken to leave her beloved Scotland."

"Hmm, I've never heard that part of the story. I thought she was excited to come here and fall in love with Judge Tremington. That's how we learned it in school."

Again that smile, like she knew something I didn't. "That may be the official version, and maybe that's the story Margaret wanted people to hear. But in private, she told a different version." Julie paused, grinning.

"Okay, I'll bite. How do you know what Margaret thought in private?"

"See, when you do an internship in a museum, you get to go into the archives and see all kinds of cool stuff the public never sees." She pointed to a door with a small sign that read, "No Admittance." "That door is the gateway to a world of treasures guaranteed to boggle the mind." She held a dramatic pause until I started to fidget. "One of those treasures is Margaret Oliphant's diary, which she kept from the age of eleven."

It was worth the wait. "Wow. Have you read it?"

Julie's face fell. "I've paged through it, but I haven't really studied it. It's very fragile, and no one has scanned it yet to produce a digital version. I'm working on that project. Of course, I want to read every page while I'm scanning, which would take a really long time. I might have to extend my internship."

"When will the digital images be available to the public?" I couldn't say why, but I was suddenly overcome with curiosity about Margaret Oliphant's experience coming to America as a teenager and marrying Judge Tremington. Maybe sewing wedding dresses all the time brought out the romantic in me. I always asked my clients to tell me about their first date.

"I don't know, it could be years. Historical scholarship isn't exactly breaking news, you know. But if there's something you're interested in, I could email you some of the digital images."

"Really? I'm a sucker for how-we-met stories. I'd love to see the pages from when Margaret met Judge Tremington and fell in love with him."

"Okay, I'll see what I can find."

I fished out my business card again and handed it to her. "If there's anything about the making of her wedding gown, please send me that too."

"Okay." She tucked my card into the front pocket of her overalls. "Have you seen her wedding gown?"

"What? Don't tell me Margaret Oliphant's wedding gown is one of the treasures hidden behind that door?"

Julie laughed like a little kid coming downstairs on Christmas morning. "We're working on restoring it right now. It was packed up in a trunk that was recently fished out of the attic in one of the dorms at Oliphant University. Who knows how it ended up there? Margaret's diary was in the trunk as well. Both pieces are destined for a special addition to the local history exhibit upstairs, which will be opening in a week and a half. But I could probably get you in to take a peek at the wedding dress if you want."

"I would love that! I'm so glad I met you today. I don't have time right now, but if you could arrange a time for me, that would be awesome."

She agreed to be in touch, and I headed out of the museum, well pleased with my trip to the Tremington.

I caught the next bus home so I'd be in time to meet Pete for our trip to the jail. He found me waiting on the porch swing when he drove up.

He waved out the window of his pickup, calling me over. "Let's get this over with. Hop in."

I clambered into the passenger seat and threw my brother a critical glance. He held the wheel tightly, reining in a lot of tension with his grip. Poor Pete. I knew the last thing he wanted to do was go to the jail, even if he was just visiting. After spending a few days there under suspicion of a different murder, no one could blame him if he avoided the place like the plague.

"Thanks for setting up this visit with Aileen," I said. "I'm sure she'll appreciate it."

He gave me a tight smile as he pulled away from the curb. "You never know what Aileen will appreciate."

We drove the next few blocks in silence, until Pete's tension made me nervous. I started talking at random. "I saw Corgi making the haggis for the ceilidh this morning. It smelled good, but the deer stomachs they're using to contain the stuff looked positively disgusting. They were all pale and lumpy, and I'm not even going to tell you what they smelled like." I felt like I was babbling, but my inane conversation was better than the apprehensive silence. The topic of haggis lasted us all the way to the jail.

Pete pulled into the one open parking place. It seemed somehow ominous that all the parking spaces at the jail were full. The whole point of living in a small town was to avoid the high crime typical of a big city. I hoped Laurel Springs wasn't sliding down that slippery slope toward more and more crime.

Pete and I got out of the truck and pushed through the double doors to the jail. We entered the tiny reception area that had two orange plastic chairs facing a desk behind a bulletproof window. The chairs were occupied by a couple of tough-looking teens who scowled at us as we walked in. I had the fleeting thought that if I were walking in with McCarthy, he would probably call out a friendly greeting to the youths, who he probably knew from one thing or another. But Pete and I didn't have that kind of rapport with them. We sidled past them and pressed the button on the window. It only took half an hour for us to get in to see Aileen.

A stern officer met us at the side door leading from the reception area and ushered us into a large room with numerous round tables guarded by half a dozen prison guards. Orange jumpsuit-clad inmates sat at the various tables, talking with their visitors: lawyers, family members, or the like. In some cases, it was hard to distinguish the inmates from the visitors; they all seemed to have the same look of hopelessness in their eyes. I scanned the room looking for Aileen.

I totally did not recognize her. The only reason I noticed her at all was the fact that she sat alone at one of the round tables. She looked like she'd been put through a car wash. All traces of makeup were erased, down to the black nail polish that normally coated her fingernails. Her jet-black hair lay limp on her shoulders, devoid of any gel or styling. If the guards could have stripped off the hair dye, I'm sure they would have. She wore a regulation orange jumpsuit instead of her normal flamboyant clothing. I wouldn't have been more shocked if she had been naked. All her rock-star trappings had been stripped away, leaving nothing but the vulnerable human behind. I turned away to hide the tears threatening to overwhelm me.

Pete managed better than I did. He waved and called out, "Aileen!" He led me through the maze of tables and found a chair for me to sit down facing her. He pulled out a grin and said, "Wow, one day in the clink and you're a changed woman."

My mouth fell open in astonishment at his insensitivity, but Aileen just snorted. "Yeah, you wish, Moron!"

"No, not really," he murmured. He laid his hands palms up on the table. "I tried to bring you in a bottle of hot sauce, but they wouldn't let me. How are you managing with the food?"

"It's bland. Everything about this place is bland. I'm holding out for a deranged serial killer or something, but so far they're all bland."

Privately, I hoped Aileen never saw any deranged serial killers, but I didn't see the need to dash her hopes. "So, how long are they going to hold you here, Aileen?"

She scowled at me. I guess I'd broken the joking mood or something. "They're waiting for me to come clean about my relationship with Ladd Frigging Foster. There's nothing clean about that lowlife."

"So all you need to do is tell them about your relationship and then they'll let you go?" I couldn't imagine any reason not to comply with that request. "Sounds pretty straightforward to me."

"I don't do 'straightforward,'" she shot back.

I twisted my hands together under the table. Aileen seemed like her own worst enemy at this point. "It looked like you knew him back at the Games, like you two had some kind of history together."

"That's what it looked like, huh?"

I held her gaze. "Yeah, that's what it looked like. Is that the way it was?"

She leaned forward and reached for my neckline, prompting a guard to bark, "No contact." She leaned back in her chair and threw her hands behind her head. "What, are you wearing a wire or something? Collecting information for the man?"

"Oh, come on! 'The man'?" I tried to keep my voice down, but Aileen's scornful glare pushed all my buttons. "You know you're a suspect in Ladd's poisoning, right? You may be innocent until proven guilty, but if you keep acting like you're guilty, it's not going to get you anywhere!"

Pete laid a hand on my forearm. His frown warned me to slow down. "Why don't you want to talk about Ladd Foster?" he asked.

Aileen continued to glare at me. "He's not worth my time."

I tried to pull away from Pete, but he held on. He couldn't shut me up, though. "Exactly! He's a worthless piece of dung—certainly not worth spending even one minute in jail for. He's also dead, and you're one of four people who could have done him in. Of course the police want to know about your relationship with him! I want to know about your relationship with him. You came within seconds of smashing him over the head with your guitar in front of half the town. Now you're hiding out in jail and refusing to say one word about him." I threw up my hands. "Why should the police even look for anyone else?"

Pete pulled me up from the table by the arm and hustled me away from Aileen before she could take a breath to reply. "Don't ever start a fight in the jail," he hissed in my ear. "Get it together right now!" He pulled me to a halt as a guard loomed right in front of us. "Sorry. She's kind of upset. We're leaving."

The shaking in his voice did more to shut me up than anything else he could have done. I whispered, "I'm good," and walked with him down the hall. I kept quiet while the guards cleared us to exit. We walked out through the double doors, and Pete breathed in a lungful of fresh, unchained air. "I am never taking you there with me again!"

"I'm sorry," I mumbled, following him through the lot to his truck. "She makes me crazy. You'd think she likes being in jail." I could feel myself getting worked up all over again. "What's wrong with her?"

Pete unlocked the door and slid in to the driver's seat. "Are you headed home or shall I drop you off somewhere else?"

I hopped into the truck and checked the time. "The ceilidh doesn't start until seven thirty tonight, so home sounds good." I kept my eye on the road as he pulled out of the lot. I felt like a driver's ed teacher taking notes on his skill level. He passed. "Are you free to give me a ride to the ceilidh?"

He gave an exaggerated sigh, to let me know I was imposing on him. "Are you going to behave yourself?"

I dropped my head in my hands, totally trusting him to maneuver the streets in safety. "Yeah. It just freaked me out to see Aileen all ordinary like that. It's like they sucked out her spirit, leaving a zombie behind or something."

Pete started laughing so hard he almost lost control of his truck. He swerved into the oncoming lane and quickly overcorrected, sending us sharply in the other direction. Ignoring my loud gasp, he straightened out and drove carefully the rest of the way home, still chuckling.

He pulled up to the curb in front of the house and I unclenched my hand from the door handle. He laid a hand on my arm before I could escape from the truck. "It was weird seeing Aileen without her rock-star getup, I'll give you that. But she's no zombie. She's got some plan going with this silence thing, and there's no way we're going to force her to talk. You'll just have to find out what's between her and Ladd Foster some other way." He gave me his crooked smile that I could never resist. "I hope I can count on you to figure that out, just like you can count on me to get you safely to your ceilidh."

Chapter 8

True to his word, Pete drove me to Hollystone where the Laurel Springs Pipe and Drum Corps was hosting the ceilidh. This stately eighteenth-century mansion, once the mayor's residence, sat on the northwest corner of Oliphant University and served as the university's admissions office. I supposed the elegant rooms filled with period furnishings were designed to impress prospective students and their tuition-paying parents. Once the students enrolled in the university they never had occasion to enter Hollystone again, and the gracious reception room was available for local parties and events.

I paused on the wide porch flanked by imposing white columns and adjusted my flowing silk skirt. It was my version of the little black dress: a black silk shantung skirt that fell just below the knee, combined with a black tatted lace tunic with a wide neckline and fluttery cap sleeves. Over my shoulders for a wrap, I wore a length of lightweight fabric in the pale purple and green plaid with white accents of the Isle of Skye tartan. I had other fabric that would have made a more striking shawl, but I thought I'd pay a tribute to Morris Hart's *Over the Sea to Skye*. Secretly, I wondered if the author would even recognize the tartan, assuming he was here, of course. I wore my thick brown hair down, with only a single pewter comb catching it up in the back. It was a welcome change from the bobby pins that normally pulled my hair away from my eyes so I could concentrate on my sewing.

The subdued sound of bagpipes floated out the open door. Wishing I had brought along a few earplugs, a necessary accessory when one lived with a metal band in the basement, I entered the spacious reception room. A small crowd milled around a lavish refreshment table set with silver and decorated with sprigs of heather. I saw Corgi, decked out in his kilt, hovering around the food. Another group of people surrounded a lone musician sitting on a chair, bending over the bagpipes in his lap. I edged closer, fascinated.

These bagpipes looked nothing like Corgi's, which he held with the drones over his shoulder and the bag under his arm with a blowpipe to inflate it while he played notes on the chanter attached to the bottom. This piper held the drones across his lap with a bellows under one arm and the bag under the other, both elbows pumping as his fingers flew on the keys of the chanter. The volume was much less than that of the Highland bagpipes, making this instrument far more conducive to an indoor gathering. A couple of tiny girls wearing leggings and bright pink and purple tutus ran over and started spinning and hopping around to the sprightly music. The crowd chuckled dotingly.

A flash exploded beside me. "Paddy McLear is the best Uilleann piper I've ever seen."

"Uilleann piper?" I said, taking note of the fact that McCarthy was snapping pictures of Paddy McLear rather than me. Maybe I should have gone with the Royal Stewart plaid instead of the Isle of Skye.

McCarthy was dressed up, for him, in a dusky green sport coat covering his customary white button-down shirt. I was surprised and pleased to see him wearing the yellow tartan bow tie I'd coerced him to wear at the Highland Games. With his dark blond ponytail combined with the green coat, he looked more like a leprechaun than a Scot. He waved a hand at the bagpipes.

"Uilleann pipes are Irish bagpipes, known for their mellow tone. You have to have the coordination of an athlete to play them, though. Paddy makes it look easy." He fired off a couple more shots of Paddy and the Uilleann pipes, and then aimed his lens on the tiny dancers. They were bumping into each other by now, dizzy from all their spinning.

I left him chatting with the girls' parents, getting permission to publish the photos in the newspaper, no doubt. I wandered over to the refreshment table and snagged a glass of punch. With so many children and teens in the crowd, I felt reasonably confident the punch would be free of whiskey. I took a quick sip, just to make sure. Ginger ale and fruit juice with dollops of ice cream floating on the surface, but no alcohol. Perfect!

Satisfied, I scanned the crowd. A lot of the same people I'd seen at the Highland Games were here tonight. Gillian lounged on one of the antique upholstered chairs, giggling with her friends. She wore her wide plaid skirt with the ruffled petticoats, along with a white ruffled blouse and velvet vest, a sign that she would be dancing later. Ryan King held court in the center of the room, berating the Phillies for trading his favorite player. He'd worked himself up over this issue until his voice could be heard over the general conversation. Looking at his red face, I remembered how Gillian had described him as having a terrible temper. I resolved to steer clear of him.

Morris Hart had gathered a small crowd around him on the other edge of the room. I half expected him to be wearing a kilt with his dinner jacket, but he wore a conservative gray suit and a plaid tie like any other professional. I took a drink of punch and joined the group. He was talking about his book, of course.

"Some critics have suggested that Stu Rohan can be seen as Everyman, but that's patently ridiculous. He is distinctly unique, as the sole legitimate heir of Bonnie Prince Charlie. He carries the hopes of a displaced multitude on his shoulders, of course, but his journey is his alone. Anyone saying anything else hasn't read the book."

I hadn't gotten to that part in the book yet myself. I was about to slip away to avoid any more spoilers when Hart laid eyes on me. He interrupted himself in midstream, his face paling a bit. He shouldered out of the crowd of fans and grasped both my hands. He held me thus at arm's length and looked me up and down as if he could hardly believe I was real.

I was so startled, I just stood there for a few seconds, letting him ogle me as if I were a diamond necklace at a high-priced auction. Then I pulled against his grip, my face flaming under his rapt attention.

He dropped my hands at once. "I'm sorry, please forgive me." His own face reddened. "This has never happened to me before. Is your name, by any chance..." his voice dropped to a whisper, "Catherine?"

"No. It's Daria Dembrowski," I said, puzzled. "We met at the Highland Games yesterday. You must have me mixed up with someone else."

He continued to stare, although he tried to cover it up. "Have you read my book?" Without even letting me answer, he went on, "My dear, you are the perfect image of Catherine in *Over the Sea to Skye*. It is as if the character I breathed into life is standing before me in the flesh." He reached out and touched my arm, as if to reassure himself that I wasn't a ghost.

The crowd of people surrounding Hart all stared at me as well, whispering behind their hands. It was just about to get weird when I spied McCarthy on the edge of the crowd. He flashed me an amused smile before raising his camera for a crowd shot.

Feeling grounded again, I smiled at Hart. "I can't wait to get to the part about Catherine in your book. I hope she's a good guy."

Hart laughed a shade too loudly, still rattled by the apparition of one of his characters intruding into real life. "She's the romantic interest. You haven't read the book?"

"I've started it," I said, relieved to see the crowd melting away. McCarthy focused his camera on Hart and me together as we talked.

"Well, I don't want to give anything away. Just…don't take it personally when things happen to Catherine." He couldn't keep himself from staring even now. "She is a creation of my imagination, but you…you are, in fact, real." He shook off his fascination and laughed more naturally. "*Skye* is my twelfth novel, and this is the very first time I've met one of my characters in real life. I am sorry. I'm sure this is bizarre for you."

I smiled and nodded, wondering how we were going to get past this awkward moment. "I have a housemate who wears black leather and chains on a daily basis. People don't usually stare at *me* when we go out."

He laughed and indicated the refreshment table. "Will you forgive me enough to join me in a drink?"

"Of course."

McCarthy winked at me as I walked with Hart over to the refreshments. I'd planned to limit my alcohol intake in un-Scotsmanlike fashion, but I accepted a small glass of whiskey from him nonetheless. If I was careful, it would last me all night.

"I've started reading your book, but I'm only on the third chapter," I said. "I read in the newspaper that your visit to Laurel Springs has to do with more than just promotion of the book."

Bolstered by a healthy drink of whiskey, he was able to turn his attention to this more general discussion of his work. "Well, it's all promotion really, but I am here to do more than just sign books. You've read about the quest for the ring, of course?" Accepting my nod as his due, he went on. "History and fiction are interwoven in *Skye*. One thing that really is historical is the lost ring of Bonnie Prince Charlie. You know about the Jacobite Rising and the Battle of Culloden? Of course, you're up to the third chapter. So you know Charlie went down in spectacular defeat and had to flee for his life across the sea to the Isle of Skye: 'over the sea to Skye,' in the words of the old ballad. He was aided by the lovely Flora MacDonald, who disguised him as her maid and took him to Skye in an open boat. Charlie was twenty-five years old at the time, a handsome, dashing figure returning to his rightful kingdom to try to recover the throne. You can imagine that he turned the heads of any number of young women. But I won't go into details because you're not up to that part yet. Suffice it to say that he had a ring, an heirloom of the House of Stuart, which was never seen again after the Battle of Culloden. Historians suspect it found its way to the finger of one of his admirers, but which one? That's the subject of heated debate. I have my own favorite, like other historians, but unlike them, I am poised to produce the ring." He paused a beat, enjoying the dramatic nature of this statement.

"Wow." A chill ran down my back as I pictured this romantic bit of history coming to life in the twenty-first century. Hart was a very good storyteller.

He continued. "I've traced Bonnie Prince Charlie's ring to eastern Pennsylvania, of all places. My dear, I suspect it is in the neighborhood, even as we speak. I have opened this quest for the ring to my readers, who can follow clues on my website to discover the ring for themselves. Call it a promotion, if you will. I like to think of it as a treasure hunt."

I took a small sip of whiskey, trying to suppress the sputter it caused. "So, if I go to your website I can figure out where Bonnie Prince Charlie's ring is? What's to stop me from picking it up and keeping it so no one else can find it? Or is it like geocaching, perhaps?"

Hart drew back, apparently affronted by this suggestion. "How does geocaching have anything to do with this historical quest?"

My second sip of whiskey went down more smoothly. "Well, geocaching is a treasure hunt as well. You follow the GPS coordinates and the riddles and clues online to get to the hidden object. Then, when you find it, you record your name in the logbook and leave the object where you found it for the next person. That's what made me think of it in relation to your quest. When people succeed in finding the ring, they could leave it for the next person to find. Otherwise, your promotion will be over once the first person finds the ring."

Hart chuckled as he topped off his glass, and mine as well. "I confess, I didn't think about staging a logbook. My plan was simply to reward the first person to find the ring. It is meant to be a short-term promotion, after all."

"Well, you've got me hooked. I'm going to go home tonight and look up your website."

He tossed back the whiskey like a pro. "And best of luck to you in the quest! I would love to have Catherine's doppelgänger be the one to find the ring. It would be too perfect!"

I wasn't sure I wanted to be anyone's doppelgänger, whatever that meant. I didn't get the chance to find out, because Patrick Ames clapped his hands together, calling for attention.

The muscular athlete wore a Highland kilt on this occasion, rather than the utility kilt he'd worn at the Games. It was the blue and green plaid of the Campbell clan, paired with a velvety green jacket and a thin black tie. His Glengarry cap, a trim hat made of thick wool with a checkered band running around the edge and a soft red pom-pom on the crown, finished off the picture of a Scottish gentleman.

"Does everyone have their cup of Atholl Brose to toast the haggis?"

I looked around in anticipation of the traditional Scottish drink Corgi had told me about. Breanna's older dancers circulated throughout the crowd, bearing trays of small plastic cups. Gillian was the one to serve me. She held out her tray to Hart and me. "Whiskey or no whiskey?" She inclined her head at the cups, which contained a thick, milky liquid. Some of the cups held a yellowish liquid, while in the others the contents were white.

"Whiskey, of course," Hart said, plucking two of the whiter cups off the tray. He handed one to me.

"Of course," I muttered, lifting the cup to my nose to take a whiff. It smelled sweet and tangy at the same time, as if someone had added alcohol to the milk left over from a bowl of oatmeal topped with lots of sugar. I hoped Gillian was planning to choose the no-whiskey kind for her own toast.

Once all the guests had been served, Patrick called for our attention again. Affecting a thick Scottish accent, he proclaimed, "And now, the honor guard will pipe in the haggis!"

Those who were sitting down stood up as a couple of bagpipes struck in. Playing a regimental march, the bagpipers processed slowly through the room, following another member of the Laurel Springs Pipe and Drum Corps, who bore a silver platter containing the haggis. I was expecting to see five medium-sized lumps resulting from the five deer stomachs I'd seen at the church, but there was only one large browned mass on the platter. I was still trying to work out how five deer stomachs could equal one large sausage when the haggis arrived at the front of the room, flanked by the two pipers who brought their march to a dramatic climax. Patrick held out an old book and began to read in his fake Scottish accent. I couldn't understand much between the accent and the Scottish words, but I gathered he was reading Robert Burns's poem, "Address to a Haggis." Patrick drew out his words when it came to the description of the haggis, "...warm-reekin, rich," and then when he got to the end, "Gie her a Haggis!" he plunged a knife deep into the warm, reeking mass. The crowd applauded, and we all raised our cups and drank a toast. The Atholl Brose tasted like oatmeal and honey with just a hint of whiskey. It was very good.

Corgi stopped by to say hi after the toast. Dressed out in his kilt and sporran, he looked like a dapper Scot, despite his ordinary black dress shoes. He looked askance at Morris Hart and whispered in my ear, "All this ceremony around the haggis is what you would find at a Burns supper in January, not necessarily a run-of-the-mill ceilidh following a games. I hope Morris Hart doesn't think we're putting on airs."

I glanced at Hart as well. "I'm sure he's not judging us." I watched Patrick slicing up the haggis for the dancers to distribute throughout the room. "I thought you had five deer stomachs, but there's only one big haggis," I said to Corgi. "What gives?"

He laughed out loud. "We sewed those five stomachs together to make one big case for the haggis. Talk about nasty! I had to shower and wash everything I was wearing when I got home." He drifted away from my side, still chuckling.

I accepted a small piece of haggis from a young dancer and allowed Hart to refill my glass of whiskey at his insistence that "haggis wasn't meant to be eaten dry." He got that right. I took a nibble, which tasted like the smell of Mohair's cat food. But a good drink of whiskey made it much more palatable. If I didn't watch out, I'd soon be drunk.

Hart's gaggle of admiring fans had grown throughout the toasting of the haggis. He fielded a number of questions on his process of writing and whether or not Stu Rohan was based on a real-life acquaintance of his. I faded back to the edge of the crowd, keeping an eye on Ryan King, who had clearly had quite a bit more whiskey than I had. I wondered what had gone through Gillian's mind when she declined to answer my question about whether her dad had ever killed anyone. I frowned as I watched him. Did he seem to be a murderer? He discoursed with Hart in an excited voice, speaking rapidly and laughing out loud at the end of every sentence. Hart didn't care—the two of them were soon swapping outrageous jokes and slapping each other on the back. McCarthy circled around the edges of the crowd, taking it all in through the lens of his camera. Through it all, the Highland bagpipes droned from the hallway, and the little girls ran and danced and spun underfoot.

Suddenly, the sound of the bagpipes stopped, and Breanna stepped up to the podium. Her face was flushed, whether from the warmth of the room or a bit too much Atholl Brose, I wasn't quite sure. But when she began to speak, in a halting, anxious tone, I knew it was nervousness that colored her cheeks.

"The Highland dancers have a special performance to honor our distinguished guest, the author Morris Hart. Usually the girls dance to a recording or, if we're lucky, live bagpipes. Today, they'll dance to the accompaniment of our own Isabelle Craig singing 'The Skye Boat Song' as a tribute to Mr. Hart's most recent work."

A thin girl who couldn't have been older than eleven or twelve walked up to the mic as the dancers lined up in front of her. Paddy McLear arranged himself and his Uilleann pipes on a chair off to the side and launched into a soft Celtic waltz tune. The dancers lifted their wide plaid skirts, showing the white ruffled petticoats underneath, and bowed to the crowd. As they started to dance, Isabelle sang in a sweet, clear voice:

Speed, bonnie boat, like a bird on the wing,
Onward! the sailors cry;
Carry the lad that's born to be king
Over the sea to Skye.

Clearly the "old ballad" Hart had mentioned, the song had several stanzas, detailing Bonnie Prince Charlie's voyage across the sea with the help of Flora, who watched over his weary head. Young Isabelle's lovely voice combined with the lyrical dancing and the lilting tune to bring a tear to my eye. By the end of the song, I wished with all my heart that Charlie could indeed come again to regain his lost throne.

Isabelle held the last note, the dancers bowed to Morris Hart, and the song was finished. Hart clapped enthusiastically, causing Breanna to flush with pleasure. She shepherded her dancers off the floor, and the crowd began chattering again. Suddenly, I found Ryan at my elbow.

"So, missy, what's your story?"

I flinched, taken aback by his loud voice so close to my ear. Ryan's face was flushed red and he slurred his words. He held an overflowing glass of whiskey that slopped onto my skirt as he prodded me with an unsteady forefinger.

I pushed his hand away and swiped at my skirt, while simultaneously dodging a bit farther away from him. "What do you mean?" I tried to stall for time, racking my brain to recall whether I had committed any offense against him or his daughter. I didn't think I had even interacted with Gillian tonight, other than to accept a glass of Atholl Brose. And in that case, Morris Hart had picked up the glass.

Ryan leaned close to my face, favoring me with an onslaught of whiskey breath. "Did you do it on purpose, coming here looking like Catherine in that book?" He waved a vague hand at my clothing, slopping more whiskey in the process. I managed to avoid this deluge.

"Just a happy coincidence," I said, trying to keep my tone light. "Have you read the book?"

"Why, sure, I've read all of Hart's books. He's a master. I'm on my way to find the missing ring." He leaned in close again to whisper in my ear, "Hart says it's within a fifty-mile radius. I'm guessing it's...."

Ryan didn't get the chance to tell me the location of the ring, if in fact that was what he was going to say. He was interrupted by a loud tattoo on the snare drum to get the attention of the assembly. A tall man I recognized as the pastor of the downtown Baptist church stood at the podium. "I don't think it amiss to take a moment out of our frivolity to remember our fallen friend." He called up a lone Highland bagpiper to stand by his side. "Yesterday we lost a vibrant soul, who left this world too soon. Let us take a moment to honor Ladd Stuart Oliphant Foster."

The piper began a slow rendition of "Amazing Grace," as the guests stood silently, baring their heads and trying to quell the antics of their children as best they could.

Ryan contained himself until the piper brought the tune to a decisive end. Then he growled on a gust of alcoholic breath, "I won't mourn that son of a bitch, pardon my French." He leaned in close again. "It was God's judgment for putting the moves on my teenage daughter. God smote him! Nothing to mourn about that."

Nothing for me to say about that either. I merely nodded and sipped my whiskey, wondering if Ryan had helped God out with that judgment and celestial punishment. He certainly had the opportunity to add the torch fuel to the flask of whiskey in the VIP tent, and he was violently angry with Ladd for consorting with Gillian. Did that make him a murderer? The thought made me shiver and draw a bit farther away from him.

Ryan drained his glass and then weaved off, looking for a refill, no doubt. He didn't say goodbye and I certainly didn't pursue him. I needed to find out more about him, but in his drunken state he wasn't much use to me.

The chattering of the crowd intensified in the absence of any music. A number of musicians were setting up in the corner, with fiddle, guitar, and one bagpipe to keep up the Scottish theme. The fiddle player, a tall woman with a long white braid trailing down her back and well-worn riding breeches tucked into knee-high leather boots, called out over the crowd. "We're going to have some Scottish country dancing now. Form two long lines!"

I gulped down the rest of my drink and dropped the glass on a sideboard before joining the line of women. I felt a rush of disappointment when McCarthy waved to me from the sidelines. He focused his lens on me and snapped what was probably a stunning photo. I wished he would just shelve that camera and dance with me instead.

I found myself facing Patrick Ames for the first dance. After a few words of instruction, the musicians struck up the tune, and the fiddle player began to call the steps. We all skipped gracefully through the sprightly, energetic dance. Patrick wasn't my partner so much as the one I kept returning to as we wove in and out through the line of dancers and then swung together in the center. I was out of breath, laughing, by the time the music stopped.

I smiled up at Patrick. "You dance as well as you throw the caber, Mr. Ames."

"Call me Patrick," he said. He steered me over to the refreshment table. "Did you see the athletic events at the Games yesterday, Miss..."

"Daria. I did. I've never seen anyone throw a caber before."

He ladled out two glasses of punch. "Well, no one's ever seen a caber toss like that one before. Let's hope we never see another one like it!" He handed me some punch and then extracted a silver flask from his horsehair sporran and added a large dollop of whiskey to my glass before I had the chance to object.

I looked at the glass. The last thing I wanted to do was drink anything coming out of the flask of one of the people I suspected of murdering Ladd Foster. Patrick Ames was among those who had cycled through the VIP tent during the time Ladd's flask was contaminated. He was also alone with the flask just before it disappeared. He was high on my list of suspects. The fact that he poured a dram of whiskey into his own punch as well did not change my mind in the slightest.

I twirled the glass in my fingers, hoping he didn't notice that I wasn't drinking. "I understand you and Ladd Foster were long-standing rivals in the athletic events. When did that start?"

He scowled at the mention of Ladd's name. "We first met at the Whidbey Island Games ten years ago. We were evenly matched and could have enjoyed a friendly rivalry, except for the fact that he cheated. He substituted heavier stones on my turn in the hammer throw, so of course I couldn't throw them as far as he threw the lighter ones. You would think it would be easy to see that kind of cheating, but no one actually saw him make the switch. When I called him out on it, no one believed me."

"Well, couldn't they weigh the stones or something?"

"Exactly!" Patrick exclaimed with as much passion as if the switch had taken place the day before. "For some reason they couldn't, or more likely wouldn't, make the effort to verify the weight of the stones. They suggested a new match, and I said he shouldn't get a chance to throw against me after that kind of cheating, and in the end, they just disqualified both of us. That was the moment when I vowed to best Ladd Foster at every opportunity

I got. And I have, even up to yesterday. If he hadn't collapsed, if he had succeeded in throwing the caber all three tries, I still would have beaten him. Anyone could see that!"

I shrank back from his righteous fervor, disturbed by the fact that he was still concerned about winning when a man lay dead from murder. Did his compulsion to win extend to committing the murder himself?

I was so distracted by this thought that I lifted my glass to my lips and took a big swallow of punch. The whiskey hit me with a jolt. I had not wanted to drink that! I started coughing and sputtering. I slipped away from Patrick and practically ran for the bathroom, pausing only long enough to dump the punch out into the trash. Once there, I rinsed out my mouth and spat into the sink under the astonished gaze of a pair of young Highland dancers. "Sorry," I mumbled.

The smaller girl wrinkled her nose at me. "I didn't like the haggis either."

The girls skipped out of the bathroom and I examined my face in the mirror. My cheeks were flaming, whether from embarrassment or alcohol, I wasn't sure. My stomach was churning, but I didn't imagine I'd been poisoned by Patrick Ames's whiskey. I wasn't much of a drinker, and I'd had two or three shots so far this evening, topped off by a slice of haggis that had been baked in some old deer stomachs. Blecch!

After a few more minutes in the bathroom, tidying my hair and "freshening up," as they say, I came out to see that the country dancing had finished. The Laurel Springs Pipe and Drum Corps were marching in, bagpipes skirling. Unlike some of the other groups that had competed at the Highland Games, our homegrown band didn't have matching kilts or jackets. A colorful variety of tartans paired with black jackets of several different cuts gave them a pleasing informal look that might never win any competitions, but we loved them. The crowd cheered enthusiastically as the band circled up and launched into their traditional repertoire. Corgi played with them, although I noticed he didn't participate in all the tunes.

Of course the best part was watching the dancers. Gillian led the line of girls out to the dance floor, a professional smile lighting up her face. They had all changed into their kilts for the Highland dances.

McCarthy appeared at my elbow as the girls set up their swords for the sword dance. "Are you all right? Last time I saw that kind of reaction to a drink, a man collapsed."

"I'm fine. Patrick Ames spiked my punch with whiskey from his flask. I didn't want to drink it, but I forgot."

I rarely saw McCarthy at a loss for words, but this was one of those times. He gaped at me until I started to laugh. "He wasn't trying to poison me! He put some in his own cup too. It's just that I didn't want any more whiskey, especially not from someone's personal flask. The fruit punch is delicious just the way it is."

McCarthy chuckled and linked arms with me to walk me over to the refreshment table. He ladled me a cup of punch and then handed me a small plate piled with cheese and crackers. "Try this fine Irish cheese—just don't tell the Scots. All this whiskey on top of nothing but haggis isn't the best idea."

The cheese was strong and tasty, and the unspiked fruit punch was cool and refreshing. I didn't really think I was drunk, but I was sure it was a good idea to eat some real food. "What did you think of the haggis?" I asked McCarthy.

"I've had worse. It looked like something Aileen would enjoy." He scanned the crowd. "Aileen didn't make it, then?"

I shook my head, my mouth full of cheese and crackers. "She's stuck in jail, refusing to cooperate," I mumbled. "Pete and I stopped by, but we couldn't get anything out of her. It's like she's covering something up." I shifted my plate and slopped some punch onto my hand.

McCarthy passed me a napkin and took my plate while I mopped myself up. "Well, it looks like the Twisted Armpits are going to go on without her. Are you up for that dance tonight?" he asked.

I popped the last cracker into my mouth as the Pipe and Drum Corps marched out of the room, followed by the line of dancers. Their recessional tune gradually faded off into the distance, to make way for the Twisted Armpits. The metal band had set up their gear along the far wall, so all they had to do was pull out a few amps and position their mics while Corgi slipped back into the room. He blew up his bag, and the band launched into a very different style of music than anything we'd heard so far that evening.

McCarthy fired off a couple of photos of the band while I ditched my plate and cup and wiped off my hands. Then I let him lead me onto the dance floor. An unusually small crowd of dancers gyrated to the driving metal beat of the band. It looked like the Twisted Armpits were out of their element. Older people drifted off to the edges of the room, and parents began gathering up their young children to go home. Some of the kids held their hands pressed over their ears.

Over the past year, I had developed more of a taste for the Twisted Armpits. Call it necessity or a survival mechanism, but I often found myself actually enjoying their music, especially when that meant dancing with McCarthy. As in other aspects of his life, he threw himself into dancing with gusto. He bounded off the floor as if gravity didn't apply to him personally, and he took me with him. Tonight in particular, I was soaring above all the other dancers, high on a mix of whiskey and the pulsing beat of the Twisted Armpits, even without Aileen. I hoped the song would never end. But it did, of course, and the pipe major from the Laurel Springs Pipe and Drum Corps pushed past Pinker and commandeered the mic. "Give it up for the Twisted Armpits!" When the polite applause died down, he went on. "Thank you for coming tonight, ladies and gentlemen. I'd like everyone to join us in a chorus of 'Auld Lang Syne' to conclude our ceilidh."

The crowd linked arms and started swaying to the sentimental tune, as if we were all one big, happy family. One big family that included a murderer!

The song came to an end and people started hugging each other like long-lost relatives. McCarthy faded from my side, snapping a series of photos of the lovefest. I stood alone, watching Gillian gathering up her backpack and departing with her father. That's when Morris Hart approached me. His hair was churned up and his eyes were rimmed with red from too much Scottish cheer.

"My dear Catherine, I would be honored to escort you home, or out for a few drinks if that's what you desire." He reached for my arm, misjudged the distance, and caught me in the waist instead. He was clearly more in need of a designated driver than a few more drinks. I wondered if he remembered I wasn't really Catherine. Probably not.

I gently removed his hand from my waist. "I'm sorry, I've got other plans." I didn't really, but I didn't want to encourage him. I'd learned that being a nondriver could put me in a position of vulnerability, having to depend on someone else to take me home and then trusting them to leave again when we got there. I wasn't in the habit of asking men to come up, and I feared that might be what Hart had in mind. He felt like he'd met the incarnation of the female lead in his novel—what could be more satisfying for him than to pursue a romantic encounter with that person? But that person was me, and I had no intention of being the object of his literary/romantic fantasy! I folded my arms as a protective gesture and said, "It was really lovely to meet you, Morris. I'm looking forward to finishing your book and trying to find that ring myself."

"My dear..." He reached out and patted me on the cheek, a move my grandfather used to employ every time he gave me a dollar to spend at the dollar store. As a romantic gesture it failed miserably, but it did call up positive memories that left me feeling kindly toward Hart, who was, in fact, old enough to be my father. I smiled at him and turned away, leaving him alone and looking slightly forlorn. He probably thought that being a bestselling author entitled him to get everything he'd ever desired.

I found McCarthy standing behind me, a smile tugging at his lips. Before I could react, he said, "Can I get a picture of you holding a sprig of heather from the table decorations before they get put away?" He led me over to the edge of the room, away from Hart.

He positioned me against the wood paneling of the wall, holding a sprig of bedraggled purple heather that looked like some small children had used it to play keep away. His eyes twinkled as he snapped several photos. "Should I caption these, 'Catherine of the Isle of Skye'?"

I rolled my eyes. "I think not. I haven't even gotten to that part, so I don't know if I should be flattered or horrified that he thinks I'm his character. I guess I need to read faster." I replaced the heather on the table. "Let me see."

McCarthy obliged, holding out his camera so I could scroll through the pictures he'd just taken. I felt as tired as the heather looked, but somehow his photos managed to exude charm rather than exhaustion. "Pretty nice. But these still don't need to be on the front page of the newspaper."

He grinned. "No, these are for my ongoing collection, the Daria Photos. I have no intention of changing the name to the Catherine Collection, by the way. So, do you really have other plans, or would you like a ride home?"

"I thought you'd never ask." I grabbed my tartan fabric wrap and shoulder bag and walked with him out the door.

It was only a five-minute drive from the Highlands, where Hollystone was located, to my downtown neighborhood. There was no need for haste, but McCarthy sped through the quiet streets as if he were trying to beat his personal best in a car race. I just hung on for dear life.

We arrived home without incident, to my relief. McCarthy pulled up to the curb and cut the engine. "So, my nosy seamstress friend, did you unmask a killer tonight?"

"Not yet. I've narrowed it down to Patrick Ames, Ryan King, Morris Hart, and Aileen." He looked surprised at this matter-of-fact statement, so I told him about the parade of people going in and out of the VIP tent during the time Ladd's flask was in there unattended. "I didn't really learn anything tonight except that Patrick Ames cares very deeply about being better than Ladd, Ryan King is a big Morris Hart fan and thinks God smote Ladd for messing with his daughter, and Morris Hart is a really good storyteller but has a few issues concerning reality versus fiction. And Aileen wasn't there, through every fault of her own, so there's nothing to say about her."

"Sounds like a good start."

"Yeah. I'll get back to it tomorrow." I leaned over and tweaked his yellow tartan bow tie. "Did I tell you that you look like a leprechaun tonight?"

"Top o' the evening to you!" McCarthy's fake Irish brogue made me laugh. "But ye'll no be getting me pot o' gold, lassie."

"Save it for St. Patrick's Day." I opened the car door. "Thanks for the ride." I blew him a kiss and shut the door behind me. He pulled out with a jaunty toot of the horn and drove off.

The house was quiet. Pete's room was dark—he'd probably already gone to bed. With Aileen in jail, there was no blaring music or bustle of the band. Feeling a strong sense of letdown, I trailed up to my bedroom and tucked myself in with *Over the Sea to Skye*. I made it through two and a half paragraphs before falling fast asleep.

Chapter 9

I had big plans for Monday morning. I wanted to finish the fringe on Breanna's wedding sash before her two-thirty fitting, and I planned to do some serious research on kilt-making before Corgi's fabric arrived. If time allowed, I might even make a muslin—a mock-up of the garment out of inexpensive muslin fabric to make sure of my technique before starting work on the costly tartan wool.

But I could spare a half hour or so for reading.

I curled up in my favorite chair with a cup of tea and *Over the Sea to Skye*. I was soon sucked into the drama of Stu Rohan learning from his mysterious informant in the parking garage that his DNA test identified him as the last living heir of the Stuart bloodline, descendant of Bonnie Prince Charlie and his line of Scottish kings. Stu barely had time to absorb this information before he was whisked off to Paris to join a group of conspirators bent on retaking the throne of Britain. That was where he met Catherine, whose physical description did sound a lot like me, I had to admit. I hoped I would like her character, if I was going to be mistaken for her by Morris Hart fans.

My half hour stretched into an hour and a half, as the group searched old texts for clues to the whereabouts of Bonnie Prince Charlie's ring, one of the crown jewels that would prove Stu's claim to the throne. I paid close attention to this part, because it probably had to do with the treasure hunt for the ring that Morris Hart had spoken of. I hadn't gotten a chance to check his website yet, but I couldn't tear myself away from the novel.

I probably would have forged on until the end without stopping if it weren't for the telephone ringing. It was Breanna. "Daria, I have a conflict today at two-thirty. Is there any possible way we could push my fitting forward to, say, now?"

I groaned inwardly. Clients always thought that because I worked out of my home, I was available to them at the drop of a hat. I supposed I fostered that attitude by accommodating them, as I was about to accommodate Breanna. I did like to keep my clients happy. "Um, sure. How soon can you get here?"

"I'll be there in three minutes." I could hear the relief in Breanna's voice as she hung up.

I popped a bookmark in my book and dashed downstairs. Three minutes didn't give me time enough to finish Breanna's sash, but I could lay out her dress and get the cider bubbling on the sideboard to create the cozy, relaxing atmosphere I liked to provide for my clients. It sounded like she could use a little bit of cozy right now.

I had just enough time to open the ruffled white organdy curtains in my fitting room and get the hot cider going before the doorbell rang. I took a deep breath to get myself into a relaxed mental space and let Breanna in.

She bustled in with one eye on her watch, her red hair mussed by the wind, as if she'd driven over with all her windows open. She headed straight for my fitting room. "Thanks for squeezing me in. I can't get away from work this afternoon, so it's really helpful to get this done on my lunch hour."

"No worries." In addition to teaching Highland dance, Breanna worked in the registrar's office at the university. I imagined she didn't have much flexibility in that job.

I held up her gown, displaying the full skirt as she exclaimed with pleasure. "Go put it on." I steered her to the curtained-off corner of my fitting room. While she changed, I pulled out her sash and tidied up the threads. With any luck, she wouldn't even notice that the fringe was incomplete.

Breanna emerged from the dressing area and posed in front of my three-way mirror. I took up my pincushion and dressmaker's chalk and pinned and adjusted the fit of the bodice. Even though she had a limited amount of time available, this part of the fitting was so important. I couldn't cut any corners or the finished product might sag or pull in all the wrong places. Plus, it was the dressmaker's due to engage in a good gossip.

"I had such a good time at the ceilidh last night," I said as an opener.

"Oh, I'm so glad you came. What did you think of the girls dancing to Isabelle's singing?"

I pulled a pin out of my mouth long enough to reply. "It was lovely. I had a tear in my eye by the end, seriously."

She beamed, as if making me cry was her main goal.

"Here, lift up your arms a minute." I checked the tension on the side seams. "I really liked watching Gillian King in the sword dance. She's learned a lot in these past few months, hasn't she?"

Breanna held up her arms obediently. "She has, but it's been a struggle all the same. I'm always afraid she's going to skip out in the middle of dance class or take up smoking while wearing her dry-clean-only kilt. Her father wants me to be a strict authority figure. I'm not sure I can be strict enough for what Gillian needs."

"What about her mother?" I tried to remember if I'd ever seen Gillian with a woman at church.

"Oh, she's not in the picture. It's just the two of them at home. Ryan does his best, you can't fault him for that." She craned her neck to try to see the back of the gown.

"I chatted with Ryan at the ceilidh," I said, moving to pin up the flowing hem. "He seems like a nice guy."

Breanna laughed with a small flinch that pulled the pin right out of my fingers. "He can be Mr. Congeniality himself, but he can also be the world's biggest jerk. There was one time when Gillian sassed me throughout the entire dance practice, when she first started coming. Well, I don't put up with that kind of disrespect. When her dad came to pick her up, I told him that she would have to shape up or she couldn't continue dancing. He started yelling at her like nobody's business. Right in front of the younger girls, too. I was afraid he was going to haul off and clobber her. Since then, I'm a little more careful about what kind of comments I make to Dad."

I lowered my head, intent on the hem near the floor. "Do you think he ever hits her?"

"If I did, I would have to report it. As a teacher, I'm a mandated reporter for child abuse. I've only witnessed yelling, never anything physical." She turned counterclockwise at my request. "I have no reason to suspect it either. We do a lot of quick costume changes in Highland dance, with little thought for privacy. I've never seen any suspicious marks on Gillian's body."

"Well, that's good." Indeed, I felt a strong rush of relief. It sounded like Breanna was looking out for Gillian. But even the reassurance that he probably wasn't beating his daughter didn't answer my question as to whether Ryan King was a murderer. "Gillian was telling me that he's run off all of the boys who tried to date her. She said he even broke the nose of one boy when he brought her home late from a party. That sounded kind of violent to me."

"Well, that's a matter for law enforcement. I wouldn't be surprised if Ryan has a criminal record. They've only lived in Laurel Springs for a couple of years. When I've asked Gillian about Cleveland, where they used to live, she totally clams up, so I just let it be." She pirouetted around so I could see the entire sweep of the hem. "I'm not a social worker, you know. I teach dance in my free time, that's all."

"Well, you do a fantastic job of it. I did want to ask you who makes the girls' costumes. If you ever have need of a seamstress, just let me know."

She laughed and assured me that I would be first on her list if she ever needed professional help with the costumes. I unpinned the back of her gown and steered her to the changing area. While she dressed, I considered what I'd learned about Ryan, if anything. Breanna's suggestion that he might have a criminal record piqued my interest. Indeed, if he went around breaking kids' noses, he probably did have some kind of an assault record. I wondered how I could go about researching that.

Breanna breezed out of the changing area, paused for just an instant to set up her next fitting appointment, and dashed out the front door. On to the next thing.

I carried her gown upstairs and started right in on the alterations I needed to make to the bodice. I liked to get to the changes as soon as possible after a fitting because it was easy to forget or to lose pins or markings if I let the garment lie for any amount of time.

I worked on Breanna's gown for the next hour or so, until I felt comfortable leaving the rest for later. Then I headed downstairs to look into lunch. The house was so quiet. I was used to Pete being gone much of the day, but Aileen was usually around, making noise and commotion at every turn. With a pang, I wondered how she was faring in jail.

I grabbed a quick lunch and headed out the door for a walk around the neighborhood in the sunshine. I enjoyed the quiet downtown streets in the early afternoon, before kids got out of school to liven things up. I hurried past the brown house with the gingerbread trim where the two Dobermans lived. I had been told they were the gentlest of family dogs, but I had a hard time believing it. Their frenzied barking shattered the peace and quiet until I had passed by and no longer posed a threat. Was Ryan like those Dobermans, all bark and no bite? Or was he capable of the kind of ferocious behavior the breed was known for?

I headed for Cramer's Pond, the popular downtown park and duck pond that was my favorite place to unwind. The playgrounds were bustling with small children and their parents, while a few older people walked methodically around the pond. I sought out a secluded park bench and sat down to enjoy the sun. I pulled out my phone to do a bit of research.

When I looked up Ryan King, I found a typical number of hits for various people with the same name, but I couldn't hone in on the one I was looking for. I wasn't interested in paying for the people-finding services, so I couldn't come up with anything specific for him. I did try to search the archives of the Cleveland newspaper, *The Plain Dealer*, but all I came up with was a couple of obituaries. No luck there. I resolved to ask McCarthy if he had any tricks up his sleeve when it came to researching individuals, and moved on to my next topic, the rivalry between Ladd Foster and Patrick Ames. I searched for the Whidbey Island Highland Games from ten years ago.

I was able to find news articles and even YouTube videos from the Games. I watched a younger, slimmer Ladd throwing the caber, followed by several tosses by a similarly younger Patrick. There weren't any videos of the two of them arguing. News articles focused on the surprise ending to the Games, when Ladd outstripped the heavily favored Patrick and captured the title as winner of the heavy athletics. The article went on to insinuate that Patrick had cheated, without mentioning any wrongdoing on Ladd's part. I imagined Patrick would resent that kind of negative publicity. It wasn't hard to see how their lifelong enmity was born. I shivered, reflecting that the enmity had indeed lasted until the end of Ladd's life. Had Patrick had a hand in that ending?

I spent some time doing Internet searches on each one of them by name. I learned that they'd competed against each other in over twenty games throughout the past ten years. In most of those games, there was some report about one or the other of them cheating, although proof was never forthcoming. I wondered why they both hadn't been thrown out of the sport for good. I also noticed that one particular name showed up in almost all the articles: Herman Tisdale. The name sounded familiar—it took me a few minutes to remember that he was the announcer from our own Highland Games. Evidently, he was a former athlete who had competed alongside Ladd and Patrick until he retired four years ago. It looked like he was keeping his hand in by running the Laurel Springs Highland Games this summer. I wondered what he could tell me about the Ladd-Patrick rivalry. I resolved to track him down at my earliest convenience, and then I shelved that idea and looked up his phone number to call him on the spot. No time like the present! I introduced myself and asked if we could meet to talk about his time competing in the heavy athletics. I might have misled him into thinking I was doing a story for the newspaper. At any rate, he agreed right away to meet me in an hour's time.

I sent a text to McCarthy, asking if he'd like to come along to meet Tisdale. I figured if I brought a *Daily Chronicle* photographer along, Tisdale couldn't accuse me of arranging a meeting under false pretenses.

He texted me back: "Nosy seamstress has a lead? Happy to come along for the ride!"

I slipped my phone in my pocket with a smile and got up from the park bench to head home. As I strolled down the sidewalk, I tried to think of what questions I wanted to ask Herman Tisdale. Good thing I wasn't really a newspaper reporter, as the thought of coming up with interview questions made me anxious. I resolved to just let things happen naturally.

McCarthy showed up forty-five minutes later and followed the detailed directions Tisdale had given me to get to his home on the south side of town near the Southern Reserve. It took us an extra ten minutes to find the house once we located his street. For some reason, half the houses had no visible numbers on them, leaving visitors to guess which one was which. We ended up knocking on three doors before we hit on Tisdale's house. He lived in a small ranch house with neatly mown grass and an army of mossy garden gnomes lining the stone path to the front door.

Tisdale answered my knock. On close inspection, he was a brawny man of late middle age with thinning hair and a perpetually red nose. He wore corduroy trousers and an oversize Phillies T-shirt that revealed his thick, muscular arms. He acknowledged McCarthy and me with an exuberant smile.

"Come in, come in! Always a pleasure to talk with representatives of the media!"

He led us into a small living room bursting with jumbled bookcases, no less than three leather recliners, piles of newspapers and magazines, and an elegant silver tea service laid out on the coffee table. He waved at the recliners and carefully poured us each a cup of tea from the steaming pot.

I sat down gingerly, balancing my tea and hoping the recliner wouldn't flip me backward without warning. I had a good view of the rows of built-in shelves flanking the doorway. They contained an impressive collection of trophies, cups, and ribbons I assumed were from his days as a competitor in various Highland games.

"Thank you for seeing us, Mr. Tisdale," I said.

"Please, call me Herman. You said you wanted to know about my history as a Highland athlete."

I gave him my most winning smile. "I'm particularly interested in the Whidbey Island Games that took place ten years ago. I've heard there were only three athletes who threw the caber that day: you, Ladd Foster, and Patrick Ames. What was that competition like?"

"That was the first time I'd ever been to Whidbey Island. Only time, for that matter. I had to take a ferry to get there, and I was seasick the whole way. If I hadn't planned it so that I got there a day ahead, I would have been useless in the heavy events." He leaned forward and shook a finger at me. "Always plan a day to acclimate when you're traveling cross-country. That's the best advice I have to give you." He paused, and I realized he expected me to take down this quote. I pulled out a notebook and jotted it down. McCarthy watched me with a secret smile in his eyes.

"So, tell me about the caber toss," I went on. "What did you think of your competitors?"

"Well, that was Patrick Ames's debut, you know. He was an up-and-comer, just like Jamie Deakens this past weekend. Patrick was one of the best rookies I'd ever seen. He handled that caber like he was used to throwing logs around his backyard for fun."

I briefly wondered how one trained for the caber toss, but that wasn't what I'd come here to learn. "What about Ladd Foster?"

A look of profound sadness filled his eyes. "Laddy was one of a kind. You'll never meet anyone so full of life as he was." He set his teacup down on the floor. "Ladd and I were drinking buddies in those days. Whenever we showed up at the same competitions, we would do everything we could to beat the other on the field, and then we'd close down the bars together afterward. And when I say 'everything,' I mean everything. Laddy was the dirtiest cheater I've ever met." He chuckled. "There was that one time—in Dunedin, Florida, I think it was—when he sabotaged one of the cabers by drilling a hole in it beforehand. He'd arranged with a couple of teenagers to stage a fight on the field as a distraction while he pulled out the wood plug he'd stuck in and inserted a steel bar. So the caber was a good ten pounds heavier for all his competitors than it was for him. None of us saw what happened. Guess who won the caber toss that day?"

Realizing it wasn't a rhetorical question, I said, "Ladd?"

Tisdale slapped his knee. "You got it! He crowed about it over drinks afterward. The thing about Laddy was, you could never hold stuff like that against him. You just had to take it as a challenge to try to get him back the next time."

I wasn't sure I could be so unconcerned about habitual cheating. "What about Patrick? Did he hold stuff like that against Ladd?"

"Oh, Patrick." Tisdale blew out a gusty sigh. "Patrick had this idea that he was going to make a fortune, or even just a living, as a Highland athlete. I told him if you want to make it big in sports, pick football, for crying out loud. But he wanted to be the Terry Bradshaw of caber tossing or something. So of course he didn't take kindly to Ladd's cheating. He was always trying to get the officials to disqualify him. But Laddy could be pretty sneaky, so you couldn't always prove he was cheating. You just had to roll with it, I guess. Poor Patrick, he never learned how to do that." He picked up his teacup and poured himself a refill. "You saw him this weekend with the pole push, right? Ladd wasn't even cheating yet, but Patrick went into the match with a chip on his shoulder. All that struggle and fighting—it was all Patrick."

McCarthy was taking notes in his small spiral-bound notebook. "Do you think Patrick could have had something to do with Ladd's collapse?"

Tisdale frowned. "They say somebody poisoned Laddy's whiskey. What a horrible way to go! But it must have been somebody who knew Ladd well, to know he would be taking a wee dram now and again during the competitions. Could it have been Patrick?" He pursed his lips. "It's possible. I hate to say it, but it is possible." He scratched his head and reconsidered. "I wouldn't have thought it of him, though. He's still trying to make it in the caber-tossing business. Committing murder doesn't get you any sponsors, does it?"

"What about Ladd? Was he trying to make a living as a Highland athlete?" I asked.

Tisdale laughed. "Ladd? I doubt it. Laddy had a hand in all kinds of different things. Back in the day, he had a band he was touring with. He played banjo and guitar and sang too. He had a nice baritone voice, for all that. At one time, we all thought he was going to make it big, but that fell through. He broke up with the young woman he was touring with and moved on to take up sailing. He said he wanted to sail around the world. There was always something with him." He shook his head sadly. "I'm going to miss him, and that's the truth."

I took pity on him at the sight of his mournful face. "I saw a bunch of trophies in the living room. What can you tell us about those?"

Tisdale led us back to the living room and posed with his trophies while McCarthy took a series of photographs. He lovingly described each trophy and the event it was associated with and told a snappy anecdote about nearly every one. When the litany was finished, I figured it was about time to wrap things up.

"Thank you so much for having us here this afternoon," I said. "If you think of anything else about the Highland Games we might need to know, or about Ladd Foster, please be in touch."

I shot McCarthy a glance, which he correctly interpreted. He pulled out a card and handed it to Tisdale. "You can reach me at the Laurel Springs *Daily Chronicle*."

Tisdale turned the card over and over in his hands, seemingly reluctant to let us go. I took a deep breath to resist my natural impulse to get on with it and simply waited. McCarthy followed my lead.

After a full minute of silence, Tisdale shoved McCarthy's card into his pocket. "You'll be printing an obituary for Ladd in the newspaper, right?"

I had no idea.

McCarthy, sensing my hesitation, stepped in. "Usually the family provides the obituary, oftentimes through the funeral home. I haven't heard if Ladd's family has approached the paper." He paused, waiting for Tisdale to make the next move.

"I don't know if he has any family, to tell you the truth. He's lived in Boston for the past five years or so, working as a trainer for some college crew team or something. I don't know if there's anyone here to speak for him."

"Taffy Deroue is the obituary editor at the *Chronicle*," said McCarthy. "I'll pass on to her some of the stories you've told us today about Ladd. She might want to talk to you when she goes to put together something about him."

Tisdale nodded and opened the door for us to go. "Thank you for coming today. It was a pleasure to relive some of the good old days."

I thanked him for his time and followed McCarthy back down the gnome-lined path to the car.

I was all strapped in and McCarthy was just about to peel out from the curb when Tisdale appeared at my passenger-side window. He must have hurried down the path—his face was red from exertion to match his habitually red nose. I ran the window down and he handed me a CD. "Ladd only made two albums when he was touring with his band. This is the second one, which I thought was better than the first. Maybe you could share it with your obituary editor. I don't need it back. I got a couple extra copies when they came out, to give as Christmas gifts." He waved off my thanks and stood on the sidewalk watching us drive away.

I turned the CD case over in my hands. It was titled *Far and Away*, by the Royal Pains. The cover image showed a path winding through a field and over a stone arch bridge. The flip side listed the names of the songs, names like "Shade," "Lie on My Empty Pillow," and "Never Again in This Life." The band consisted of Ladd Foster on guitar, banjo, and vocals, and Penny Morrow on guitar and vocals. She must be the young woman Tisdale spoke of. I wondered if we might be able to contact her to find out more about Ladd and who might want to kill him.

I held out the CD to McCarthy. "Shall we have a listen?"

He glanced at the dashboard clock. "I don't have time right now. I've got a meeting at six thirty. Why don't you take it home and check it out, and then we can give it to Taffy tomorrow?"

I slipped the disc into my shoulder bag. "What kind of a meeting do you have at six thirty? A dinner meeting?"

He grinned at me. "'Nosy' really is your middle name."

He left it at that, which only served to make me curious. I wasn't about to let him see that, however. I just smiled and said, "Yup, I come by it naturally."

He dropped me off at my house and sped on his way, leaving me feeling a bit at a loss. I had, in fact, thought we might grab a bite together and talk about this new picture of Ladd Foster that Tisdale had given us.

I was touched by Tisdale's obvious fondness for Ladd, even in the face of his perpetual cheating. Outrage over persistent cheating was on my list of possible motives for murder, especially when it came to Patrick Ames. Now I began to question that thought. Could one man really be driven to murder by an offense that another found endearing? It took all kinds, I supposed. Most people didn't resort to murder, no matter how far they were pushed. The question was, was Patrick Ames the kind of man who could consider murder as a solution to the problem of Ladd's incessant cheating?

I shook my head and opened the front door to hear the familiar sound of heavy metal music coming from inside. It took me a few minutes to realize the significance of that sound. I hurried inside to see Aileen plugged into her amp in the middle of the living room, facing the TV broadcasting the Phillies game.

I flung down my shoulder bag and waved my arms in front of Aileen to get her to stop playing guitar. "You're home!"

She played a final crashing chord, and the room rang with the sudden silence. "They couldn't keep me forever. We've got rights in this country, you know."

"It's so good to see you!" Aileen looked like she was back to her old self. She was dressed all in black: a tight black leotard that clung to every curve, black leather pants with steel rivets coursing down the seams, and fingerless black gloves that reached her upper arms. Why she needed gloves on this warm summer day was beyond me. Her jet-black hair was moussed into dramatic spikes all over her head and her face was heavily made up with black mascara and eye shadow. The only color about her was a pair of high-heeled red sandals that were the same exact shade as her bright red lipstick.

I was so happy to see her back to normal that it was all I could do to refrain from hugging her on the spot. "What did they say? Why did they let you go?"

She sat down and cradled her guitar on her lap. "They kept asking me what Ladd Foster was to me, and I kept declining to divulge that information. I'm sure I could have held them off until doomsday, but they didn't get the chance to get fed up with me and kick me out of there. Somebody sent a lawyer over to tell them there was a time limit on holding someone without formally arresting them." She strummed a few chords. "Was that you?"

"Did I send a lawyer? No, it wasn't me. Sounds like a good idea, though."

She snorted. "If I'd known about that time limit, I would have let them go past it and then sued them for false imprisonment." She shrugged as her strumming sped up. "Still, it's good to be shut of that place. Your brother spent seven whole months in jail. Two nights was plenty for me."

"Yeah, no kidding." We sat without speaking for a minute, thinking of Pete surviving an extended jail stint for drug use. He never spoke of it, but it was now part of his history.

Aileen played a series of crashing chords on her guitar, her way of changing the subject, I supposed. "I missed the ceilidh. Did the band suck without me?"

There was only one right answer to that question. "Pretty much. But the good news is, I'm making Corgi a new kilt. He'll look really sharp by the next time you guys play."

"You're a kilt-maker now? That can't be an easy thing to make."

"I'll figure it out." I couldn't stand this small talk anymore. "Aileen, tell me about you and Ladd Foster. I'm trying to figure out who killed him, assuming it wasn't you."

She stood up and churned out a blistering guitar riff. I sat quietly, biting my tongue and sitting on my hands to keep from ripping the guitar away from her and hitting her over the head with it. Why wouldn't she just answer me?

"He's the definition of lowlife," she finally growled. "I'm glad he's dead. We're all better off without him. I don't want to talk about him ever again."

I sighed. "Okay, just answer me one question. Did you put torch fuel into his whiskey flask?"

She glared at me. "If you need to ask me, you don't deserve an answer." She threw her guitar over her shoulder and marched out of the room.

I dropped my head in my hands. I supposed I could have been more subtle with my question, instead of essentially asking Aileen if she was a murderer. I was unlikely to get another chance to bring up the subject. When I went upstairs after supper, Aileen's door was closed. I knew better than to disturb her.

I lingered in the doorway of my workroom, looking over my projects. I still needed to finish raveling the fringe on Breanna's sash and I had yet to start work on the tiny tartan bows for her headpiece. Then there was Corgi's kilt. I wasn't expecting the tartan fabric for another day or two, but I could work up a muslin to get some practice on making the pleats. I tried to avoid pleats when I could because it was always very time-consuming to get them spaced just right. With the plaid tartan fabric, there would be no room for error. Some practice might be a good idea.

But not right now.

I closed my workroom door deliberately and headed for my bedroom. I curled up in the padded rocking chair in front of the bricked-over fireplace and cracked open *Over the Sea to Skye*. I was transported to Paris, where Stu and Catherine ditched their group of conspirators and headed off on their own to a monastery in Alsace, looking for Bonnie Prince Charlie's ring. I could feel the tension building as I read. The stakes were increasing for Stu, even as he appeared to be falling in love with Catherine. I found myself liking Stu a lot, so Hart's admonition not to take it personally when things happened to Catherine made me nervous for the two of them.

Finally, I realized this wasn't a book to read under the covers at night unless I was prepared to keep going until I finished it at three thirty in the morning. Then I would have to stay up the rest of the night hoping no international intrigue was going to assail me in the staid little town of Laurel Springs. I laid the book aside. It was already eleven thirty and I had accomplished absolutely nothing all evening. As I drifted off to sleep, I found myself thinking about Morris Hart, and wondering if I would run across him again.

And who was McCarthy having dinner with anyway?

Chapter 10

I woke up the next morning ready to get my hands on some tartan fabric and start making a kilt. But I had to wait until the mail was delivered.

The morning was cool and sunny, but the weather forecast was for rain starting around lunchtime. I decided to start my day off with a walk and save my sewing for the rainy afternoon. Neither of my housemates was around. Pete was already off to work, and Aileen was still sound asleep, so I stepped out by myself. I strolled down the shady streets adjacent to Cramer's Pond, and then, on an impulse, I hopped on the bus to the Commons, just a short bus ride away.

The Commons was a pedestrian mall created by blocking off a few downtown streets, bricking them over in a decorative pattern, and installing wrought-iron lampposts and benches to give it an old-fashioned aura. The shops on the Commons leaned heavily toward scented candles, stained-glass creations, and expensive couture kinds of clothing that someone like me could never afford. My custom-made historical sewing business would fit in nicely on the Commons, but I couldn't afford the high rent for a storefront either. Maybe someday…

Even if I couldn't afford to buy, I always loved window-shopping on the Commons. I indulged in that passion without shame. I did have a bit of an ulterior motive, however, as I headed for Letty Overby's antique shop. I was looking for a good gossip, and if Letty couldn't provide that, nobody could.

The bell jangled as I entered Letty's shop, Treasures of Yesteryear. The shop was filled to bursting with antiques of all descriptions, from the crowded shelves of jewelry and bone china to the racks of vintage clothing to a jumble of wooden barrels and iron plows in the corner. Despite the open window, the shop smelled dusty and musty. It was a pleasant mustiness, however, evoking old comic books and Grandma's faded felt hats, more than dirt and decay.

Letty bustled out from the back room, dusting her hands on her slacks and calling out a cheery hello. She added my name to her greeting when she noticed who had entered her shop.

"Daria, how good to see you! Out for a stroll on this fine, sunny morning? We're supposed to get a deluge by this afternoon, you know."

"Yeah, I thought I'd grab some sun while I can get it." I fingered a few of the antique textiles spread out on a wide shelf. "Do you have any handkerchiefs I can look at? I need a few more to use as christening bonnets."

Letty reached under the counter and pulled out a box overflowing with handkerchiefs of every description. If I couldn't find a nice batch for some future christening bonnets, there was no hope for me.

I sifted through the piles, pulling out some possibilities when I saw them. "Looks like you've gotten back into the swing of things after the Highland Games."

Letty leaned both elbows on the counter, a sure sign she was ready to gossip. "I don't know about you, but I lost money on that venture. I'm not sure if I'll do it again. Those booths were so expensive, even with the two of us splitting the cost."

"Yeah, but think of the experience. I sold a bunch of tartan bow ties and I had a great time. That was worth it in my book."

"Well, I suppose the exposure itself was worth it. Some people go out of their way to avoid walking on the Commons, for fear they'll get sucked into spending some money or something. But I have had some new customers as a result of the Games." She pointed to a handkerchief I'd rejected. "That one is half off. Guess who came in this morning, looking to sell some jewelry?"

I placed the handkerchief firmly in my reject pile. "No idea. Anyone I know?"

"Ryan King. You know, Gillian's father. He just left, as a matter of fact. He brought in these pieces of jewelry." She indicated a tray containing an array of necklaces, dainty bracelets, and even a wedding band and engagement ring. "He said they belonged to his wife and he couldn't bear to have them in the house any longer. He didn't know how to get rid of them until he saw my booth over the weekend."

"No kidding." I bent over the tray and fingered the jewelry. "Did he say what happened to his wife?"

"Well, of course I had to ask him. If there was a nasty divorce or something, he might not have had ownership of the jewelry to begin with. The last thing I want is a lawsuit for selling items that rightfully belong to someone other than the seller. So I asked him." She picked up a stray handkerchief and placed it on my yes pile. "Want to know what he said?"

"Yes!"

She smiled and folded up a few more handkerchiefs. Then she leaned on the counter once more. "He said she died two years ago, when the family lived in Cleveland. I said that must have been a terrible tragedy and he said, and I quote, 'you have no idea.' So you know me, I asked him if it was cancer or what. She must have been a fairly young woman, with a fifteen-year-old daughter. With younger women, it's usually cancer. He didn't want to go into specifics, poor man. He just said it was a terrible shock, and when the investigations were over, he couldn't have gotten out of town quicker. He's been in Laurel Springs for two years, no more."

I stood still, the handkerchiefs forgotten. "He said that? 'When the investigations were over'? What investigations? That's not a typical thing to say after someone dies."

"Hmm, good point. I didn't think about that. Maybe she died in a car accident."

Or maybe she was murdered. I thought about Gillian's reaction when I said her father had never killed anyone, right? Maybe he had. The very thought gave me a chill. "Did he mention his wife's name?"

Letty shook her head. "He clearly didn't want to talk about her."

I sifted through the necklaces, hoping to find a locket with a picture or a name. I came up empty, but I did find an engraving inside the wedding band. It read, "Ryan and Melissa, till death do us part."

"Look, her name was Melissa." I held the ring in the palm of my hand. "You're not really going to sell this as an antique, are you?"

"Well, people do buy wedding rings, if you can believe it. I suppose they're cheaper than a brand-new ring from a jeweler. It's a bit harder to sell one that's personalized like this." She studied my face. "You have some objection to my selling this?"

I stroked the ring gently, feeling like I should call it "my precious." "I was just wondering if he'd given any thought to Gillian. You would think a girl would want her mother's wedding ring, especially if she died in tragic circumstances."

Letty considered the ring. "I have no way of knowing whether he consulted with his daughter."

I laid the ring down on the tray with the rest of Melissa King's jewelry. "Maybe you could just hang on to all this stuff for a few days before you put it up for sale. If Ryan comes in and asks why it's not displayed, you could tell him you had to send them to the cleaners or something."

"Or I could just ask him straight out if he might want to save these things for Gillian. I don't mind asking those kinds of tough questions. I could call him up right now and tell him I wanted to make sure before I sold any of it."

I laid a hand on her arm, afraid she was about to pick up the phone and do just that. "Maybe just hang on to it for a bit. I'd like to talk to Gillian to see what her feelings about her mom are. I'd hate to stir up Ryan's grief if Gillian doesn't even care about her mother's things." I placed my pile of handkerchiefs on the counter. "Let me talk to Gillian and I'll get back to you about the King family jewelry."

Letty gathered up my pile and began punching buttons on her old-fashioned gilded cash register. "I'm in no hurry to put these things out." She waved a hand at her display cases, filled with vintage jewelry. "There's plenty for people to choose from." She held up one of the necklaces, a delicate silver chain strung with beads that looked like garnets. "This one would look perfect with your complexion."

I couldn't help but agree. "Tell you what: if Gillian has no interest in her mother's things, I'll buy this one for myself."

Letty laughed and laid it back with the rest. "Don't feel like you have to, of course. But you couldn't find a prettier necklace to pick up the depths of your eyes."

"You are without doubt the best saleswoman in town." I paid for my purchases and waved on my way out.

I'd spent a good forty-five minutes in Treasures of Yesteryear, so I figured it was time to head home and get to work on my sewing. I only had to wait a few minutes for the next bus, which drove up just as the raindrops began to fall.

By the time the bus let me off on my street, the few drops of rain had become a deluge. It was only one block from the bus stop to my house, but I was still wet to the skin by the time I dashed through the front door. I threw down my bundle of handkerchiefs and ran upstairs to change. I was just coming out of the bathroom with a towel around my wet hair when the doorbell rang.

When I got to the front door there was no one there, but a big package sat on the doorstep. I ripped it open to reveal four yards of heavyweight wool in the Ancient Guthrie tartan. Time to make a kilt!

* * * *

I grabbed a quick bite for lunch and then holed up in my workroom to get started on Corgi's kilt. Usually, the first step in sewing is to wash the fabric, to preshrink it before running up the seams. I'd never had the experience of having a garment come out all puckered from shrinking around the stitches after the first wash because I religiously adhered to this important step. But not today. Technically, wool was washable, but only if you wanted to shrink it into felt. That wasn't my intention. Once Corgi's kilt was finished, it would be dry-clean-only.

I started by laying the whole cloth out on the floor and finding the midpoint. Luckily, the plaid was straight on the grain of the fabric, so I could use the pattern as a cutting guide. I took a deep breath, prayed I wouldn't make a foolish mistake, and began to cut lengthwise along the midpoint until I had two lengths of four yards each. Together, they would become the eight-yard kilt.

My online instructions would have me hem the fabric next, but I intended to use the selvage for the top edge of the kilt, thus eliminating the need for a hem. I would hem the bottom of the kilt once it was all constructed and Corgi had tried it on. So, I proceeded directly to the pleats.

The first pleat was the most important because all the others would build off it. The tartan lent itself to a six-inch pleat. I took a sturdy piece of cardboard and marked it at six inches, to use as a guide for measuring. It took me a good fifteen minutes and numerous false starts just to pin up the first pleat. I took a picture of it on my phone, to commemorate the process and to celebrate the first step. Then I continued to the next, and the next one after that.

It wasn't long before I realized I needed something to distract me from the strain in my back as I crouched over the fabric laid out on the floor. I stood up and stretched, and then rooted in my shoulder bag for the CD from Herman Tisdale. I wasn't a big fan of country music, but a bit of Ladd Foster's band would do nicely to keep my mind off the tedious pleats.

I popped the disc into my CD player and knelt back down for the next series of pleats. I had long abandoned my first thought that I could get them all pinned up this afternoon. At this point I was just shooting for completing ten of them.

The twangy sound of the banjo predominated in Ladd's music. He did have a pleasant baritone voice, like Tisdale had said. His bandmate, Penny, had a rich alto voice that complemented his. Her voice sounded somehow familiar to me, although I couldn't think why. I rarely listened to country music, so I wasn't likely to recognize any country artists. I folded and pinned, and pulled out pins to reposition them, and listened to the love affairs and laments of the Royal Pains as the raindrops pounded on my windowpanes. It was just enough to keep my mind off the pain in my back, not to mention murder.

When the CD finished, I was still short of my goal in my pleating. I hadn't been able to identify why Penny's voice sounded so familiar, but the nagging question was distracting me from concentrating on my work. After three false starts before I succeeded in pinning up the next pleat, I decided to take a break. I pushed Play on the CD again to listen to the catchiest tune, "Flowers of the Forest." I leaned back in my work chair and closed my eyes, focusing on the voice of Ladd Foster, now dead, and his bandmate, Penny. She mostly sang harmony, but on this song she had a lead part. Her voice soared above the guitar, clear and full. She reminded me of... I just couldn't tell. It was so close but still elusive.

The sound of my phone dinging interrupted my thoughts. It was McCarthy. "Are you doing anything this evening? I've got a gig at the Printed Page at seven. Your buddy Morris Hart is doing a reading and the Highland dancers are opening for him. We could grab a quick bite to eat beforehand. What do you say?"

I surveyed the blister on my forefinger, caused by shoving pins into the thick fabric. My pleats could wait. "Sure. Just don't call me Catherine."

He laughed and said he'd be right over.

I nipped into my bedroom to change and tidy up my hair, as if McCarthy would even notice. Most of his focus would be on photographing the events at the Printed Page. Maybe I would get a chance to ask Gillian about her mom once the Highland dancers were done.

McCarthy texted me from the car: "Ready?" That's how it was, going out to eat with McCarthy. Dinner with him didn't even have the appearance of a date. I ran down the stairs and out the front door, dodging the raindrops on my way to the Mustang idling at the curb.

McCarthy gave me a cheery hello. He was dressed up in a sport coat and slacks instead of his customary jeans.

"Wow, is this a formal occasion, then?"

"With the Printed Page, you never know." He peeled out from the curb and zoomed through the relatively heavy traffic, the closest we ever came to rush hour in our small town. "Sounds like this is a pretty big event, with the dancers and all."

I nodded, preoccupied by the trepidation that always overtook me in a car.

McCarthy glanced over at me and slowed down a little bit. "Any word from Aileen?"

I gave a start. I should have told him. "She's out of jail and back home. It's good to have her back."

"Is she still taking the high road when it comes to talking about Foster?"

I blew out an exasperated breath. "Yeah. I don't know what's the matter with her. I'm going to have to find out what that whole thing is about without her cooperation."

He glanced sidelong at me. "She'd better watch out. You've got that determined look on your face. Something tells me that you're not feeling shy about getting into her business. But a word to the wise, my nosy seamstress. Aileen is a force to be reckoned with. You might want to watch out yourself."

I looked at him in surprise. "You don't think she murdered Ladd, do you?"

For once, he was serious. "I don't know, Daria. It's not impossible."

When I stared at him, incredulous, he backpedaled a bit. "I'm not saying she did it. Just that she's a force to be reckoned with. She obviously hated the guy. She held off from bashing him over the head with her guitar, maybe because so many people were watching. Who's to say she didn't sneak off in private and slip some poison into his whiskey?"

"Well, it doesn't sound like Aileen, for one thing. Privacy isn't one of her big values. When has she ever tried to hide or cover up anything she does?" As soon as I said it, I realized that was exactly what she was doing. She was trying to hide her prior relationship with Ladd Foster. Was there some clue in that relationship that would reveal her as a murderer?

McCarthy just concentrated on the road. He circled around the Commons, looking for a parking place, finally settling for street parking a couple of blocks away. "We've got time for dinner at City Lights as long as they're not busy." He offered me his umbrella, and we hustled along the sidewalk at a brisk walk.

Lucky for us, City Lights wasn't busy. A small storefront a block from the Commons with a gritty urban atmosphere, the café specialized in gyros, Greek salads, and the best hummus west of Philadelphia. We slid into a tiny booth and placed our orders.

McCarthy leaned back and threw an arm across the back of the booth. "So, my nosy seamstress, what have you discovered about the case today?"

"I haven't come to any conclusions." I nodded to the waitress as she deposited my soda on the table. "Mostly, I've been pinning up plaid pleats, if you want to know the truth." I showed him the pictures I'd taken of

Corgi's kilt in progress. "I do have a couple of leads, but I need to track them down before they're really worth talking about."

His eyes crinkled up at the corners when he smiled at me. "You sound like a regular private eye."

"That's more than you can say. What has the obnoxious photographer discovered?"

McCarthy chuckled at my usual characterization of him. "I've been behaving myself all day at the Amish quilt show, followed by a children's matinee at the symphony." He clenched his hands together beseechingly. "I must confess I've come up with exactly nothing in terms of cracking the case of who killed the caber tosser. Please have mercy!"

I drew my eyebrows together in a frown while trying to suppress my laughter. "All right. This once, I'll forgive your lamentable inaction. Don't let it happen again."

The arrival of our food interrupted this charade. We dived in with one eye on the clock. At half past six McCarthy hustled me out of the restaurant. "I want to get set up before the event starts." We hastened down the sidewalk to the brick walkway of the Commons and on to the local bookstore, the Printed Page. The front window held a display of Morris Hart novels, with *Over the Sea to Skye* prominently displayed. Inside, a handful of customers browsed through the bookshelves, while the staff set up more copies of Hart's bestseller on a table in the open area off the front door. Hart hovered next to the table, seeming ill at ease. His face brightened considerably at the sight of McCarthy and me.

"Hey, there, Catherine. Nice to see you here. I was afraid the rain would keep people away."

I couldn't help smiling at him. "My name's really Daria, you know. I'm still not done with the book, but I have met Catherine by now."

"You get what I'm talking about, then? You're the spitting image of Catherine. You could play her in the movie." He cocked his head and surveyed me as if I were a curious piece of artwork. "Do you act, by any chance?"

I laughed. "Only if you count high school musicals." He seemed to be sober today, unlike the last time we'd talked. I was sorry he persisted with this idea of me being the incarnation of his character, as if he was only interested in me as Catherine, not Daria. If I wanted something from him, I could use this Catherine likeness to my advantage. But there wasn't anything I wanted from Morris Hart.

I faded off into the background as the staff consulted with McCarthy about the photographic coverage for the newspaper and Hart prepared to do his reading. The Highland dancers were gathering in the children's section, preparing for their opening performance. The girls wore their Highland outfits: kilt, ruffled blouse, and velvet vest. I was scanning their ranks for Gillian when I heard her loud voice.

"It's not my fault. The button was loose and it came off, that's all. It's right here. I didn't lose it."

"You should have sewed it back on at home." Breanna stood with her hands on her hips, frowning. "You can't go on with your vest gaping open like that. It looks awful."

Gillian tossed her head. "I don't know what you think I'm supposed to do about it."

Breanna bristled at this belligerence, as if she were at the end of her rope with Gillian.

"Seamstress to the rescue," I called out, rummaging through my shoulder bag as I hustled over to join them. "I always carry a sewing kit in my bag. I'll have that button back where it belongs before you know it."

"Thanks, Daria. You're a lifesaver," Breanna said. She turned away without a word to Gillian. She probably figured silence was better than a lecture.

Gillian shrugged out of her vest and held it out to me, along with the button.

I regarded the vest. "Do you know how to sew?" I offered her my pincushion.

She rolled her eyes. "Who's gonna teach me how to sew?" She shoved the vest at me.

I plucked out a needle and threaded it for her. "I usually use a double thread when I sew on buttons." I showed her how to tie the knot so it wouldn't look too big and messy. Then I picked up the vest and showed her the broken threads that marked the place to put the button. "You have to get these out first, and then use the stitch marks left behind as a guide to sew the button back on." I handed her the vest, needle, and button.

Under my watchful eye, she succeeded in sewing her button back on. There was a faint shine of accomplishment in her eyes as she put the vest on and buttoned it up.

"Nice job," I said. "If you're interested in learning to sew, just let me know. Maybe we could work something out." She could learn to sew and I could learn what she thought about what happened to her mom in Cleveland.

"Gillian! Right now, ready or not!" Breanna called. The other girls were all in line with their swords held upright, ready to march.

Gillian jumped up to follow them. "Thanks" was all she said.

I didn't press the matter. She was like a wild animal—I needed to gain her trust. I just hoped she would think things over before leaving the bookstore, because I didn't know when I would run into her next.

I joined the crowd that had gathered to watch the Highland dancers. Most of them were parents of the dancers, including Ryan. I sidled through the crowd until I was standing next to him.

He gave me an automatic glance and then did a double take as he recognized me. "You're the girl who looks just like Catherine. Are you going to go on tour with Hart?"

Not on your life! "No. I just came to watch the dancers and listen to the reading." I directed his attention back to his daughter. "Gillian looks better and better every time I see her."

"Better than what?" he growled. "What are you judging her on?"

"I'm not judging her," I said, taken aback. "I meant her dancing is getting better. She must be practicing. That's all." Like Hart, Ryan seemed to be completely sober, but he still made me uncomfortable every time I talked to him. But I pressed on. "I was just helping her sew a button back onto her vest. I'm a seamstress." When he didn't respond, I prattled on. "I'm making Breanna Lawton's wedding gown, you know. She's going with a Celtic motif that should be quite lovely." I paused to clap as the girls bowed at the end of the sword dance. "Sometimes I give sewing lessons to high school students. It's a great way for them to stay out of trouble while learning a useful skill. One girl even made her own prom dress, with my help." I smiled at him, as if I had just shared the most important secret he would hear all week. "I love watching the sword dance, don't you?"

Ryan just nodded and stared after me as I moved away through the crowd.

I wormed my way to the edge of the crowd, looking for a good place to stand. I'd planted seeds with both father and daughter. Now it was time to leave them to germinate on their own. I shuffled around until I had an unobstructed view of Hart. I wondered why the bookstore hadn't set up chairs, for goodness' sake. At least the rain hadn't kept everyone away. There was a good-sized crowd staying after the dancing to hear Hart's reading.

Hart opened his copy of *Over the Sea to Skye* to someplace in the middle. If he was reading a portion I hadn't gotten to yet, I resolved to skip out on him. I didn't want any spoilers.

He chose a section I had already read; just last night in fact. The sound of the familiar words read in Hart's deep, slow voice became something akin to poetry. I was enjoying the sensory experience so much, it was a good ten minutes before I realized he was reading the section in which Stu meets Catherine for the first time. With a start, I saw that his eyes kept flashing to me, as if I were on the receiving end of a private, intimate reading of his words. People in the crowd began to notice and turn to stare at me. I didn't know whether to feel flattered or annoyed or just plain embarrassed by the overt attention. Just when I thought it couldn't get any worse, it got worse.

Hart closed his book with a snap. "Before I take any questions, I have a fascinating tale to tell you. I've been an author for over twenty-five years and this has never happened to me before. I was doing a book signing over the weekend at the Highland Games here in town, and I met a special young woman. She could be the incarnation of the character I created out of mere imagination." He flung out an arm in my direction. "Let me introduce you to the perfect image of Catherine in the flesh."

I gave a little wave, but that wasn't enough for Hart. He held out his hand, inviting me to join him at the front.

Realizing that a refusal would only bring me more attention, I walked up to his side. He grasped my hand and leaned in close to whisper in my ear, "Tell me your name."

"I'm Daria Dembrowski, a seamstress here in town," I said to the crowd with as much poise as I could muster. "Like Mr. Hart, this is a first for me too. I've never been the embodiment of somebody's character before. But I haven't finished the book yet, so don't give away what happens to Catherine in the end." I turned to Hart, silently imploring him to take some questions from the audience, hopefully ones that had nothing to do with the miraculous appearance of one of his characters in the flesh. In the background, McCarthy's camera clicked merrily away.

Hart grinned from ear to ear, clearly delighted to share the stage with the incarnation of his character. He kept hold of my hand while he addressed the crowd. "If you have read *Skye*, you'll recognize Catherine in Daria here in a heartbeat. If you haven't read it yet, you'll keep her image in your mind while you read." He gazed at me in silence for a moment and then shook himself. "Could we get a picture for the newspaper?" he called out to McCarthy.

We posed for a picture, taken by a grinning McCarthy, and then Hart turned to the questions from the crowd. I slipped back to my place on the edge of the action.

McCarthy sidled up beside me. "I said I wouldn't call you Catherine, and I didn't. Remember that."

I rolled my eyes. "At least when you print that picture you can include my business title. I'll take it as a bit of free publicity."

He laughed. "There you go. Spoken by a savvy seamstress, as well as a nosy one."

Hart's question-and-answer session lasted for over an hour. I learned he tried to write every day, if only just a few paragraphs, and that his dog, Muse, had a special chair next to Hart's desk, where the Scottie could snooze and provide inspiration. "Whenever I don't know what to write next, I write a few words to describe Muse's appearance or actions. It usually gets me over the hump," he said.

The mental picture of a fluffy black dog named Muse acting as just that for his master caught my fancy. I'm a cat lover myself, but I could well appreciate the devotion of an artist for his pet. I found myself feeling drawn to Morris Hart.

When he was finished with the questions, Hart sat down behind a mountain of books and began signing copies for his fans. McCarthy continued taking photographs, while I browsed through the bookshelves, wondering if I should just ditch McCarthy and head home on my own. But I found a table filled with books on Scottish history and culture, compiled by the bookstore staff to supplement Hart's novel, no doubt. I was soon lost in a book about genealogy and the history of the Scottish clans in America. As I paged through it, I almost wished I had Scottish heritage myself.

"That's the definitive work on the Scottish diaspora." Morris Hart leaned over my shoulder to turn a few pages. "Here's the section on Count Roehenstart, Bonnie Prince Charlie's illegitimate grandson. Charlie had no legitimate offspring, you know, so I've traced his descendants through Roehenstart, whose sojourn in Philadelphia provided much of the inspiration for *Over the Sea to Skye*." He pointed to the page, and then let his hand come to rest on mine. "I'm glad you waited around. Maybe you'd like to go somewhere and talk about Scottish royal roots over a drink or two."

I slipped out of his embrace. "Actually, I was waiting for Sean McCarthy. We came together."

Hart looked over his shoulder, where McCarthy was engaged in an animated conversation with the bookstore owner. "McCarthy, the photographer?" He glanced at my left hand, looking for a ring, no doubt. "Are you two a couple, then?"

Good question. I felt McCarthy's eyes on me as I fielded Hart's inquiry. "Sean's a close friend. We do a lot of things together."

"Close friends like Stu and Catherine?" Hart persisted.

I had already gotten to the part where Stu and Catherine ended up in bed together within twenty-four hours of their meeting, so it was clear to me that my relationship with McCarthy wasn't on a par with that. But I didn't feel like I needed to discuss that with Morris Hart. I settled for what I hoped came across as a secret smile and said, "I'm sorry I'm not available this evening. How long are you in town for?" Maybe I should have left off that last bit, but I had to admit there was a heady romanticism involved in being the living image of an author's creation. I would have enjoyed spending some time with Hart, if I wasn't afraid that what he most wanted was an intimate encounter with his Catherine. I totally wasn't interested in that.

I glanced over at McCarthy to see that he had his camera out and pointed at me. He winked at me, a big grin on his face. If he had caught my secret smile on film, I would never hear the end of it.

He dropped his camera around his neck and came over to join us. "I really enjoyed the reading," he said to Hart. "How goes your search for the ring?"

"I'm homing in on it, but it's proving to be more elusive than I had anticipated." Hart shifted his attention back to me. "I'm planning to be in town for another couple of days, until I wrap up my quest. Maybe we could plan a date together, you and I? We could meet for coffee, or lunch perhaps?" His gaze flicked to McCarthy and away again, as if he were testing how McCarthy would take this suggestion.

I was interested in this question as well, but McCarthy didn't rise to the bait. He merely watched quietly, waiting to see what I would say.

Well, if he didn't care…

"Let's meet for lunch. Tomorrow?" It would be a good opportunity to get to know Hart better, and try to figure out if he had any motive for killing Ladd, or if I could take him off my list of suspects. I eyed him dubiously. What kind of restaurant would a bestselling author frequent? "We could meet here at noon and then find someplace to eat on the Commons."

A delighted smile lit up Hart's face. "Tomorrow it is!" He turned away without another word. He snagged his blazer and umbrella from the signing table and sauntered out the door, leaving me alone with McCarthy.

I expected some barbed comment about Hart, but, as usual, McCarthy surprised me. He laid a hand on my arm and pointed to a chair in a corner of the children's section. Huddled on the chair with her head down on her knees was a forlorn Highland dancer. Her sheathed sword dangled from a cord around her wrist. It was Gillian.

Chapter 11

I glanced around, but Breanna and the other dancers had long gone. I didn't see Gillian's father anywhere.

"Do you think she got left behind?" McCarthy said.

"I guess there's one way to find out." I went over and stood next to her. "Hey, Gillian. You're still here."

Her head snapped up. "Duh." She scowled at me and then dropped her head on her knees once more.

"Is your dad around?"

Her head shot up again. "What do you care? Leave me alone!"

I exchanged a helpless look with McCarthy. He drew me away from her. "Do you know where she lives? The store is about to close and it's still raining buckets out there. Can she get home on her own or does she need a ride?"

I was an expert on the bus schedules in Laurel Springs, but I didn't know where Gillian lived. Reluctantly, I approached her again.

"Do you need a ride home? We can drop you off if you want."

Gillian glared at me. "What makes you think I need anything from you?"

I gritted my teeth. "Nothing. See you." I spun on my heel and walked away. I grabbed McCarthy's arm and pulled him straight out the door. "If she wants a ride, she'll follow us. If she doesn't, then she can figure it out on her own."

Outside, the rain cascaded off the roof and pelted into the puddles forming on the brick walkway. McCarthy opened his umbrella and held it over the two of us. "How long does it take a sulky teen to realize she needs a hand?"

"Probably longer than we'd like." I scootched closer to him under the umbrella. "I'm guessing there's a power struggle going on between her and her dad and we've stepped into the middle of it. If we go back in, we lose. If we stay here too long and she comes out and we're waiting for her, we lose. If we just leave, we'll feel guilty, so we lose." I brushed at my shoulder, which was rapidly getting soaked.

McCarthy put an arm around me, drawing me even closer. "If we're going to lose anyway, I'd rather just lose now and get it over with. Come on." He opened the door and ushered me back inside, shaking the rain from his umbrella on the way in.

Gillian hadn't moved. McCarthy walked straight up to her and squatted down in front of her. He turned on his two-hundred-watt smile. "I'm Sean McCarthy from the Laurel Springs *Daily Chronicle*. I was wondering if I could get one last photo of you for the newspaper." He waved a hand at me. "You know Daria, right? She's doing a piece on kilt-making for the newspaper, and we'd like to run a picture of a real-live person wearing a kilt. I got some shots of the dancers during the sword dance, so just one posed picture would wrap things up." He glanced at his watch. "We've got four minutes before the store closes." He flashed that grin again. "What do you say?"

Gillian bought it, like I knew she would. She wiped an arm across her eyes and stood up. She tucked in her blouse, straightened her kilt, and stood where McCarthy told her. She even smiled at his coaxing.

He fired off a series of pictures. Just in time. The lights went out and then flashed on again. A quick glance at the checkout desk showed me that the remaining staff members were all looking at us and tapping their feet.

As if he had all the time in the world, McCarthy replaced the cover on his lens and said, "I'll need to get a parent's permission to run these pictures in the paper. Is your mom or dad around?"

"Um, no, my dad took off." Gillian looked about to shut down again, but McCarthy wasn't done yet.

"Do you need a ride home? I'm taking Daria home, so I could easily drop you off as well." He pulled out his phone. "Let me just give your dad a call so he knows you're riding with me. What's his number?"

Gillian stared, but only for a second. Then she gave him her dad's number. She muttered under her breath, "He'll never go for it. He told me to walk home."

We both watched as McCarthy dialed and then launched into a genial conversation with Ryan. He introduced himself and talked easily about photographing the girls for the newspaper and the special shots he'd taken of Gillian. He emphasized the fact that he needed Ryan's written permission to print any pictures of his daughter and mentioned my name several times. They even talked about the Phillies game Ryan was evidently watching. Finally, McCarthy hung up and turned to us with another big smile.

"All set. We'd better get going before the bookstore staff decides to charge us rent." He gave them a cheery wave goodbye, turned up his collar, and handed me his umbrella to hold over Gillian and myself. We made a dash down the brick sidewalk awash with water. By the time we made it to the car, Gillian was gasping with laughter at the rain and her reprieve from walking home in it.

It was a short drive to Gillian's house on the north side of town, but it would have taken her a good twenty-five minutes to walk. She had the grace to thank McCarthy for the ride when she gave him directions.

I was bursting to know what had transpired between Gillian and her dad to cause him to leave her behind to walk twenty-five minutes in the dark and rain, but I restrained myself. Instead of questioning her, McCarthy and I engaged in some cross-talk from the front seat about the size of the crowd despite the weather and the fun of seeing the Highland dancers in the unlikely setting of the bookstore.

"What's the most surprising place you've ever danced?" McCarthy asked over his shoulder, keeping his eyes on the road.

"One time three of us danced on the back platform of a caboose. The train wasn't moving, but the platform had all these little slots in it so you could see the ground. It was freaky." Gillian leaned back and closed her eyes. "Did my dad sound mad when you talked to him on the phone?" she asked in a small voice.

"Not really. Did the two of you have a fight or something?" McCarthy kept his eyes on the road.

Gillian groaned. "Or something. He's always ragging on me about my makeup or how I fix my hair." She leaned forward, gripping the front seats with both hands. "Do you think this makeup makes me look like a slut?"

McCarthy didn't miss a beat. "Well, I can't tell when I'm driving. But I didn't feel like I was photographing a slut back at the bookstore." He flashed her an encouraging smile. "Sometimes dads get a bit overprotective when their daughters grow up."

She snorted and flounced against the backseat again.

We drove in silence for a few minutes, then, just as we turned onto Gillian's street, I said to McCarthy, "Remember those girls I'm giving sewing lessons to? One of them is making a skirt to wear once school starts back up. She's really proud of herself to be able to make something she can really wear."

McCarthy glanced sideways at me, but he went with it like I hoped he would. "Good for her. She's got the best teacher in town."

"I've got one more open slot," I told him.

McCarthy threw a warm glance over his shoulder as he pulled into the driveway of Gillian's house. "What about you, Gillian? What would you want to make if you were taking sewing lessons from Laurel Springs' premier historical seamstress?"

She unbuckled her seat belt slowly. "I'd make a peasant shirt, with embroidery all over it."

I'd expected a snide response, so this charming suggestion took my breath away. I turned full around in my seat to look at her. "I could teach you how to make the blouse and how to do the embroidery. Last month, I made a full set of embroidered curtains for a client. It was a ton of fun."

She opened the car door. "I might like to try that."

McCarthy opened his door. "Come with me," he whispered to me.

I got out on the other side and walked with the two of them to the door. "Let's talk with your dad about the possibility of sewing lessons," I said. "No time like the present."

Gillian grasped the door handle, only to find it locked. She punched the doorbell, and we could all hear the bell jangling throughout the house.

The door flew open to reveal the scowling face of Ryan King. However, his face instantly cleared at the sight of McCarthy and me flanking Gillian. McCarthy launched into his spiel. "Mr. King, so nice to see you. Let me show you the photos I took of your daughter." He fiddled with the buttons on the back of his camera and held it out.

I leaned over his shoulder to see the pictures. They were amazing. In half a dozen shots, McCarthy had captured the best of Gillian's personality. A viewer could tell from the quirk of her mouth or the movement of her hair that she was a girl of spirit, but her habitual sulky belligerence was completely absent. When I saw her mischievous grin, I realized I rarely saw her smile at all. McCarthy could work wonders with his camera.

Ryan merely nodded and signed the paper McCarthy held out to him. "Thanks for bringing her home." He held the door open wide, inviting us to leave. It was my last chance.

"Mr. King, I was telling Gillian about the sewing lessons I'm giving to some high school students. It sounds like she might like to join in. Would that be all right with you?"

I caught a surprised look on Gillian's face, which instantly vanished when her dad turned to her and said, "You want to learn how to sew?"

She nodded without saying a word.

"How much do you charge?" he said to me.

It was a delicate question. If my rates were too high, he would just say no. If I said it was free, he'd get suspicious and say no. "It's fifty dollars for the whole semester. I think Gillian would get a lot out of it."

Ryan stared at her for a long minute, and then he agreed to let her take sewing lessons from me. We arranged the details and fixed it up for her to start the following day.

I was well satisfied when McCarthy and I took our leave and settled into his car for the drive to my house.

He turned to me. "What was that about? You've never talked about giving sewing lessons before."

"You've never talked about doing a story on kilt-making either. I suppose I'm committed now?"

He laughed as he accelerated down the road. "Okay, I guess we're a couple of liars. I was just trying to get her home safely. What's your ulterior motive?"

"I want a chance to talk to her in private about her mother. Evidently, her mom died in Cleveland, and then Gillian and her dad moved here. I want to know the whole story. It's easier to talk about tough subjects when your hands are busy with other things, like sewing."

"Nosy seamstress" was his reply.

It wasn't until we pulled up at the curb in front of my house that McCarthy referred to Morris Hart. "Well, Catherine, you're home."

I whacked him on the arm with my shoulder bag. "You said you wouldn't call me Catherine." I pushed open the car door and then let it close again. The rain continued to come down in buckets. "Thanks for the evening, Sean." I leaned over and gave him a quick kiss. "I'd better get back to work on Corgi's kilt." I pushed the car door open again and scrambled out with a quick "'Bye!" over my shoulder. I dashed for the front porch. Once under the porch roof, I turned to wave goodbye. He was already driving down the road.

The house was quiet, a sure sign Aileen was out. Pete's truck was absent from the curb, so I knew he was out as well. I had nothing to distract me from working on Corgi's kilt.

I puttered around in the kitchen, feeding Mohair and clearing up the pile of dirty dishes that always seemed to occupy the sink. Finally, I had nothing else to do. I headed upstairs to my workroom.

Corgi's kilt lay on the floor exactly where I'd left it. No gremlins had come in and finished the pleats while I was out. I switched on my CD player for another round of the Royal Pains and knelt down to tackle the pleats. I'd been at it for twenty minutes and had only completed three pleats when the front door banged. Big feet clattered on the stairs, and Pete appeared in my doorway, home from work at ten o'clock at night.

"Is that the kilt for Corgi, then?"

I nodded. "These pleats are the hardest part. How was filming in Amish country today?"

"It was fine, except for the moment when I stepped in a cow patty. It was great entertainment for the crew." He paused, listening. "That's Aileen."

I tried to stop laughing long enough to listen. "I didn't hear anything downstairs." Aileen never came in quietly. There was never any doubt when she got home.

"No, on the CD. That's Aileen singing country music on your CD player."

I dropped my pins. "What? Aileen?"

I knew he was right. No wonder I thought Penny Morrow's voice sounded familiar. But what was Aileen doing singing with Ladd?

Pete picked up the CD cover and turned it over. "The Royal Pains, with Ladd Foster and Penny Morrow. Must be a pseudonym. And Ladd Foster's the guy who died at the Highland Games, right? The guy Aileen didn't want to talk to the police about?"

I nodded, still trying to take it all in.

Pete sat down on my chair and started scrolling through his phone. He held it out to me so we could both watch the online videos he found. They were live clips of the Royal Pains at several small venues. Ladd Foster was easily recognizable as the younger man I'd seen in the clips from the Whidbey Island Highland Games. His bandmate, Penny Morrow, was unmistakably Aileen, despite her dyed blond braids, which bounced on her shoulders to the rhythm of the music. She was dressed in a spangly blue-checked blouse and a ruffled blue skirt that grazed the top of her tooled leather cowboy boots. She wore a lot of mascara and eye shadow skillfully applied to make her eyes look wide and innocent. She strummed the same guitar as the one she'd used to threaten Ladd at the Highland Games. She looked like she was barely nineteen years old.

Pete played a handful of videos before letting his phone drop into his lap. We sat in silence, staring at each other, stunned.

"She was in a band with him. A country music band." He jumped up to pace around the room. "We're not supposed to know this. She'll kill us."

"Why? Because she killed him with torch fuel in his whiskey?"

Pete fell back into his chair. "Daria! That was a figure of speech." He locked eyes with me. "Do you seriously think Aileen killed Ladd Foster?"

"Did you seriously think you'd ever see Aileen in dyed blond braids shimmying to 'Flowers of the Forest'?" I flung out my hands. "I don't know what to think. She could have done it. She was in the VIP tent at the right time. She'd just had a fight with him and threatened him with her guitar." I waved a hand at the CD. "She has a history with him. It's pretty obvious she hates him." I stared at the CD cover with unseeing eyes. "I wonder what color her hair really is."

Pete groaned at this random comment. But I persisted. "Pete. What do we really know about Aileen? Is her real name Aileen or Penny? Which one is a stage name? Ten some years ago, she was in a country music band with Ladd Foster. She's since remade herself into the lead singer in a metal band. How much farther could you go, musically? What happened between her and Ladd? It must have been momentous, to make her go to jail rather than talk about it. It must have been more than just embarrassment about an early musical venture." I gulped. "It must have been bad enough to give her an ironclad motive for murder."

Pete sat chewing on his fingernails, an old nervous habit he had largely conquered of late. I sat back on my heels, looking at him for guidance. "What are we going to do?"

"Nothing." His reply was instantaneous. "We're not going to do anything. We know something we're not supposed to know. We have to forget it. If Aileen wants us to know about her history with Ladd, she'll tell us. Otherwise, we don't know anything."

I snorted, sounding just like Aileen. "That's ridiculous. We can't forget something like this. Shouldn't we tell the police?"

"If you tell the police, they'll come back and detain Aileen again. Even if they wave the CD in her face, she still might not talk to them. And she'll never talk to us again if we throw her under the bus like that." He twisted his hands together. "I don't want to make an enemy for life out of Aileen."

"Don't tell me you're afraid of her. You just said she couldn't have killed Ladd."

"I'm not afraid of her." He looked away, suddenly clamming up.

I studied his face, reddening under my gaze. *What was going on?* He was hiding something from me, so of course I wanted to know what it was. "What is it you're not telling me?"

He ignored this question, countering with one of his own. "Where did you get this CD anyway?"

I decided to let him get away with it, for now. I told him about Herman Tisdale and the fictional obituary McCarthy and I were putting together. A pang shot through me at the realization that we had lied to Tisdale, just like we'd lied to both Ryan and Gillian. Is that what my nosy nature was transforming me into, a systematic liar? And now Pete was insisting we cover up knowledge that could have a bearing on the case. Aileen called Pete "Moron." She could just as easily call me "Liar." It was a sobering thought.

Finally, Pete got up to leave, after telling me to hide the Royal Pains CD and hand it off as soon as possible. Sensible advice.

I shoved the CD deep into my shoulder bag to give to McCarthy tomorrow. I contemplated the kilt that was slowly taking shape on the floor and abandoned it for the night. Time to curl up in bed with *Over the Sea to Skye*. I wanted to finish the book before meeting Morris Hart for lunch tomorrow.

I checked my email before heading off to bed. There was a quick message from Julie Lombard at the Tremington, asking if I could stop by at ten the next morning to take a look at Margaret Oliphant's wedding dress. I said yes in a heartbeat.

Chapter 12

I made a cup of relaxing herbal tea to drink while I finished *Over the Sea to Skye*. It did little to alleviate the tension.

Stu and Catherine got a tip from one of the old Alsatian monks and traveled across the sea to America, following the tracks of Count Roehenstart, illegitimate grandson of Bonnie Prince Charlie. They landed in Philadelphia, where they struggled against mysterious would-be assassins in their quest for Charlie's ring. These foes captured Catherine, leaving Stu to choose between freeing her and beating his opponents to the ring. I did find myself identifying with Catherine by this time, so it was hard for me to read the part where she was tortured with Stu as a helpless witness via phone. "Don't take it personally," Hart had said. I could hardly help it. But Stu figured out how to do the impossible. He rescued Catherine, and together they recovered the ring and headed back to England, where Stu deposed the aging Queen Elizabeth and claimed the throne as the descendant of Charles Edward Stuart and his grandson, Count Roehenstart. The novel ended with Stu accepting congratulations from the president of the United States, even as the mysterious adversaries massed in the shadows in the hopes of overthrowing this new claimant to the British throne.

I laid the book down at three-fifteen in the morning. The ending was satisfying, while leaving enough unanswered questions to make readers anticipate a sequel. Truly, Morris Hart was a master at his craft.

I turned out the light, but I was so keyed up by the excitement of the novel that I knew I wouldn't fall asleep anytime soon. I toyed with the idea of getting up and working on Corgi's kilt but decided against it. Maybe I wasn't sleepy, but I definitely was tired, and in no fit state to struggle with pinning up pleats.

I heard Aileen rustling around in her bedroom, across the hall from mine. She had come home well after two-thirty, presumably from a gig. I imagined she found it hard to settle down for bed after a late-night session of metal music in a crowded bar. I pictured her in the midst of the Twisted Armpits, dressed in full leather and chains with her hair in dyed black spikes all over her head, howling to the thrashing music. Such a different image from the fresh young thing who'd harmonized with Ladd Foster in the Royal Pains video clips.

Aileen or Penny? Who was the woman sharing a house with my brother and me? Was she a murderer?

On my list of suspects in Ladd's death, Aileen was the only woman. They say poison is a woman's weapon, presumably because of a lack of physical strength for stabbing or strangling. It seemed like an outdated notion to me. It was hard to imagine a woman lacking the strength to pull the trigger of a gun. When it came to Aileen, it was a completely ridiculous idea. I couldn't think of a single thing she couldn't do. If she wanted to kill someone, I had no doubt she could accomplish it with one swing of her guitar. She had refrained from whacking Ladd with her guitar at the Highland Games, but that could have been because of the crowd of onlookers. A bit of torch fuel slipped into his whiskey had achieved the same result. Was it Aileen who did the poisoning?

I snuggled down in bed, too tired to think about murder any longer. I guess the very fact that I could sleep was an indication that I didn't see Aileen as a threat, at least not to me.

* * * *

It was hard to get up the next morning, but there was no way I was going to miss the chance to see Margaret Oliphant's wedding gown from the 1700s. To a historical seamstress with a healthy business in wedding gowns, this was practically the Holy Grail. I hurried through my breakfast, keeping quiet so as not to wake Aileen, and caught the bus to the Tremington Museum.

The museum doors were just opening when I arrived. Julie had told me to find her in the basement, so I headed downstairs. I hoped it would be easier to find a staff member than it was to find any given item in the chaos of the basement. But I didn't need to worry. Julie met me at the elevator. She wore the same bib overalls as she had the other day, along with a long-sleeved, tie-dyed shirt that gave her a decided hippie aura. "Hey, Daria, nice to see you. Ready to go where no tourist has gone before?" She led me to the door marked "No Admittance."

"Seriously, nobody gets to come back here?" I felt a little thrill when she unlocked the door and pushed it open.

I took in the wide, stainless-steel table in the middle of the room, surrounded by deep shelves covered with any number of random artifacts. There were broken pots that looked like they came from some ancient gravesite, piles of faded textiles, a collection of bones spilling out of a cardboard box, various household items in differing states of disrepair, and a pile of framed pictures that could have contained the *Mona Lisa* or a crayon drawing from a local third grader, for all I knew. Several chests of drawers were crowded along the wall, from the wide, shallow drawers that held maps to the tiny drawers that must have contained jewelry. I looked around in delight. Honestly, the staff workroom wasn't all that different from the public areas of the basement, except that the items here in the back were in much poorer shape than the ones displayed out on the floor. Julie and I were alone in the midst of this historical treasure trove.

"This place is awesome," I said. "What a fun place to work. Where does all this stuff come from?"

Julie pulled on a pair of thin cotton gloves. She handed a second pair to me. "People bring stuff from their attics and barns. People leave things to the museum in their wills. There's a staff member who actively searches for things to put in the exhibits. Some of these things have been here for decades, waiting for someone to catalog them, or clean and preserve them, or even just to open a box and see that they're here." She grinned. "It's a fantastic place to work."

She lifted a soft package wrapped in tissue paper from a shelf and laid it on the table. She unwrapped the paper to reveal the heavy folds of a wedding gown. She put out a hand to stop me from touching it. "We can't pick it up in its present state. The fabric is almost to the point of shredding." She gently shifted the bodice so I could get a better look at the gown. I had expected to see ivory-colored silk or satin, but Margaret Oliphant's wedding dress was made of gold brocade with intricate embroidery covering the bodice and overskirt. The underskirt layer was a pale blue silk that was heavily spotted with water damage. Lace ruffles that had once been white adorned the ends of the sleeves and the low neckline.

"It's beautiful," I said. "Will you be able to get out those water spots?"

Julie shook her head. "Not unless you know something I don't know." She carefully spread out the skirt until the dress lay unfolded the length of the table. "According to the historical record, Margaret Oliphant was a petite woman, probably no more than five feet tall. She was seventeen years old when she wore this dress. Judge Tremington was a good twenty years older than her."

I longed to finger the intricate embroidery but restrained myself. "Are there any pictures of their wedding, or even any portraits of Margaret as a young woman?"

Julie rooted through the drawer of a filing cabinet until she found a small pamphlet. "This is a program from an exhibit on the Tremingtons' family life that was on display in the 1960s." She leafed through the program and showed me a color photograph of a portrait painted in the eighteenth century. It depicted a couple sitting together on a stone bench in a garden. The man was dressed in a waistcoat and fine white breeches, with long graying hair tied up in a queue and a tricorn hat held under one arm. With his other hand he held hands with a short young woman wearing the very dress that lay on the table before us. Margaret's auburn hair was tightly pulled away from her face, and her gold damask skirt was carefully arranged to cover her feet and ankles. The pale blue satin shone under the artist's skill.

"It wasn't hard to identify this dress as Margaret's wedding gown," Julie said with a chuckle. "When the dress is ready to go on exhibit, this picture will go with it."

I studied the dress on the table. Something about it made me uneasy, something more than the sadness I felt at such beauty now faded and lost. I circled the table to view it from all angles. The proportions weren't right. Margaret was a petite woman, barely five feet tall. That was easy to see in the portrait, and the length of the skirt bore it out. But the width of the waist was greater than I would have expected, given her petite stature. I spanned the waist with my hands hovering just above the dress, and then I brought my hands to my own waist. Since I was only five-foot-three, I figured I might have similar proportions as Margaret. But that waist was quite a bit bigger than mine. A second glance at the picture assured me that Margaret wasn't a heavy girl, unless the artist had taken liberties when painting the portrait. She was seated at an angle, in such a way that her waist wasn't readily visible to the viewer. I turned to Julie. "Was Margaret pregnant when she got married?"

Chapter 13

Julie's eyes opened wide. "You can tell this from looking at her dress?"

"Was she?"

"Well…that's a fair question. The Tremingtons' only child was born two years after their wedding, kind of a long time for a dutiful wife. But there's a record of Margaret taking an extended holiday roughly four months after the wedding. She was gone for several months, ostensibly visiting family. That's curious, because her family was in Scotland and she didn't go to her father in Philadelphia. Some scholars have speculated that she was gone long enough to carry a baby to term, but she didn't come home with a child. She could have had a stillbirth, or she could have fostered the child, which raises all kinds of questions as to why she would abandon Judge Tremington's baby. But it's been nothing but speculation, until now." Julie rubbed her hands together like a pirate contemplating his chest of gold. "Now we have her diary. I haven't gotten that far, but I'm dying to know what she writes about this journey so soon after her wedding day. I'm almost positive there's more to this story."

I found myself consumed with curiosity as well. "Can I see the diary?"

Julie lifted a brittle leather volume off a shelf. Embossed on the front cover was an image of a unicorn encircled by some words that could be Latin. It looked familiar to me, although I couldn't think why. Julie saw me looking. "That's the Oliphant crest. It says '*Tout Pouvoir*,' which is translated from the French as 'provide for all.' Those Oliphants sound like good socialists to me." She carefully opened the book, revealing fragile pages closely written in a flowing cursive hand. "I'm working on scanning the diary page by page, and then I'll type it up from those images to produce a transcribed version for scholarly use. It's so tempting to stop and read, but it takes forever because of the old-fashioned handwriting and the spelling variations." She turned to the middle of the book. "Here's the part about her journey to America and meeting Judge Tremington." She pointed to a paragraph and read aloud. "He is a good man, my father says. A good provider. Rich. My father does not say that he is bald around the ears and has teeth as brown as an old shoe. But that does not matter. He will be my husband, although he will not be my love. My love is lost to me forever."

Julie paused. "That doesn't sound like Margaret falling in love with Judge Tremington, does it?"

So much for romance. "No, it doesn't. What comes next?"

"The next entry is a list of goods she bought in Philadelphia, where the ship docked, and then she writes about learning how to bake an apple pie." She carefully turned a few pages. "Here's a description of her wedding dress, and further on she writes about the ceremony and the guests. I can make copies for you if you want."

"That would be awesome. So, what about her 'love'? Does she write about him?"

Julie smiled. "Just hints and side comments. I haven't seen any place where she wrote his name. He was someone she knew in Scotland. He probably died in the Forty-Five. She makes mention of a book of poetry he gave her, and a ring. Sadly, those two items weren't in the trunk where we found her diary and wedding gown."

My eyes kept returning to the thick-waisted dress on the table. "So, is it possible her lover in Scotland fathered a baby who was born during Margaret's extended absence?"

Julie chuckled. "You sound like a historical detective or something. Technically, it is possible. The passage to America could take anywhere from six to eight weeks, depending on the weather. If she were pregnant before she got on the ship, and she married shortly after arriving, she would have been anywhere from two to four months pregnant on her wedding day."

Caught up in the excitement of someone else's life story, I said, "She would have begun to show at three to four months. That would explain the wide waistline of her wedding gown."

"Then four months later, when she left town, she would have been seven or eight months pregnant. Would wide skirts hide that fact? There wasn't any mention in the primary sources of her being pregnant."

I indicated the voluminous skirt lying on the table before us. "I'll bet this could hide a pregnant belly. Is there anything in the parts about her lover in Scotland that indicate he got her pregnant?" I didn't know why this interested me so much, but it did. McCarthy always said I was nosy.

Julie glanced at the wall clock. "I've already scanned the parts that mention this mysterious lover. I haven't read them all, because, like I said, the handwriting is so hard to decipher. But I can email you the scanned images and you can see for yourself." She took down my email address. "Let me know what you find out. I need to get to work now, but you're welcome to hang around as long as you want."

"Is it okay if I take pictures of the gown?"

She nodded. "Sure. Then I need to put it away."

I paced around the gown, taking photos from all angles. I didn't have any use at present for pictures of an authentic eighteenth-century wedding gown, but the opportunity was too good to pass up.

I finished up with my eye on the clock as well. I was meeting Morris Hart on the Commons at noon. I needed to get out to the bus stop.

"Julie, thanks for letting me come here and for showing me all this cool stuff."

She smiled, her gloved hands stroking the crinkled pages of Margaret Oliphant's diary. "Come back any time. There's always something new to see."

I let myself out, well pleased with the historical mysteries we had explored together. Maybe I should have pursued a career in history instead of becoming a seamstress. I guess a historical seamstress was as close as I was going to get.

I had to wait a good ten minutes for the bus. When it finally arrived, it was packed, so I had to stand. I often do my best thinking on buses, but today wasn't one of those days.

I got off the bus a couple of minutes after noon and hustled to the Printed Page to meet Hart. He was waiting for me.

"Catherine! I was beginning to wonder if you were going to show up, or if you were nothing but a dream."

"Here I am, in the flesh. Sorry I'm a little late. My real name is Daria, you know."

He chuckled and put an arm around my shoulders. "Thanks for keeping me honest. I do like to think of you as Catherine." He touched my hair lightly. "You look so much like her."

I slipped out from under his arm. "I finished reading your book last night. It kept me up until three a.m."

He beamed at me. "I always love to hear that kind of feedback. That's my goal, of course: to keep you on the edge of your seat until you devour the last page." He seized my hand. "Where should we go for lunch? Do you favor tacos and Mexican rice, like Catherine?"

I tried to disengage my hand, but he held on tight. "Um, sure, tacos are good. There's a nice Mexican restaurant along here." I led the way to Over the Wall, a tiny storefront on the main stretch of the Commons that was a favorite with college students and tourists alike. The rough stone walls were painted in bright blues and oranges and hung with mini sombreros and garlands of flowers. Tiny bulbs of white lights crisscrossed the ceiling, giving the space a whimsical feel. Hart continued to hold my hand as we stood in line to order at the counter. I could feel his eyes on me, and I wondered if he was waiting to see if I would order Catherine's favorite dish. I couldn't remember what he'd written about in the novel. I felt so self-conscious, not wanting to try to be like Catherine, and not knowing whether I was heading in that direction. I should have said I wanted pizza instead.

Finally, I decided to just get what I liked and stop worrying about Catherine. I ordered two carne asada tacos. Beside me, Hart said, "I'll have the same as the lady."

He paid for our meals and then we found a tiny table in the corner. He leaned both elbows on the table and looked into my eyes. "So, Daria, is it? Tell me honestly, did you like *Over the Sea to Skye?*"

I leaned back in my chair. "I liked it very much. I don't read a whole lot of thrillers. I have to confess, I haven't read any of your other books. But I really enjoyed this one. I especially liked how you wove history into the story."

Hart never took his eyes off my face. "What did you think of Catherine?"

"I wasn't sure about her at first. I thought she might be one of the bad guys." I chuckled. "You told me not to take it personally when things happened to Catherine, but it did creep me out when she got tortured."

"Could you almost feel the hot iron on your skin?" He reached over and took my wrist, turning my arm to expose the underside. "But look, there are no burn marks here."

I pulled away from him. "Right. I'm not Catherine."

He must have heard the exasperation in my voice because he leaned back and dug into his food. "So, Daria. That's not a Celtic name. What's your connection to the Scottish community here?"

I took a deep breath, thankful for the change of subject. "Daria is a Greek name. It's kind of funny, because my last name is Dembrowski, which is Polish all the way. My parents just liked the way it sounded. I don't have any Scottish roots. I was at the Highland Games to sell my handiwork. I'm a historical seamstress."

I was in the middle of explaining what a historical seamstress was all about when I remembered that Morris Hart was on my short list of murder suspects in the death of Ladd Foster. Now was as good a time as any to find out about his relationship to Ladd.

"It was a sad ending to the Games, with Ladd Foster's death," I said. "He seemed to know so many people there. Did you know him?"

Hart took a big bite of his taco, leaving me to wait a few moments before getting an answer. "I met him at the Games. He came up to talk to me about my book. Said he was a fan. That's about it." He took another bite and mumbled, "Terrible what happened to him, and in front of children, too."

I remembered seeing Hart frowning while talking with Ladd, and later avoiding him when they passed each other at the VIP tent. Those two interactions hadn't seemed like those of a fan approaching one of his favorite authors. Strange…

"I talked with Ladd a few times at the Games," I offered. "He came to check out my booth and flirt with the woman sharing it with me. He seemed like a real character who was into just about everything."

He shrugged and took another bite of his taco. "I couldn't really say. I saw him heckling his competitors in the heavy events, but that was all."

I leaned forward, elbows on the table. "You're a mystery writer. You must come up with all kinds of ways for people to meet their deaths, and motives for murder. Do you have any theories about who might have killed Ladd or what their motive could be?"

He chewed thoughtfully. "I hadn't really thought about it. It's kind of a pitfall of the field, if you know what I mean. Crimes happen every day, and as a mystery writer, I do pay more attention to them than the average person. There's nothing I can think up about murder that hasn't happened in real life. If I study the ways and means people use to kill one another, I can come up with some fantastic plots for my work. But I can also get overwhelmed by the sheer evil that exists in the world. Sometimes I need to protect myself from the real-life crimes that are so much more horrible than anything I can dream up. I suppose this is one of those instances when I'm distancing myself from a crime. I haven't given it any systematic thought since Saturday."

"Okay. That makes sense. I guess you don't really want to talk about it, then?"

Hart smiled at me. "I'm in a delightful little Mexican restaurant having some excellent tacos with a beautiful young woman who embodies my heroine. Why would I want to talk about a real-life murder?"

Why indeed?

Chapter 14

We lingered over our lunch for the next hour or so, talking about Hart's novel, Scottish politics—of which I knew next to nothing—and my progress on Corgi's kilt. Finally, I put down my napkin with a sigh. "I need to get back to work. Corgi is counting on me to finish his kilt on time."

Hart stood up and stretched. "I'd like to see this kilt in the making, if I may."

I had anticipated this request, but I still didn't know what to say. I didn't really want him coming to my house. His fascination with my likeness to Catherine and his insistent physical contact were both red flags to me. I had very much enjoyed our lunch together in this public place, but bringing him home with me was something else altogether. To make matters worse, I didn't have my own transportation. My plan was to take the bus home, but what would I do if he offered me a ride? "No, thanks, I'll take the bus" was a pointed brush-off, but accepting a ride came with all kinds of expectations I wasn't interested in fulfilling. Time to lie.

I got up and led the way out of the restaurant. "Oh, no, I just realized I'm meeting Gillian this afternoon for a sewing lesson," I said. That much was true. "We're meeting at the library. I won't be able to get to Corgi's kilt until later today."

Hart nodded, a disappointed look on his face. "Too bad. I'll walk you to your car."

I thought about having him accompany me to some random car, but he might get suspicious when I didn't get in. "Oh, I didn't drive today. I'm on the bus." I waved in the direction of the bus stop. "It's been lovely having lunch with you."

He grasped my hand, as if to keep me from flying away from him. "The least I can do is offer you a ride to the library." He tucked my hand under his arm and walked me down the sidewalk. "My car's around the corner." I bowed to the inevitable and accompanied him to his car, a sleek Lexus, as befitted a successful author. He opened the door with a flourish and handed me in as if I were a film star. I certainly wasn't used to such gentlemanly attentions.

I took a deep breath, and by the time he got in the car, I had a smile on my face. "Do you know where the library is?"

He nodded and started up the car. The engine was incredibly quiet, and the absence of road noise screamed luxury more than anything else about the vehicle. I leaned back in the comfortable seat and resolved to enjoy the short ride.

"I was at the Tremington Museum this morning," I said, hoping to keep the conversation away from my home. "I learned some things about Margaret Oliphant Tremington, the wife of Judge Tremington, who was one of the founders of our town. Margaret came to Pennsylvania from Scotland after the Forty-Five." I glanced at him, making sure I was using this term correctly. "Her father fought with Bonnie Prince Charlie in the uprising, so they had to flee the country. It's amazing how her story intersects with your novel."

Hart regarded me with interest. "Margaret Oliphant Tremington? The local university bears her name, I understand. What did you learn about her story today?"

"I got to see her wedding dress. It was recently discovered in an attic at the university, so it's under reconstruction right now." I told him about the water-stained dress and the portrait that showed it on her special day.

"I understand Judge Tremington and his wife had only one child, a son named Finnley," Hart said, maneuvering the car past a couple of kids skateboarding in the middle of the road. "Did you learn anything about him at the museum today?"

"No, I didn't learn anything new about Finnley. But I know from what I learned in third grade that he continued his father's work, becoming a lawyer who practiced in Philadelphia. The Tremington descendants mostly live in Philly now. They still support the museum financially, and I think the board of trustees has a seat reserved for a member of the Tremington family." Of course, the child I was interested in was the potential baby born before Finnley. But I didn't know how much I wanted to share my speculations about Margaret's pregnancy with Morris Hart. It almost seemed like spreading gossip, especially since I hadn't actually read her diary entries yet. But it couldn't hurt to mention the discovery of her diary, could it?

"I did get to see another artifact that was found along with Margaret's wedding dress—her diary. A staff member is going to email me some pages from it. It'll be fun to see what she says about the dress and the wedding ceremony, now that I've actually seen the dress in real life."

He turned around to look at me. "The museum has Margaret Oliphant's diary? You got access to excerpts from it? That's fantastic!"

I couldn't help grinning. "Yeah, it was pretty cool."

He pulled up to the loading zone in front of the library. The Laurel Springs Public Library was one of the oldest buildings in town. Originally a modest circular building with a domed ceiling to match, it had been added on to until it encompassed half a city block. It housed the best collection of local newspapers in the region. Today, I only needed it for cover.

Hart leaned both elbows on the steering wheel and contemplated me. "I would love to see pages from Margaret Oliphant's diary." He touched me gently on the leg. "And of course, I'd love to see you again. Could we get together another time and you could show me what you get from the staff member at the museum?" He pulled a card out of his wallet and pressed it into my hand. "Call me anytime. I'll be in town at least through the weekend." He pulled out another card and a pen. "How can I reach you?"

I gave him my cell phone number and hopped out of the car before he could do anything silly like try to kiss me or something. "Thanks for the lift and for a lovely lunch. I'll be in touch." I hurried into the library with a cheerful wave.

When I got inside, I headed straight for the ladies' room. I felt like a fool for hiding from him, but I really didn't want Morris Hart to know where I lived. His fascination with my resemblance to Catherine was just weird enough that I could imagine him standing under my window with a guitar to serenade me in the twilight. Sure, it would be romantic to be serenaded in the twilight, but Morris Hart wasn't the man I would choose for that honor. I smiled to myself, trying to picture McCarthy serenading me with a guitar. I couldn't. He'd be more likely to pop out of the bushes with his camera clicking away and yell, "Surprise," and then tease me about how my eyes go bug-eyed when I'm surprised.

I chuckled at my reflection in the mirror. After brushing my hair about a hundred strokes, I figured it was safe to come out. Plus, it was time for me to get home to meet Gillian, assuming she was really going to come by for a sewing lesson. I nipped out of the restroom and took a peek out the window. I didn't see any luxurious Lexus in the vicinity. I walked boldly out the door.

The library was only a few blocks from my house. I walked fast the whole way, hoping to avoid being seen by Hart and to get home in time for Gillian. Lucky for me, I achieved both goals.

I heard a knock on the door less than two minutes after I came in. I'd barely had time to fill up Mohair's empty water bowl. I went to the door to let Gillian in.

She stood on my front step, scantily dressed in a flowered halter top and denim short shorts. A canvas backpack was slung over her shoulder. Her pretty strawberry-blond hair was braided into a thick plait that hung over her shoulder, tied at the bottom with one of my tartan bow ties. She looked like what she was, a sexy child. I breathed a prayer of strength for her father as I watched him pull away from the curb and drive off.

"Hi, Gillian. I'm glad you came." I held the door wide so she could come inside.

She came in and stood awkwardly in the front hall. "Yeah, well, my dad dropped me off. I don't know if I'd be here otherwise."

I forced a smile at the ungracious response. "Well, you're here now. Let's do some sewing."

She dropped her backpack on the window bench in the hall and I led her upstairs to my workroom. I indicated a wooden chair for her to sit on. "You had your first lesson yesterday, when you sewed your button back on. Today, we can start a project that's not too hard. You said you were interested in a peasant blouse. Want to start with that?"

"Wait, you remembered that?" She fidgeted in her chair. "Yeah, that's what I want to make."

I pulled an oversize shopping bag out of the closet and dropped it on the floor. Lengths of fabric spilled out the top.

"I've got a bunch of remnants here, left over from any number of sewing projects. Let's see if there's something here you could use."

"Great, so I get the leftovers." Despite her grumbling, she did come over and start rooting through the bag. She was soon immersed in the fascinating task of finding the perfect bit of fabric for her project.

After several false starts, we settled on a lightweight white muslin, which would look great with embroidery, if that was what Gillian wanted to pursue. I threw the fabric over my ironing board and turned on my iron. "Normally, the first thing you do when you sew anything is wash the fabric, assuming it's washable. That way you take care of any shrinkage before you cut and sew your garment. But this fabric is a remnant, what's left over from another project, so it's already been washed." I indicated the iron. "Have you done much ironing?"

She shook her head, so I showed her how to handle the iron safely and still accomplish a wrinkle-free effect. I expected more grumbling, but she passed the iron across the fabric without complaint.

While she ironed, I rooted through my store-bought patterns to see if I had anything resembling a peasant blouse. I figured it would be easier to start with a pattern because she was a beginner. By the time she was done ironing, I had half a dozen options for her to choose from.

"Let's try this one," she said, pointing to a simple pullover blouse that had elastic at the neck and three-quarter-length, set-in sleeves. With no buttons, it was a good first project.

I showed her how to press the pattern pieces on low heat, and how to find the straight grain of the fabric and lay the pattern pieces and pin them on before cutting. I've always suspected I take at least twice as long as other seamstresses when it comes to cutting out my projects. I try to be meticulous at the cutting stage to prevent a host of issues later on. But my friends always accused me of being obsessive about getting everything just right.

While we worked on pinning and cutting, bent over my cutting board laid out on the floor, I tried to come up with a natural opening to segue into the topic of Gillian's late mother. It was a tall order. I didn't want to be too blunt and scare her off, but I wanted to talk to her about the jewelry Ryan had consigned to Letty's shop. In the end, Gillian herself gave me the opening I was looking for.

"You make a living with your sewing, right?" When I nodded, she followed up with another question: "Who taught you how to sew in the first place?"

I sat back on my heels and watched her push in the pins. "My mother taught me. She learned from her mother. It was my grandmother who originally owned this Singer sewing machine." I pointed to my antique treadle machine with the black head decorated with gold tooling. "It still works like a dream. I'll let you use it after a while." I reached down and repositioned a pin so it wasn't at risk of getting cut in two when she got to the cutting part. "I liked working with my mom on sewing, even if she did criticize me sometimes. I miss her."

Gillian's head shot up. "Where is she now?"

I took a deep breath. It had happened years ago, but that fact didn't make it any easier to talk about. "In heaven, I hope. She died of cancer when I was in college. It was hard coming home on school breaks and seeing her getting worse and worse. Cancer's such a cruel disease."

Gillian sat back and dusted her hands. "It could be worse."

I pushed back a reflexive feeling of defensiveness. "How could it be worse?"

"You could come home from a sleepover and find that your mom had been carted off in an ambulance and nobody would even tell you for the longest time what was going on." Gillian's voice trembled.

"Is that what happened to you?" I asked in a low voice.

She nodded without a word, a single tear snaking down her cheek. Then she snatched up my pincushion and began stabbing pins into the pattern until it was so well secured that even a tornado couldn't have budged it.

Again in that low voice, I said, "What did your mom die from?"

She continued shoving pins into the fabric. "They said she choked. That's all they told me." She looked me in the face, all of a sudden seeming much younger than she really was. "I don't know if that means she choked on her food or somebody choked her around the neck. Or maybe she hung herself. Nobody would ever tell me."

"Did you ask your dad?"

"My dad," she scoffed. "My dad didn't even call me at the sleepover. I didn't find out until the next day that she was dead. He told me to never speak her name again." She dropped her gaze and concentrated on the pins. "He probably killed her."

I gasped, shocked. "Gillian…"

"You don't know! There were police rooting around the house for months afterwards. I thought my dad was going to get arrested and I would have to go live in some stinking foster home. Finally, they decided he wasn't guilty and told us it was okay to leave town. We moved that weekend. We've never talked about my mom again." She covered her face with her hands. "He probably killed her."

I didn't know what to say. She was right; I didn't know anything about what had happened to her mother that day. "I'm sorry." It seemed like such a feeble comment.

She scrambled to her feet and ran out of the room. I started to follow her when I heard the powder room door slam downstairs. She probably needed a few minutes to get herself together.

While waiting for her to come back, I picked up Breanna's scarf to finish pulling out the threads to make the fringe. It was a mindless task, but it needed to be finished. No time like the present.

I reflected on the tale Gillian had told me. I admit I was shocked. Even though I suspected that a young teen's conclusions were probably more sensationalized and emotional than the stark truth, I couldn't shake off her suspicions. Everything I'd heard about Ryan King, as well as my own observations of his altercation with Ladd at the Games, made me believe he could be a murderer. If he had killed once, he might be more likely to kill again.

Gillian took a good twenty minutes to get settled down and return to my workroom. I was just about to go after her when I heard her moving around downstairs. She appeared in the doorway a few minutes later.

Her eyes were red, but otherwise she had regained her customary rebellious demeanor. Rather than move on to other topics of conversation, she chose to pick up where we left off. "So you see, there are worse things than cancer."

I tried to keep my voice neutral, to cover the surprise I felt over the fact that she still wanted to talk about this painful subject. "I guess so."

"I'll bet your dad didn't get mean after your mom died." It almost sounded like a challenge in a game of one-upmanship. I could feel myself taking the bait.

"My dad was always mean. After Mom died, he was still mean. Nothing much changed."

I didn't really want to go into my whole family history with this volatile teen. My father could have been a poster child for the head-of-the-household alcoholic. While never being physically abusive, he managed to terrorize our whole family with his alcoholic rages. Indeed, my own experience was uncomfortably similar to Gillian's. We just dealt with them differently. She acted out, while I had tended to avoid conflict and retreat to my room when things got hot. I'd relied on my brother to share the experience with, although Pete's method of coping had been to numb his feelings by hanging out with the potheads and beer guzzlers in high school.

I shook off the bitter memories. Pete and I were doing just fine now, and we didn't have to have anything to do with Dad unless we chose. Gillian had a few more years to navigate before she reached this level of independence. She was an only child, alone in her dread that her father might have killed her mother. My heart went out to her.

She stood silently in the doorway, seemingly touched by my last comment.

I beckoned her into the room. "But enough about me," I said, "Let's get going on this project before you have to go." I studied the patterns laid out at my feet. "It looks like you've only got a few pins to go and then you can cut." I resisted the impulse to stick them in and pointed instead.

Gillian popped in the last few pins and settled into the rhythm of cutting. She worked in silence for a few minutes, and then she said, "Did you figure out who killed Ladd Foster?"

I almost dropped Breanna's scarf. "What do you mean?"

Her scissors snicked through the light fabric. "You told me you were trying to figure it out. What did you come up with?"

I laid Breanna's scarf on my desk. "I haven't landed on anyone yet. What about you? Do you have any idea who did it?"

Snip, snip, snip.

"I've narrowed it down to four suspects," I said. Maybe I shouldn't tell her this, but I continued nonetheless. "Patrick Ames, Aileen, Morris Hart, and…your dad." I watched her closely to see how she would react. She didn't flinch. "They were the only ones who went into the VIP tent during the time when Ladd's flask was in there unattended."

Snip, snip, snip.

"That's what you told the police, then?" she mumbled, her eyes on the fabric.

I tried to remember if I'd told the police my suspicions. I left it with a nod.

"It sounds like you don't suspect me, then."

Was that relief I saw on her face? "*Should* I suspect you?"

"No!" She made her final cut and stood up. "I'm done."

"Here, let's put these pieces away for next time." I pulled out a plastic shoebox, and together we folded up the blouse pieces and stowed them inside. I fished a roll of masking tape out of my desk drawer and used it to mark the lid with her name. I stashed it on a shelf and turned to face her. It might be risky, but I decided to push her. "You think your dad killed Ladd Foster, don't you?"

"What do you know? You don't know anything!" She turned and fled down the stairs.

I followed more slowly. Obviously, Gillian suspected her father of murder. By my calculations, he had a one-in-four chance of being the culprit. I wondered where the police were in their investigation. They hadn't pestered Aileen since releasing her from jail. Did that mean they'd ruled her out as a suspect? I wondered if they were building a case against Ryan King, and if so, what would become of Gillian?

She had mentioned a fear of being sent to a foster home if her father were arrested in her mother's death. She was probably entertaining that same fear right now. Which was worse, I wondered, living with a father you suspected was a murderer or being removed from that home to an unknown foster-care placement? Poor Gillian. She had a lot of anxiety to cope with right now.

I found her on the porch swing, pumping her feet against the floorboards to propel the swing higher than it had any business going. In my experience, porch swings were for gently swaying, not soaring to touch one's toes to the ceiling. I hoped it could withstand the onslaught.

I sat down on a wrought-iron chair in front of her. "I'm sorry. Nothing like a murder to bring out the worst in all of us. You did a great job cutting out your blouse today. I hope you'll come back another time to sew it. Then we can work on embroidery if you want. In the meantime, why don't you draw pictures of what you want the decorations to look like? I think the neckline, the bottom of the sleeves, and the hemline are the best places for embroidery."

Gillian continued to propel the swing forward. "When should I come back?"

"Let me check my planner." I popped inside to fetch it. When I stepped back outside, I said, "We could make it a weekly thing until the blouse is done, and then go from there. Want to come back this time next week?"

We fixed an appointment time, and then waited for Ryan to pick Gillian up. I avoided talking about murder of any kind, and she simply swung on the swing until she wore herself out. Finally, Ryan arrived and collected her just before suppertime.

I went back inside the quiet house, wondering what was up with Pete and Aileen. I hadn't seen either of them all day. Of course, I hadn't been home much, other than for my sewing lesson with Gillian. I groaned inwardly. Upstairs, a half-pleated kilt called for my attention. I could tell I was procrastinating. I usually enjoyed a challenge, but pleats were one of those things I routinely avoided if I could. Tonight was the night to finish them up. But first, supper.

I resisted the impulse to pull out a cookbook and discover a new recipe, preferably one that took a long time to prepare. Instead, I rooted out some lunchmeat and sourdough rolls and made myself a quick sandwich. I lingered at the table with a cup of tea, stroking Mohair's head while she snuggled in my lap. But in the end, I couldn't put it off any longer. I had a lot of work to do.

Corgi's kilt was actually more like one-third finished, which meant I had at least twenty pleats to go. I set a timer for half an hour, to challenge myself to see how many pleats I could finish before the time was up. I steeled myself for the task.

I was only ten minutes and two pleats into my work when the phone rang. I almost didn't answer because I was on a roll. But I've never been good at ignoring the ringing of a phone, so I picked up. It was McCarthy.

"How's the nosy seamstress this evening?"

I smiled at the sound of his voice. Talking to McCarthy was as invigorating as a plunge into cool water in the sunshine.

"I'm knuckling down to finish pleating Corgi's kilt tonight. I haven't gotten much work done today."

"Too busy lunching with famous authors? How did that work out for you?"

Was McCarthy checking up on me? "We went to Over the Wall on the Commons. Evidently, Catherine likes tacos and Mexican rice."

He started to laugh. "Sounds like you had lunch with Catherine. Or maybe Hart was the one who had lunch with Catherine."

"Don't be ridiculous. I told him several times that my name is Daria. We even discussed the cultural roots of my name, for your information."

McCarthy laughed harder. "You had to tell him several times? He's definitely fixated on Catherine." His voice sobered. "Seriously, Daria, it's a little creepy how he's got this obsession with you because of his novel. Better keep an eye on him, that's all I'll say."

I had the exact same thought, but I wasn't about to tell McCarthy that. What did he know about the tightrope a woman walks when it comes to going out with men? His attempt to caution me only served to put me on the defensive. "Duly noted. Is that what you wanted to talk to me about? Because I have a kilt to pleat, remember?"

He could probably hear the frostiness in my voice. "Well, I'll let you get back to work. I was just wondering if you'd learned anything new in the Foster case."

I sat back on my heels, abandoning my effort to pin a pleat while talking on the phone. "I talked with Gillian—she came over for her sewing lesson today. I wanted to ask her about her mother's jewelry, but she launched into a story about how her mother died. She's worried that her father might be the murderer. She thinks he might have killed her mom in Cleveland." I told him what Gillian had said to me. "Is there any way to look into Gillian's mother's death? It's weird that her own daughter doesn't really know how she died."

"Do you know exactly when she died?" The smile had left McCarthy's voice. "What was her first name?"

"I don't know the date. Letty said they came to Laurel Springs two years ago, after the investigations were over. Wait, Letty has her engagement ring. I saw the inscription. It was..."

I closed my eyes and tried to picture the golden ring with the inscription, "Ryan and ..."

"Melissa. I think it was Melissa."

"Melissa." I could hear him writing down her name. "I'll look into it and let you know what I find. My chance to be nosy."

"Oh, right, like you never get a chance to be nosy. I'm pretty sure that's a job requirement when you work for the newspaper."

"Probably. You should look into journalism—you've got the perfect temperament for it."

We laughed together, and then he said goodbye and hung up.

I bent over my pleats once more. I vowed to keep working no matter what.

I made it through ten more pleats before I gave up. My hands were cramped and my back and knees ached. Time enough tomorrow to finish the job.

A quick glance at the clock showed me that it was well after ten o'clock. I tidied up my workroom and closed the door behind me on the way out. The house was dark and quiet. I checked my phone to see if there were any messages from Pete or Aileen, but there was nothing. I locked up the doors downstairs and retired to my bedroom.

I checked my email, to see that Julie was as good as her word. She'd emailed me a huge file of scanned images from Margaret Oliphant's diary. I nipped downstairs and popped up a big bowl of popcorn and then settled down on my bed to read.

Julie was right; the old-fashioned handwriting was very hard to read. I was glad I had persisted in learning cursive writing in the third grade, even though my teacher had made it optional because he didn't see much use for beautiful penmanship when a computer could do the trick. But my cursive training certainly helped me to read this historical document.

Margaret had a straightforward style of writing. She made little attempt to sustain a narrative, tending instead to simply write down what happened on any particular day. Her diary flowed in chronological order from one day to the next, with the same weight placed on a trip to the market to buy a chicken as the construction of her wedding dress. So, I almost missed it when she wrote, "I think I might be with child."

Chapter 15

I checked back to see the date of that entry. It was May 14, 1746, and Margaret was on a ship to America as she wrote. She was seventeen years old.

I flipped back to the start of the ocean journey. Margaret and her father, Jock Oliphant, left Scotland the week after the disastrous Battle of Culloden. She was seasick at the start of the voyage, recovered, as did most of the other passengers, and then got sick again in calm seas. She told her father it was stress and motion sickness, but she confided in her diary her suspicions that her nausea had another cause. I tried to skim forward to see if those suspicions were founded, but it was hard to pick up after skipping some parts. I found myself slogging through passages about the ship's meager food, the crowded conditions, and the young wounded Jacobite soldier who watched her wherever she went on the ship. She wrote of him with thinly veiled contempt, saying, "His dressings must be changed every evening, and he won't suffer any save me to do the deed. I do it, though I hate it. I do it for C. E. and him only. If he were wounded, I would hope that some maid would provide such care for him."

Evidently the young soldier was not her lost love. I pressed on. Margaret's musings on her future child became more frequent, as she became more certain that she was pregnant. She wrote, "If a boy, I hope his eyes are light like his sire's, and if a girl, I hope she has his sweet smile." She hid her condition from her father, writing, "Dear Father counsels me on the benefits of fresh sea air to dispel seasickness. He knows not what ails me."

I finished off my bowl of popcorn and checked the time. It was close to two in the morning. I'd been reading for over three and a half hours. I hadn't heard either Pete or Aileen come in, but now that I stopped to listen,

I could hear Pete snoring upstairs. Aileen's room across the hall was quiet. I reflected that I'd become as enthralled in Margaret Oliphant's story as I had been in Stu and Catherine's. Margaret didn't write like a bestselling thriller author, but her simple words were just as compelling.

I felt fairly certain she was indeed pregnant on her wedding day, and Judge Tremington was not the father. Now I wanted to know who was. I scrolled back through the images, looking for some that predated the Battle of Culloden and Margaret's subsequent flight from Scotland. I couldn't find any. I resolved to ask Julie in the morning to send me those passages as well.

I flipped past the making of the wedding dress and the bride's description of the ceremony, telling myself that I could go back and read that story anytime. I wanted to find out about the child.

I found an entry in which Margaret described packing numerous trunks and traveling by stage to a remote location in North Carolina. A few pages later, I found a passage where she wrote of her tremendous abdominal pains and the elderly woman with callused hands and a mustache who was charged with delivering her baby. She wrote of missing her mother, one of the only references I'd read to any other family members besides her father. I tried to skim faster.

Finally, maybe ten minutes of dedicated reading later, I found Margaret's description of her newborn baby. "He is tiny and red with wisps of dark hair clinging to his scalp. I can see my love in his eyes." She described wrapping him in a soft cloth she had prepared and asking for the priest to perform his christening. "His name is Edward Stuart Oliphant," she wrote. "Mr. T. shall have none of him."

I bit back a smile, remembering the character from the old TV series *The A-Team*. In this context, I was sure Mr. T. referred to Judge Tremington. Margaret was resigned to be his wife, although she clearly did not love him. She didn't want her child to bear his name. But whatever happened to Edward Stuart Oliphant?

I continued skimming through the handwritten pages as the clock ticked on. Margaret got to spend three and a half weeks with her tiny baby before the time came to give him up. "Mrs. F. is a fine woman. She will take good care of Eddy. She has agreed to keep my letter, to be opened upon his eighteenth birthday and cherished throughout his generations. He shall know who he is."

I couldn't find any more about Mrs. F., and soon after this entry, Margaret wrote about the return journey to Laurel Springs and the preparations for Christmas in the New World. I skimmed to the end of the pages Julie had sent, but there were no more mentions of Mrs. F. or of Eddy. That chapter in Margaret's life appeared to be over.

I closed my computer and snuggled into bed to finish the rest of the night. I would have to stop staying up late reading like this or I wouldn't be able to function at all in the morning. I wondered who C. E. was and what Eddy grew up to become.

* * * *

I slept late the next morning. When I came down to breakfast, I found Aileen at the table, dressed in a pair of fuzzy footie pajamas that were so far off her usual rock-star style that I did a double take. She hunched over a quart-size cup of coffee and a plate full of what looked like mango slices slathered with chunky peanut butter and sprinkled with onion flakes and bacon bits. I made myself a bowl of instant oatmeal and sat down across from her.

"Did you have a gig last night? I never even heard you come in."

She slouched down in her chair and took a huge slurp of coffee. "Yeah, we've got a standing gig at Wexman's on Wednesday nights. They're trying to build a hump-day crowd." She snorted. "There are a few diehard regulars, but other than that, there's not much demand for a dance party in the middle of the week. But Corgi wants to keep it up. He's got his eye on one of the waitresses, and it gives him a regular chance to see her." She took a big bite of her mango mess. "He said he's going to stop by this morning to see how the kilt is shaping up."

I choked on my orange juice. "Did he say what time?"

She glanced at me with her all-seeing eyes. "What, the kilt isn't shaping up? You're not setting Corgi up for a fall, are you?"

"Of course not. The kilt is fine. I just have a bunch more pleats to finish before it looks much like a kilt." I gobbled up my oatmeal and jumped up from the table. "Off to work!"

She called after me, "Want me to stall him when he gets here? We can work on a few tunes if you need a little extra time."

I paused in the doorway, touched. Aileen rarely offered to help me with my sewing business in any way. This suggestion felt like an olive branch. "That would be great. You could give me an extra twenty minutes or so. Just so long as Corgi's in a good mood when he gets to me."

She got up to dump her plate in the sink and refill her massive coffee cup. "Corgi's always in a good mood. You got nothing to worry about there."

I hustled upstairs and spread the project out on the floor. I had another few yards to pleat, but the garment was starting to look less like an extremely long length of tartan fabric and more like a kilt. If I worked fast and Corgi took his time getting here, maybe I could have the pleats all pinned up by the time he arrived. I closed my door, turned off my phone, and got to work.

After an hour of dedicated pinning, my hands were cramped up and I was starting to feel the tension in my neck and shoulders. But I was within three pleats of the end. I shook out my hands, did a few shoulder rolls, and checked my phone before getting back to it. I'd missed a text from McCarthy. It read, "Let me tell you about Melissa. Lunch?"

Good old McCarthy! I texted back: "Cool. Where?"

His answer was instantaneous. "I'll pick you up. Noon okay?"

It was already 11:20 and Corgi hadn't shown up yet, unless Aileen was stalling him downstairs. Of course, we didn't have a formal appointment. I was under no obligation to rearrange my personal schedule for him. "Sure," I replied, and bent over my work once more.

Ten minutes later, I pushed in the final pin. I stood up and threw out my hands, "Ta-da!" The moment needed some kind of celebration.

I hurried downstairs with an armload of kilt, to find Corgi and Aileen bent over some papers filled with handwritten music notation. Aileen had gotten dressed for the day in a magenta bustier and some skin-tight gold lamé leggings. Her hair was gelled into a ponytail on the top of her head, with spikes sticking out in all directions like fireworks. Corgi's Phillies T-shirt and khaki shorts looked positively bland in comparison.

"Remember, the pipes are in a different key," Corgi was saying. "I can't transpose this section. It'll sound terrible."

"Okay, let me see what I can do here." Aileen looked up at me. "Are you ready for the wearer of the kilt, then?"

"Yup. Hi, Corgi." I led him to my fitting room and displayed the kilt on the sideboard. "It's full of pins right now, so I'm not going to ask you to put it on, but I would like to get a few measurements."

He looked over the kilt and fingered the heavy wool. "It's amazing. I'll be the best-dressed piper in the band." He stood still while I measured the back of his waist from side to side and compared it to the pleated section of the kilt. Perfect!

"How soon will it be done, Daria? I'd be great if I could wear it on Saturday."

I dropped my measuring tape. "Corgi! Today is Thursday. What do you think I am, a miracle worker? You said you didn't need it before the games in Ligonier in two weeks."

"Yeah, right, I know. It's just that I was talking with Patrick Ames. You know, the Highland athlete. He was telling me about this event in Valley Forge on Saturday. Some kind of parade or something."

I picked up my measuring tape and coiled it up. "When were you talking with Patrick? At the ceilidh?"

"No, he's staying at my mom's bed-and-breakfast." He gave me a sheepish look. "You know I live with my mom."

"That's okay; I live with my brother. Whatever works, right?"

Corgi grinned. "Well, Patrick is hanging around here all week because of the thing in Valley Forge. Then he's off to Ligonier and the West Coast after that. He's even going to Scotland at the end of August for the Cowal Highland Gathering, which is the biggest Highland Games in the world. What a guy!"

What a guy indeed. I wondered if Corgi could be my link to Patrick, who remained one of my main suspects in Ladd's murder. I didn't even know what I needed to find out about him. All I knew was that he had been a rival of Ladd's for ten years, he hated Ladd because of his habitual cheating, and he had been in the VIP tent with Ladd's flask shortly before it disappeared.

"So you don't want me to try this on, huh?" Corgi fingered the tartan again, clearly disappointed he wasn't going to get to model his half-constructed kilt.

I shook my head. "All those pins will impale you. So, what's Patrick like? I danced with him at the ceilidh and he seemed like a nice enough guy. How is he at home?"

Corgi shrugged. "He's kind of cold, if you know what I mean. He doesn't mix much with the other guests. He keeps his bedroom door locked whenever he's out. He doesn't even want any housekeeping services unless he's in the room. My sister does all the rooms. She doesn't like to clean in front of the guests—she says it makes her nervous."

I folded up Corgi's kilt thoughtfully. "Do you suppose he's hiding something in his room? Maybe something that might incriminate him?"

Corgi stared at me, clearly not jumping to the same conclusions I was.

It seemed so obvious to me. "He's probably got Ladd Foster's flask hidden in his room. He's concealing evidence that he's the murderer!" I barely resisted grabbing his arm. "Can you get me into his room, just to check to see if Ladd's flask is in there?"

Corgi threw up both hands, trying to slow me down, no doubt. "I can't just let you in the room of one of my mom's guests. That would be trespassing, or burglary, or something. He's given instructions that no one should go in his room if he's not there. That's that."

"That means he's got something he's hiding. We've had a murder in this town, and Patrick hated the victim. You might be hosting a murderer in your house, Corgi. Wouldn't you want to know?"

Corgi scratched his head with a forlorn look on his face. "I guess I could ask my mom. She'd probably want to get the police involved. They could get a search warrant to go in his room, but a hotel owner can't do that. She could lose her license."

I chewed my lip. If we called the police, they might not even take my suspicions seriously. Or maybe they'd already searched Patrick's room. Maybe they'd solved the murder by now, and I was wasting my time and energy. No, that couldn't be true. I was sure they would inform the public when they fingered the killer.

"Here's an idea: You let me know when Patrick is in his room and I'll drop by to see him. If he entertains me in his room, I can at least glance around and see if he's hiding anything. It isn't trespassing if someone invites you in."

"What if he wants to hang out with you in the living room? You'd be wasting your time, instead of sewing my kilt by the weekend."

I laughed. "Is this extortion? Okay, if you help me with this, I'll try my hardest to get your kilt done by Saturday." I gave him my best winning smile.

"Cool." He held out his hand to shake on the deal. "Maybe I could be vacuuming in the living room, or playing the bagpipes or something, so you would need to go to the privacy of his room to talk."

I gave his hand a hearty shake. "Now you're talking. When is Patrick usually at home?"

"He was there when I left. We could go right now and get it over with. Then you could concentrate on my kilt."

"Okay, let's do it." I grabbed my shoulder bag and hustled down the stairs, only to find McCarthy hanging out at the kitchen table chatting with Aileen.

He called out a cheery greeting to Corgi and stood up. "Ready for lunch?" he said to me.

I'd forgotten about McCarthy. "I can't go to lunch right now, Sean." I hastened to explain. "Patrick Ames is staying in Corgi's mom's bed-and-breakfast, and he keeps his room locked at all times. Well, that's suspicious, right? So we're going to go over there now, and if Patrick's home, I'm going to chat with him in his room and take a look around."

A smile tugged at McCarthy's lips. "And if he's not home, you're going to sneak in for a closer look, right?"

"No, Corgi won't let me. He says his mom will get in trouble."

McCarthy laughed out loud. "Can I come along on this reconnaissance mission? I'll be backup—I won't even set foot in the house. Then we can have lunch afterward." His face sobered. "I found out some things about Melissa King."

"Sounds like a plan." I grabbed my house keys from the hook. "Ready?"

Aileen waved her long black fingernails at us on our way out. "Have fun casing the joint."

* * * *

Corgi's mother, Sally Redmond, ran the Mountain Laurel Bed-and-Breakfast, located a few blocks away in my downtown residential neighborhood. Her stately three-story house was very similar to my own, built with numerous bedrooms and only one bathroom. She had renovated extensively when she converted it from a single-family home to a bed-and-breakfast. I'd followed her progress at the time, wondering if I wanted to do the same and run a bed-and-breakfast to make some extra money on the side. I'd chosen to rent out rooms instead, which meant I didn't need to put a lot of money into renovations. I'd never regretted that choice.

We gave Corgi a five-minute head start. I drove down the street with McCarthy, who assured me that he would stay in his car during my interview with Patrick. When we pulled up to the curb in front of the B and B, he slouched down in his seat and held a magazine up to his eyes, like he was on a stakeout. I pulled out my phone and waited for Corgi to text me.

"Can't tell if he's home or not," the text ran. "Just come knock."

I held out my phone to McCarthy. "What do you think?" I said in a deep, scary voice. "Is it a trap?"

He pretended to consider it. "Probably. Call me if you need backup." He powered his seat back to a reclining position and closed his eyes.

I whacked him on the shoulder with his magazine. "Some backup."

I hopped out of the car and knocked on the front door. Corgi answered. "Is Patrick Ames home?" I asked in a loud voice, feeling somewhat foolish.

"Let's go see," Corgi said, leading me up the stairs and down a narrow hallway. He stopped in front of the door marked "Lilac Room," and knocked.

There was no answer.

"He's probably out to lunch," Corgi said. "Everyone is gone right now."

So much for my great plan. But another plan was forming in my mind, one that Corgi would not approve of.

"Would you mind if I use the bathroom before McCarthy and I take off?"

"Help yourself." He pointed down the hall. "The guest rooms have their own bathrooms, but Mom left the original bathroom as well. It's just a powder room now."

"Thanks, Corgi." I nipped into the bathroom, reflecting that he wasn't the most perceptive person or he might have guessed my intentions.

I used the facilities and paused at Patrick's door on my way out. Wishing I had thought to bring gloves, I grasped a fold of my skirt and tried the doorknob. As Corgi had said, it was locked.

I glanced over my shoulder for any prying eyes, pulled out my wallet, and fished out my library card. I'd learned this trick from McCarthy, which is to say I didn't make it a habit to pick people's locked doors. Only when I suspected them of murder.

I slipped the card in between the door and the doorjamb and forced the lock open on the fourth try. I was lucky Sally hadn't changed the locks to deadbolts as part of her renovation. With another glance over my shoulder, I ducked into Patrick's room.

The Lilac Room was furnished in attractive shades of purple on white, with ruffled bed skirts and frilly curtains. It was very bed-and-breakfasty, but nothing like the abode of a burly Scottish athlete. I couldn't picture Patrick in this room at all. I bit back a smile and bent to my task, which was no laughing matter. I had broken into someone's room to look for evidence of murder.

I checked under the bed and in the closet, searched through the dresser drawers, and rifled through the trash. A black soft-sided suitcase lay open on the floor in the corner. I took a deep breath and sifted through Patrick's shirts, pants, and other clothing, all the while knowing I shouldn't be doing it. I patted everything down where it came from and turned to the bathroom. A quick search through the bathroom cabinets and the wastebasket yielded nothing of interest. I was about to give up in despair when I heard the door handle rattle.

Chapter 16

I ducked back into the bathroom and pushed the door closed without making a sound. My hands were shaking so much, I could barely work the lock. How could Patrick come back at this exact moment? I had to figure out how to get away before he unlocked the bathroom door. I couldn't let him find me in the middle of ransacking his room.

Although the window over the toilet was small, I thought I might be able to get through it. But what good would that do me? Patrick's room was on the second floor. But it might be my only hope. I pushed aside the mini-blinds and looked out the window.

My heart sank. The bathroom window was miles above the ground, with no tree, fence, or helpful ledge within reach. If I went out the window, I would break my leg or my neck, depending on how unlucky I was. I was racking my brain for an excuse to give Patrick when I remembered I had backup.

I ducked behind the shower curtain just in case and texted McCarthy: "Help. I'm in Patrick Ames's bathroom. He came home. Lure him out of his room."

His response was instantaneous. He texted back: "Yikes. I'm on it."

I held my breath and started counting to keep myself from freaking out. I was on fifty-three when I heard the rattle of the bathroom door handle, and a voice swearing on the other side. "What is it with this door?" He jiggled the knob and pulled on the door, and then he was gone. He was either going for a key, in which case I was in big trouble, or he was going to complain to the management that he couldn't get into his bathroom. I was probably in big trouble in that case as well. I was wondering if that orange prison jumpsuit would be comfortable when I heard a loud knock on the outer door. I longed to slip out of the shower and put my ear to the door, but I didn't dare. Luckily, I didn't have to. I could hear Corgi's voice telling Patrick that he had a visitor from the media downstairs. Good old McCarthy! He must have known Patrick would respond to any chance of media attention.

I listened as two people left the room and closed the door behind them. I counted to ten and then opened the bathroom door a crack, just to make sure the room was empty. I made sure to lock the bathroom door behind me and then flew across the room and cracked open the door to the hallway. It was deserted. With a pounding heart, I slipped out of Patrick's room and closed the door behind me. I practically ran to the bathroom at the end of the hall and locked myself in.

I washed my hands over and over in the sink, letting the warm gushing water soothe my frenzied heart rate. Finally, I thought I was calmed down enough to avoid suspicion. I flushed the toilet for good measure and emerged from the bathroom. I had been in Patrick's room for less than ten minutes. Maybe Corgi would just think I'd been taking my time in the bathroom.

I walked down the hall past Patrick's room and right down the stairs as if I belonged there. I waved to McCarthy and Patrick, who were engrossed in a photo shoot, and walked straight out the front door.

I found Corgi straddling a stool on the porch, strumming on an acoustic guitar. He looked up when I walked out. "Your plan is kind of backward at this point. Patrick came home while you were in the bathroom. McCarthy drew him out of his room just when I was ready to start vacuuming so he would have to talk to you in his room. What do you want to do now?"

I had cringed when he said "bathroom," until I realized he meant the one in the hall, not the one in Patrick's room. "I'm kind of losing my nerve. I think I'll just head out to lunch with McCarthy when he's done. I'll figure out some other way to find out Patrick's deal."

"Suit yourself." He played a few chords on the guitar. "You'll find time to fit in my kilt, though, right?"

I gave him a big smile filled with genuine relief. "Absolutely! I'm not going to promise it'll be done by Saturday, but I'll do my best."

I sat down on the porch steps to wait for McCarthy.

He eventually emerged. He thanked Corgi for the chance to photograph this "renowned athlete" and beckoned me to follow him. We hopped into his car and drove off.

McCarthy turned to me with a grin. "So?"

"Thanks for the backup. You really came through."

He shook his head, as if he didn't know what to do with me. "So, I'm wondering how you got stuck in Patrick Ames's bathroom in need of backup. Just curious."

"Okay, I was being nosy. He wasn't home, and Corgi had made it very clear he wouldn't open up Patrick's room for me, so I sort of broke in. I didn't find anything there, so I can't think why Patrick needs to keep his door locked all the time. I didn't even find any valuables." Although, now that I thought about it, I realized I hadn't checked to see if there was a safe in the room. If there was, that would be a logical place to hide an incriminating silver whiskey flask. I'd have to ask Corgi.

"So you were in the middle of an illegal search when the suspect came home and discovered you?" McCarthy's eyes twinkled at me.

"Yeah, except that he didn't find me because I locked myself in the bathroom and hid behind the shower curtain. Then you created a diversion, which allowed me to escape." I leaned back against the car seat and closed my eyes. "I hope Patrick can figure out how to get into his bathroom before it's too late." The thought of him doing the potty dance while trying to open the locked door to his bathroom struck me as so funny, I burst out laughing until the tears ran down my face.

McCarthy just drove without a word, casting sidelong glances at me as if to make sure I wasn't cracking up right there in his passenger seat. He pulled into a parking spot near the Commons and cut the engine. "Ready for some lunch?"

I wiped my eyes and took McCarthy's hand. "Seriously, you probably saved me from getting arrested for breaking and entering. Thank you for being my backup."

He squeezed my hand tight. "Happy to be of service. I'm just sorry I didn't get a photo of you crouching behind the shower curtain. That would have been a priceless blackmail shot."

I snatched my hand away. "Yeah, you wish."

* * * *

We walked along the Commons, looking for a good place to eat. The lunch crowds had dissipated because it was already close to one o'clock. McCarthy gave me a glance full of mischief and led the way to Over the Wall.

I rolled my eyes at him. Good thing I liked Mexican food.

We placed our orders at the counter and then McCarthy found us a quiet table in the corner. It happened to be the same table I'd sat at with Morris

Hart, but I didn't feel the need to mention that fact. I positioned myself with a good view of the entrance and wondered what the waitstaff must think of me, coming in to eat at the same table on two successive days with two different men. I really wasn't that kind of a girl.

McCarthy pulled out his little spiral notebook and flipped a few pages. He looked up at me expectantly. "Ready to talk about Ryan King as a suspect, or did you have thoughts on Patrick Ames first?"

I reached for the basket of chips on the table. "I don't know what to think about Patrick. He was the last person to have access to Ladd's flask before it disappeared, but I didn't find any trace of it in his room. That's not definitive, of course, because he could have ditched it anywhere. Why would he hold on to it, unless he's got some crazy need to collect souvenirs of his crimes or something?" I loaded up a chip with some salsa. "He's carried on a bitter ten-year rivalry with Ladd. I can't rule him out just because I didn't find the murder weapon in his luggage." I popped the chip into my mouth and mumbled around the edges, "Let's move on to Ryan."

"Right." McCarthy consulted his notes for a few seconds, the smile fading from his face. "I checked with a couple of sources and called in a few favors and ended up with a pretty good picture of what happened to Melissa King in Cleveland two years ago. She was Ryan's wife and Gillian's mother, as you know. Their marriage wasn't…uneventful, shall we say. There were no less than three domestics lodged against Ryan King, although in each case Melissa refused to press charges. All three calls had to do with yelling and shoving only, no weapons, so the Cleveland Police Department didn't worry too much about it."

He paused while the waiter put down our steaming plates. I'd ordered a burrito with rice and beans today. It was bursting with meat and cheese and smelled delicious. I hoped McCarthy's tale wouldn't spoil my appetite.

"Then, two years ago on August 22, when Gillian was at a friend's house for a sleepover, Ryan called 911 to say his wife was choking. By the time the paramedics arrived, she was dead. They would have taken his word for it that she choked on some food, except for the history of domestic disturbance and the bruises on her face and neck. So they ordered an autopsy and questioned Ryan, who was out of control." He consulted his notes again. "The police report said he was screaming at the paramedics and police officers who were working on his wife's body. He had to be physically restrained." He shook his head. "It sounds like it was an ugly scene."

I eased the notebook out of his hand. "You should eat your lunch first and then tell me the rest."

He picked up his fork. "There's not much else. Gillian wasn't home, so she was spared the sight of the cops putting her father in a chokehold over the dead body of her mother. But because she wasn't there, there wasn't any witness to back up Ryan's story. The autopsy showed evidence of choking on food. There was no explanation for the bruises on her face and neck, except that they didn't contribute to her death. So the police told Ryan he was no longer a suspect, and he took Gillian and left town and came here. And from what I understand, Gillian is a real handful, and Ryan keeps her in check by running off her boyfriends, with force if necessary."

"That's what she told me. There's another side to this story that your sources probably don't know. Gillian was never told how her mother died. She told me that her father told her to never mention her mother again. She thinks he killed her."

McCarthy laid down his fork again. His food was going to get cold at this rate. "What a thing to carry around."

I nodded, poking at my own food. "Picture a thirteen-year-old girl, coming home from a sleepover to find her mother dead. Her dad didn't even call to tell her what happened. It breaks my heart. It's no wonder she acts out the way she does."

We sat in silence for a moment, feeling for Gillian. Then McCarthy rallied. "So, the upshot is that he really didn't kill his wife in Cleveland two years ago. She died from choking on her food. It's altogether possible his reaction to her death was shock and grief that came out sideways. But for your sleuthing purposes, oh nosy seamstress, Ryan King does not have a history of murder."

"Well, that's good to know. You know, he told me that God smote Ladd for messing with his daughter. He was glad he died."

"You told me. But that doesn't mean Ryan killed him."

He put his notebook away and proceeded to tell me a fantastical story about a reporter colleague who was trying to get an interview with a daredevil pilot who insisted it take place in his vintage biplane. By the time he got to the part where the pilot was flying upside down and the reporter dropped his notes at ten thousand feet, I was laughing so hard, I was at risk of choking on my own food. Leave it to McCarthy to lighten the mood!

We didn't linger too long after finishing because McCarthy needed to get back to work and I needed to make some serious progress on Corgi's kilt. Whatever possessed me to say I'd even try to have it done by the weekend?

McCarthy dropped me off at home and sped off with a cheery wave. I watched him go with a smile on my face and then headed inside to get to work on the kilt. The house was quiet, a sure sign Aileen was out and about. I knew Pete was at work, like always.

I knuckled down all afternoon, working on basting the pleats so I could pull out all the pins I had so laboriously inserted. Progress. I found it ironic that I needed Corgi to come in and try on the kilt once the pleats were all basted and pressed down, after I'd denied him the chance to model it this morning. Maybe he could come back tomorrow.

Basting is a fairly mindless activity in which you stitch down your seam using a long stitch that's easy to pull out later once the final seam is sewed. I tried to skip this step whenever possible, but I knew this wasn't one of those times. So I stitched and thought about my collection of murder suspects.

I felt like I'd been snooping and asking questions and coming up with nothing. I had learned today that Patrick Ames wasn't harboring Ladd's flask in his room, unless it had eluded me, which was entirely possible. I'd also learned that Ryan hadn't killed his wife. That didn't mean he hadn't killed Ladd. I couldn't eliminate either of them as suspects.

I pricked my finger on one of the hundreds of pins holding the pleats together and had to pause to put on a Band-Aid. I couldn't really stop for a break. I wanted to get all the basting done by suppertime so I could call Corgi and arrange for a fitting tomorrow. I turned back to my basting.

So, what about motive? Each one of my four suspects had a distinct motive for murder. Patrick harbored resentment from a ten-year rivalry that was on display at the time of Ladd's death. Ryan had witnessed Ladd cavorting with his underage daughter and had gone so far as to punch Ladd in the face. Aileen had a history with Ladd and obviously hated him with all the passion of her fiery nature. Morris Hart…what motive could Hart have to kill Ladd? He was a successful author and described Ladd as a fan. Could they have had some other kind of connection that would lead to murder? Was there some dispute over something Hart had written? That seemed pretty far-fetched. I couldn't think of a single reason why Hart would want to kill Ladd.

I was more than halfway done with my basting when I heard the door downstairs and the sound of someone puttering around in the kitchen. A few minutes later, Pete knocked on the frame of my open door. He held up a small silver object that I recognized immediately. "I found this in the bin when I went to take out the recycling. Did you really mean to recycle it?" He handed me Ladd Foster's whiskey flask.

Chapter 17

I dropped the flask on my desk as if it burned my fingers. "Do you know what this is?"

"It doesn't look like recycling, that's all I know."

"It's Ladd Foster's missing flask." I couldn't believe it had been in our house all along. I grabbed a couple of tissues to pick it up and unscrew the lid to take a whiff. It smelled exactly like it had when I'd first handled it in the VIP tent at the Games. I screwed the lid back on with fingers that shook. "It smells awful. I'd say it hasn't been washed. That's good news for the police anyway." I couldn't believe I was saying that either.

Pete stared, the color slowly fading from his face. "What, this is the murder weapon?" He fumbled for the back of my wooden chair, as if he needed it to hold himself upright. "How did this poisoned flask get from the VIP tent at the Highland Games to our recycling bin?"

He knew. Why did I have to spell it out for him? "I didn't put it there. You didn't put it there. Who else lives in this house?"

He sat down slowly, shaking his head. Resting his elbows on his knees, he dropped his head in his hands. "No."

"Who else could have put it there?" I felt like I was accusing him, which was completely unreasonable. But I couldn't help it.

Pete lifted his head to look me in the face. "You think Aileen brought this home and threw it out in the trash?"

I nodded. "What else could I think?"

"No. Aileen couldn't have done it. Think about it. When I came to pick you up, the flask had already gone missing. Then the police carted off Aileen. They kept her in custody for a couple of days, right? Not to disillusion you, but cops don't let people in their custody hide items on their person or in their belongings. She couldn't have had it on her."

"She could have put it in her car before the police took her," I argued. "Or she could have stashed it in her band gear. She carries around a bunch of bags filled with cords and mics and things. No one would think twice at seeing a whiskey flask in there."

Pete ran his hands through his hair. "Okay, she could have done that. But why bring it into the house and leave it in the recycling bin for us to find? She could have gotten rid of it in any garbage can in town. Why bring it home to incriminate herself?"

I didn't have a good answer for that. I stared at the flask, wishing it could give an explanation of its movements. The unicorn embossed on the front stared back at me, as if mocking me.

My gaze sharpened. I'd seen that same unicorn before, on the front of Margaret Oliphant's diary. Julie had said it was the Oliphant crest. Interesting that Ladd Foster carried around a silver flask with the Oliphant crest. I supposed he could have graduated from Oliphant University. I made a mental note to look into that possibility.

Pete stared at the flask as well, as if it were possessed. "I got my fingerprints all over that darn thing," he said in a glum voice.

Poor Pete—the last thing he wanted was to be a suspect in a police investigation. "You didn't know what it was. I guess my prints are on it too. I hope the cops will go easy on us."

His head shot up. "We can't turn this in to the cops. They'll come back and arrest Aileen for murder."

I rolled my eyes. "We can't just put it out with the recycling. If we hold on to it, we're covering up a crime. They could bust us for accessory after the fact or something."

He twisted his hands together. "We could just ditch it somewhere…."

So much for my trying-to-be-law-abiding brother. I picked up my phone. "I'm calling the police."

"Wait! Let me talk to Aileen first." He bowed his head. "Then we'll call."

At that moment, I heard the front door slam and a clatter in the front hall. Pete flinched. "We don't get any time to think about what to say, do we?" He stood up, squared his shoulders, and picked up Ladd's flask. "No time like the present." He headed downstairs with me right behind.

We found Aileen rooting through the fridge. She had added a wispy purple cape to her earlier ensemble of magenta bustier and gold lamé leggings, so now she looked like a colorful superhero about to hit the catwalk. A motley assortment of lunchmeats, hot sauces, dried fruit, and a huge bag of fiery nacho chips were strewn about on the counter. Pete put down the flask next to the dried mangos.

Aileen popped her head out of the fridge and looked from Pete to me to the flask on the counter. She straightened up slowly and closed the refrigerator door. She locked eyes with Pete, who returned her gaze without flinching. I faded back to the doorway, feeling the tension building in the room.

"I found it in the recycling," Pete said, cutting off Aileen before she could say anything. "It's Ladd Foster's flask with the poison still in it."

Nothing subtle about that. I might have waited to see if Aileen would recognize the flask on her own, but Pete just charged ahead.

Aileen plucked a plate from the cupboard and opened a hamburger bun on it. She started loading it up with all the food items on the counter to make one huge sandwich. She piled on a large portion of nacho chips and smashed down the top of the bun. "What's it doing in our house?" she said.

"That's what…" My words died on my lips at a warning glance from Pete. He was probably remembering my lamentable behavior at the jail, when I'd almost started a brawl with Aileen during visiting hours. Maybe it would be better for him to take the lead.

"I don't know," he said to Aileen. He was standing so still that Mohair almost stepped on his foot when she padded into the kitchen.

Aileen carried her laden plate to the table and sat down. She took a huge bite and mumbled around the food. "So you came down here to ask me if I put it in the recycling bin, right?"

"Did you put this in the recycling bin?" Pete said, keeping his eyes on hers.

She washed her mouthful down with a long drink of soda. "No. I didn't."

Pete let out his breath in a rush and went to sit down at the table across from her. He reached across the table and took her hand. "Who could have dumped this thing in our house to incriminate us?"

I stared at the two of them, feeling like I was trying to keep up. "That's it?"

Aileen tore her eyes away from Pete. "If you were hoping for a full confession, sorry to disappoint. Usually it's the guilty ones who confess."

I went and sat down with them. "I wasn't hoping you were guilty. I just…I don't exactly know how we know you're not. Guilty, I mean."

She started to laugh until she almost choked on her foul sandwich. "I guess you just have to believe me. How hard could that be?"

I leaned forward, getting in her face just the tiniest bit. "It would be a lot easier if you told us about your history with Ladd Foster."

Aileen set down her glass and looked me in the eye. I tried to keep eye contact without flinching. After a couple of hours—or maybe just thirty seconds or so—she picked up her sandwich again. "You once had a scumbag fiancé who jerked you around, but I didn't hound you to tell me all the gory details. Did I?"

"Well, you kind of did," I said, glad she was willing to talk about this rationally. "Was he your fiancé?"

She almost dropped her sandwich. "Hell no." She heaved a sigh. "He was my partner, if you must know. We were in a band together."

"I know." I said, my heart starting to thump. "The Royal Pains."

Pete's hand holding hers was the only thing that kept Aileen from jumping up from the table. "It was a country music band," he said. "You sounded really good."

"What is this, some kind of intervention?" Aileen growled, glaring at Pete. "What else do you know, Moron?"

"Daria got a CD and we recognized your voice. We looked up some online videos, of Ladd and Penny Morrow in the Royal Pains. You have a really nice voice. That's all we know."

Aileen picked up her sandwich and took a bite, chewing slowly and deliberately while watching both Pete and me watching her. We sat like that in silence until the sandwich was almost gone. Aileen finally spoke. "He was a jerk. Okay? The Royal Pains were good. We could have hit the big time, but he got mixed up with gambling until we couldn't pay our band's debts. He lived like a con man, keeping one step ahead of the bill collectors and the police, laughing all the while. He dragged me down with him until I couldn't play a single gig without it ending in a police bust. I had to get out or get arrested for all kinds of fraud." She picked her teeth with the sharp corner of a nacho chip. "My only regret is that I never got the chance to hit him over the head with my guitar. If I was going to kill him, that's what I would have done, while making sure he saw me coming. I wouldn't slip some poison into his whiskey when he wasn't looking."

I believed her. After seeing her reaction to Ladd at the Highland Games, the hardest part about considering Aileen as a murderer was the clandestine manner of his death. I never was able to think of her as a poisoner. She would have knocked him out with her guitar in front of hundreds of witnesses if she hadn't been restrained by her bandmates.

"So what's your real name, Penny or Aileen?" I asked, ignoring Pete's glare. If she was confiding in us, she might as well go all the way.

She flashed me a mischievous grin. "Wouldn't you like to know?"

Suddenly, I didn't want to know. I wanted her to be Aileen, singer and guitarist in the Twisted Armpits, that raucous metal band that was so far from the music of the Royal Pains that no one would ever suspect they could find Penny Morrow there.

"No, don't tell me," I cried. I leaned over and hugged her around the shoulders, knocking over her half-full glass of soda. "I'm sorry I suspected you of murder. I don't know what I was thinking. Maybe I'm the one you should call 'Moron'."

She pushed me off and swiped at her spilled soda with the ends of her wispy purple cape. "Does that mean I'm off your list?" She looked over at Pete, who was sitting quietly with a huge smile lighting up his face. "What about you, Moron? Am I off your list too?"

He took her hand again. "You were never on any list. I'd be a fool if I thought I could put you on any kind of list."

My eyes flicked from Aileen to Pete and back again. I *was* a moron. How could I have failed to notice what was happening under my own roof? I slipped out of the kitchen to give them some privacy. I walked up the stairs to my workroom, shaking my head the whole way. Pete and Aileen. It seemed so far-fetched and so absolutely right at the same time.

Chapter 18

After a while, Pete and Aileen came upstairs and stood in the open doorway of my workroom, hand in hand.

I looked up from my basting, which was almost finished at long last. "Congratulations, you two lovebirds. Nothing like a murder to bring people together in the end, right?"

"Or something," Pete said with a smile that caught me off guard with its sheer happiness. I hadn't seen him look so contented in the whole time he'd been home from his ill-fated time in Hollywood. It was especially striking now, with him holding Ladd Foster's horrible flask in his left hand.

"What are we going to do about this, Daria? If we're not going to throw it out with the trash, we need to figure out how to turn it over to the police without getting anyone arrested."

I contemplated the revolting thing. "It could be any of us, really. I ended up with the poison all over my blouse because I was wrestling with Gillian for control of the flask. Aileen has the strongest motive for killing him."

"And I have the police record," Pete said with a grimace, "which makes me one of the usual suspects in the eyes of the LSPD."

Aileen piped in, "Eeny, meeny, miny, moe, pick a murderer by the toe. Which one of us will they pick?"

I sat back on my heels and tried to think of a way out. Nothing came to mind. "Aileen, why wouldn't you tell the police about your history with Ladd? Were you worried about your reputation as a musician?"

"Maybe you weren't listening while I was baring my soul to you, but my history with Ladd was punctuated by fraud. I don't know how he avoided a long stint in jail unless he managed to pass off all his deceptions onto me after I split. In that case, if I were to resurrect Penny Morrow, I'd probably spend the next few years of my life behind bars. No, thanks!"

"Gotcha." I stared at the flask until it blurred before my eyes and all I could see was the unicorn embossed on the front. "Aileen, do you know if Ladd went to Oliphant University?" I pointed. "That's the Oliphant crest on his flask."

She snorted. "He went to Penn State and majored in partying. He had the Oliphant crest because he was part of the Oliphant family." She contemplated the unicorn as well. "He told me some wild story one time about how he was the descendant of Scottish kings. That's why he liked the name Royal Pains." She rolled her eyes. "He was so full of himself."

I stared at her. "Ladd was an Oliphant?"

"His full name was Ladd Stuart Oliphant Foster. He used to reel it off like he was somebody special because he had four names."

Maybe he *was* somebody special. I thought about Margaret Oliphant's diary, in which she'd written of giving birth to a boy in secret and naming him Edward Stuart Oliphant. Eddy was then given over to Mrs. F. to raise. Could that have been Mrs. Foster, by any chance? Was Ladd Foster descended from Eddy, son of Margaret Oliphant and her mysterious Scottish lover? But I'd never understood the Oliphants to be royalty. Margaret's father, Jock, was a clan chieftain in Scotland, but by the time he got to Pennsylvania he was probably no different from all the other immigrants fleeing from war abroad.

"Hang on a minute." Pete broke in on my musings. "Who is Gillian, and why were you wrestling with her over Ladd's flask?"

"She's a troubled teen—one of Breanna Lawton's Highland dancers. Gillian was flirting with Ladd at the Highland Games and he gave her the flask to hold. She put it down in the VIP tent, where it was poisoned. I watched four people go in and out of the tent before Ladd collapsed: Aileen, Patrick Ames, Morris Hart, and Ryan King, Gillian's dad. Ryan had a fight with Ladd over the flirting, so he's got a good motive for murder. I think Gillian was trying to make the flask disappear because she was afraid her father was the killer."

As soon as the words left my lips, I knew how Ladd's flask came to be in our recycling bin. After I hustled Gillian out of the VIP tent when Patrick Ames came in, she must have gone back and filched the flask. She could have hung on to it all this time, only to sneak it into our house during the sewing lesson. My cheeks burned at the thought of her taking offense to my questions and running off downstairs, leaving me to feel sorry for her while she planted incriminating evidence in my house. It was even possible she'd planned the whole thing before the end of the event at the Printed Page and had stayed behind with the express intention of guilting me into offering her a ride. I took it one step further. Could she have put the torch fuel into the flask to begin with? Was Gillian King the murderer after all?

I couldn't believe it. Regardless of whatever else I could imagine her doing, I couldn't see her poisoning Ladd. She'd seemed to genuinely like him, or at least she liked the attention he'd lavished on her. Why would she kill him? I couldn't think of any reason.

Pete and Aileen were both staring at me by this point, wondering what was going on in my head, no doubt.

"Sorry. I just realized it was Gillian who hid the flask in our house." I shook my head, tight-lipped. "I was giving her a sewing lesson while she was trying to get one of us to take the fall for her father. I think she suspects him as the murderer."

"He's one of your four," Aileen said, chewing on a long black fingernail. "Maybe he did it."

I took a deep breath. "I guess that's what we'll have to tell the police. I'm not going to protect Gillian if she's ready to throw us all under the bus like this." I picked up my phone.

Pete gripped his head with both hands. "Maybe we should call a lawyer first. I don't want to bring the cops here to cart one or all of us off. Your fingerprints and mine are all over this flask," he said to me.

Aileen leaned down and picked up the flask and tossed it from hand to hand. "Mine are too." She dropped it back onto my desk.

I started to laugh, with only a hint of hysteria lurking underneath. "We're all in this together, is that it? I'm going to call McCarthy first. He can come over and document the whole police thing. His prints aren't on the flask."

"Good idea," Pete said. He and Aileen went back downstairs, leaving me with the flask and my phone. McCarthy answered on the first ring. He responded with enthusiasm when I told him about the flask. "I'm already there!" I could almost see the gleam in his eyes through the phone.

I paused a moment to breathe a quick prayer, and then I dialed the police department. "I've found Ladd Foster's missing flask." I gave the officer my address, and he told me that someone would be over as soon as possible.

I went downstairs with the flask to wait.

McCarthy beat the police to our house. He bounded up the porch steps and pounded on the door as if he were the prize patrol or something. His camera dangled around his neck, close at hand and ready for business.

I displayed the flask for him to photograph. "No need to put my face in the shot, though. You can take a close-up with my hand holding it if you want." I did a little wave worthy of a game-show hostess. "I'm hoping to stay off the front page."

His camera clicked away. "This is front-page news, you know. Unless something bigger comes up, I'm sure the *Chronicle* will run this on page one." He grinned at me. "You'll get your fifteen minutes of fame."

"I'd rather get ten minutes for something I accomplished that was worthy of recognition." I laid the flask down on the kitchen table in time for the arrival of the police.

Pete ushered in Officers Franklin and Butler, the two cops who had responded to Ladd's collapse at the Games. They were the ones I'd taken to the VIP tent to find the torch fuel, so they knew all the issues of the poison and the disappearing flask. Their eyes fixed on me the minute they walked into the kitchen.

"Daria Dembrowski," Officer Franklin said, pulling out her notebook and flipping a few pages. "You were on the spot, covered in torch fuel, when Ladd Foster's whiskey flask—the murder weapon, if you will—went missing. Now here it is, in your house." She slipped on a glove and picked up the flask and unscrewed it, her snapping black eyes never leaving my face. "Yup. Smells just like your blouse from the other day."

My heart sank. I was just trying to do the right thing and she wanted to pin me for Ladd's murder! I was only slightly reassured by the sight of McCarthy and his video camera capturing every minute of this exchange.

"We found the flask in the recycling bin," I said, hoping to keep Pete out of the spotlight. "I'm pretty sure Gillian King hid it there yesterday when she was here for a sewing lesson."

Officer Franklin noted this down. "I hadn't heard you were giving sewing lessons to wayward teens."

I bit my lip. Only a small-town policewoman could possibly know this level of detail about both me and Gillian. If small-town life was like living in a fishbowl, living in Laurel Springs was like taking that fishbowl and setting it up on a table in the middle of the most popular restaurant in town on a Friday night. McCarthy always called me nosy, but I wasn't the nosiest person in town; not by a long shot.

I figured it was best to tell the truth. "I offered to teach her to sew because I wanted to know more about her personal life. I didn't think I was opening my door to her so she could plant evidence to try to trap me."

Officer Franklin looked me over with her piercing gaze and then made another note in her notebook. "We'll want to question each of you separately.

This is a fine place to talk. Is there someplace the other two witnesses can wait?" She frowned at McCarthy. "Have you gotten what you need for the newspaper? Feel free to leave at any time."

McCarthy winked at me. "Notice how the police are never inviting us photogs to feel free to stay as long as we like?" He grinned at Officer Franklin. "I believe I'm here as moral support, as well as in my capacity as a member of the media. I promise I'll be on my best behavior."

I could see a smile tugging at Officer Franklin's lips, even as she tried to keep a stern demeanor. Stern was hard to achieve where McCarthy was concerned.

Officer Butler took Pete and Aileen into the living room, followed by McCarthy. Officer Franklin sat down at the kitchen table and motioned for me to take a seat across from her. I told her how we had found the flask and concluded that Gillian was the one to hide it in our house.

"Tell me about your dealings with Gillian King, and why you suspect her of harboring the flask."

I took a deep breath. "You know that Gillian was flirting with Ladd Foster at the Games, and her father punched him and told him to leave his daughter alone. I think Gillian thinks Ryan was so angry, he killed Ladd. So she's trying to protect him by throwing suspicion onto Aileen, who also got into a confrontation with Ladd at the Games."

Officer Franklin chewed on the end of her pen. "Why would Gillian want to protect her father? By all accounts, she's openly defiant of him."

"Okay, I'm just guessing here. But I think she's really protecting herself. She made some mention about wanting to avoid getting sent into foster care. It all has to do with her mother's death."

I'd managed to surprise Officer Franklin. Her head snapped up and her sharp eyes bored into mine. "What do you know about her mother?"

"Her mother died by choking two years ago, but there was some doubt as to whether Ryan killed her. I think Gillian thinks he did, so it's not hard for her to imagine Ryan killing Ladd." I thought about what Gillian must be feeling. "It's sad, really. She'd rather live with someone she suspects is a murderer than risk going into foster care."

Officer Franklin had herself under control now. "This is all speculation on your part. Please stick to the facts."

I drew myself up straight. "The fact is, nobody living in this house put Ladd Foster's flask in the recycling bin, so someone other than me, Pete, or Aileen must have done it. I'm guessing it was Gillian. She was in the house yesterday for a sewing lesson. That's a fact. She was alone downstairs at one point, so she had plenty of time to hide the flask." I looked Officer Franklin in the eye. "You can ask her."

She flipped her notebook closed. "For what good that would do."

She escorted me out of the kitchen and called Pete in. I joined the group in the living room.

"So, did you incriminate yourself or the rest of us?" Aileen said. Luckily, I caught the wink in her eye or I would have taken offense at her insinuation.

"We won't have any discussion of this police investigation," Officer Butler said before I could respond. He was standing stiffly by the mantel, like a soldier standing at ease, with feet apart and hands clasped behind his back. It was a pose that was meant to intimidate more than relax.

I sat down on the couch next to McCarthy and wondered if we could have any kind of conversation at all.

"I don't see any handcuffs," McCarthy observed. "That's a good sign." He caught Butler's warning glance and lifted his camera to snap a picture of me. "I'll call this, 'After the Interrogation.'" He wiled away the next few minutes showing me the pictures he'd taken that afternoon. As always, the images in McCarthy's photographs seemed more meaningful, somehow, than my memories of what I'd seen or done.

Pete came back into the room and said, "Your turn," to Aileen. He sat down next to me and heaved a sigh that sounded like relief, unless it was anxiety for his brand-new girlfriend.

It seemed like Officer Franklin took a long time questioning Aileen. I could feel myself getting more and more worried that she'd be led out of here in handcuffs. Pete didn't help matters. He spent the time twisting his hands together in his lap, standing up and pacing around the room only to sit back down again, and checking his watch every few minutes. If I were judging his innocence on behavior or body language, I'd have said without a shadow of a doubt that he was guilty.

Finally, McCarthy engaged Pete in a discussion of yesterday's Phillies game, and Butler joined in as well. Talk of fastballs and changeups and one spectacular catch at the wall made the time pass more quickly.

When Aileen entered the living room at long last, she wasn't wearing handcuffs. Thank goodness for that!

She plumped down on the easy chair and said, "One interrogation down, how many more to go?"

No one answered her.

Chapter 19

After Officers Franklin and Butler left with the flask, Pete and Aileen took off for a walk, leaving me at home with McCarthy. He accepted my offer of tea and followed me into the kitchen.

He sat down at the kitchen table and smiled up at me as I puttered around putting the water on and rousting out the mugs and tea bags. "So, I can't help noticing a certain bliss in the air, despite another police interrogation. I've been wondering when things would come out in the open."

I plunked down a mug and offered him his favorite Earl Grey tea. "Don't tell me you saw that coming? I live here and I was taken by surprise."

He scrolled through a bunch of pictures on his camera and then held it out to me. The photo showed Pete and Aileen at this very table, engaged in conversation over an ordinary bowl of popcorn. Aileen leaned forward, gesturing with one arm. Her face was animated; her black stage makeup couldn't conceal the intensity of whatever hilarious thing she was saying. Pete sat back in his chair laughing, his eyes lit up and fixed on Aileen as if she were the only person in the world.

There was a softness in McCarthy's face as he looked at the picture. "This was a couple of weeks ago, when I was waiting for you to come down." He turned off his camera and picked up the mug. "Sometimes you can see things better in a photograph than when it's happening in front of your face."

I sat down across from him with my own mug of tea. "Well, I just hope this new thing doesn't mess up the dynamics of our house. Nothing like romance to tear down a good friendship."

He busied himself with his tea bag, dunking it up and down in his mug. "I guess we'll see."

I was lost in thought, picturing Pete and Aileen either isolating themselves in their newfound love or breaking up with disastrous consequences to the camaraderie of our household. Things change, I reminded myself. Life is never static.

I glanced over at McCarthy, who was drinking his tea in unaccustomed silence, for him. He looked at me and said, "Do you suppose Pete will become the newest member of the Twisted Armpits?"

"No, but he's their biggest fan. Although…he does play guitar, but it's more acoustic. He and Aileen could strike out as a folk music duo and blow everyone's minds."

We laughed together over the thought of Aileen playing folk music, although I knew she could if she wanted to. She could do anything.

I realized I hadn't shared the tale of the Royal Pains with McCarthy. I would ask Aileen's permission at some point before letting him in on the secret.

McCarthy hurried through his tea and got up from the table. "I need to get these pictures off to the paper. It's not really a breakthrough in the case, but it's news nonetheless." His eyes crinkled up at the edges when he smiled that smile I loved. "Thanks for calling me for backup and giving me the scoop. You know how much I love getting news first."

"I'll let you know when I've got anything else." Suddenly, I didn't want him to leave—not yet. "Actually, I do have something you might be interested in." I got up from the table. "I got some pages from Margaret Oliphant's diary that I think might have something to do with Ladd Foster. Want to take a look?"

"Does a monkey want a banana? Of course I want to have a look." He waited while I ran upstairs and collected my laptop. I plunked it down on the table and called up the pages Julie had sent me.

McCarthy looked on with interest as I showed him the scans of Margaret's handwritten diary entries. He listened in rapt attention as I laid out my theory that Margaret had a baby whose father wasn't Judge Tremington and gave him up to Mrs. F., who may have been Mrs. Foster. I pointed out the similarities in the names of Margaret's child Edward Stuart Oliphant and Ladd Stuart Oliphant Foster. I showed him a picture of the Oliphant crest and he compared it to the photo he'd taken of Ladd's whiskey flask. He laid down his camera on the table and looked at me in something approaching awe. "This is a fascinating story, a true historical mystery. Do we know who the father was?"

I shook my head. "I need to check back in with Julie to get some earlier pages from the diary. She hasn't read all of them because wading through the handwriting is so time-consuming. She told me that Margaret didn't name her lover, although she wrote about him giving her some gifts. I can't remember what."

"Can you ask her now?"

I glanced at the clock. It was coming up on eight-thirty. With a start, I realized I hadn't had anything to eat since my lunchtime burrito. No wonder I was feeling so hungry. I pulled out my phone and began typing. "I'll send her a text and then I need to get some food." I pressed Send and pulled the refrigerator door open. "You probably haven't had any dinner yet either."

McCarthy checked the clock like I had and jumped up from the table. "I need to get these pictures over to the paper so they can run them tomorrow." He scooped up his camera and gave me a quick peck on the cheek. "Let me know what you hear from Julie." He breezed out of the room, leaving me feeling somewhat forlorn. The abrupt absence of his boundless energy left the kitchen feeling cold and empty. I called to Mohair and scrounged a bit of supper from the fridge. After filling the cat bowls, I sat down to a cold turkey sandwich with nacho chips on the side, where they belonged, and scrolled through the images from Margaret's diary again. What did it matter if Ladd was related to Margaret Oliphant anyway? Could that have had anything to do with his death?

I finished my simple dinner and scooted upstairs to try to finish my work on Corgi's kilt so I could get him in for a fitting tomorrow. I went ahead and texted him to fix a time. Nothing like a deadline to spur me on to completion.

I had only basted two more pleats when my phone rang. It was McCarthy. I let it ring a couple of times while I toyed with the idea of not picking up. I really needed to focus on this kilt. But how could I ignore McCarthy? I picked up, of course.

"Daria, I've got something you're gonna want to see. Herman Tisdale came by while I was out and dropped it off. I'm going to swing by and pick you up." He hung up before I could even remember that Herman Tisdale was the announcer from the Highland Games who had been a drinking buddy of Ladd's.

McCarthy pounded on my door before I even had a chance to set the rest of the pins in the pleat I was working on. I hurried downstairs and threw open the front door.

"I had to leave it at the *Chronicle* because it's not technically mine," he said as he swept me out the door and down the walkway to his car.

"What is it?" I asked, a bit out of breath as he hustled me into the car.

McCarthy threw the car into Drive and peeled out from the curb. "Herman Tisdale stopped by the office today to drop off a book for Taffy, who's supposed to be writing an obituary for Ladd Foster. Tisdale said Ladd gave him the book at the Highland Games and asked him to have a look and give an opinion on it. Tisdale stashed it in his car and then, in the chaos surrounding Ladd's death, he forgot all about it. He discovered it this afternoon when he was cleaning out his car, and he thought Taffy might want to look at it for material for the obit. I just happened to see it on her desk, and she told me how she came by it."

He pulled up in front of the Laurel Springs *Daily Chronicle* offices and hopped out of the car. He practically dragged me into the newsroom and through a maze of cubicles and piles of file boxes. He bypassed his own cubicle and led me to one next to the window that looked out onto the disappointing view of the dumpsters in the back parking lot. A young woman with cropped brown hair wearing a pair of tortoiseshell cat-eye glasses sat at the desk. An unlit cigarette dangled from her lips as she clicked the keys of her computer.

"Taffy, this is Daria Dembrowski, the seamstress." He turned to me. "Taffy Deroue edits the obituaries. As we suspected, no family members have come forward with an obit for Ladd Foster. But Taffy's really good at writing as well as editing them, so she's working with Herman Tisdale on Ladd's." He turned back to Taffy, barely containing his enthusiasm. "Show her what Tisdale dropped off. He said Ladd told him it had been in the Foster family for generations."

Taffy shifted the cigarette to the other side of her mouth and shuffled a few papers off a small book bound in cracked leather. It looked really old and fragile, like it should be in the Tremington Museum instead of under a random pile of papers on a newspaperwoman's desk. Taffy handed the book to McCarthy and turned back to her screen.

McCarthy handled the book gently, almost with reverence. He opened it to the title page so I could see it was a book of poetry that looked like it was in Gaelic, by someone named Alasdair.

The small volume of poetry sparked a memory. "Julie said Margaret wrote about a book of poetry and a ring her lover gave her. Those items weren't in the trunk that contained her wedding dress." I leaned closer. "I've never heard of Alasdair."

"Me neither. I looked him up. He was a poet in Scotland in the eighteenth century who wrote in Gaelic even after the Jacobites were crushed in the Forty-Five and the language was suppressed. He was known as the Great Bard, or in English, Alexander MacDonald. Interestingly, he was a Gaelic tutor to Bonnie Prince Charlie." He pointed to an inscription on the facing page, written in English. 'Remember me, my love.' Short and sweet. It was signed, 'C. E. S.'

"I'm guessing we've found Margaret's book of poetry," McCarthy said. "C. E. S. must be Margaret's lover, and the father of Eddy." I reached for the little book and gently flipped through the pages. "I remember that Margaret wrote about taking care of a wounded soldier on the boat to America. She didn't want to change his dressings, but she did it for C. E. I took that to mean her lover. C. E. S. must be the same person."

I flipped through to the back of the book, where a faded envelope was tucked between the endpapers. I eased it out and held it up for McCarthy to see, my breath coming faster. "This might be a love letter to Margaret."

He grinned at my growing excitement. Meanwhile, Taffy typed away, oblivious to the historical revelations taking place behind her.

I eased the envelope open to find two pieces of paper inside. One was a thin piece of writing paper closely written by hand in old-fashioned handwriting. The other was a thicker piece of typing paper with text that looked like it had been produced on an old manual typewriter. I started with the handwritten letter.

It wasn't a love letter.

The handwriting looked the same as what I had been reading from Margaret's diary. But I didn't have to guess. The first line read, "From Margaret Oliphant Tremington, to Edward Stuart Oliphant Foster, on the occasion of his eighteenth birthday."

I was right about Mrs. Foster.

I held my breath as I continued to read:

> *My dearest Eddy,*
> *You are a man now, and a man should know where he comes from. Your parents will have told you that you were adopted, and now I will tell you of your true parentage.*
> *You are my son, conceived in love when I was still in Scotland, before ever I met Judge Tremington. You were not born into the sin of adultery. Your father fled Scotland after the Rising, as did I. He went to France while I took ship to America. You may have guessed at your noble blood, but now I will lay all doubts to rest. You are the natural son of Charles Edward Stuart, whose name you bear, along with my own. You may never be king of Scotland and England, but in your heart, you may know that the blood of kings runs through your veins.*

*I ask that you keep your royal heritage alive through
the naming of your sons, granting each of your firstborns
throughout your generations with the names Stuart and
Oliphant, as a testament to the love between two people torn
asunder by the disaster of war.*

*I gave you birth and then gave you up, but I never gave up
on loving you. I pray you will think kindly of me, as I think ever
fondly of you, my firstborn son.*

Your mother, Margaret Oliphant Tremington

I laid down the letter in awe. I had pulled aside the curtains of time and history and gotten a glimpse into the heart of a young woman forced to relinquish her firstborn son.

I whispered to McCarthy, "Her lover was Bonnie Prince Charlie!"

He was reading the typewritten page. "What a story!" He held it out to me. "I'm assuming this is the same letter, typed out at some later date."

I glanced at it. "Yeah. And get this—Margaret's wishes are still being followed. Ladd's full name is Ladd Stuart Oliphant Foster. I wonder if he has a son."

"Nope," Taffy called out over her shoulder, without even turning her head. "He wasn't married. Unless he has a child out of wedlock, of course." She kept on typing.

McCarthy chuckled. "From what I saw at the Highland Games, I wouldn't be surprised if there are any number of Stuart Oliphant Fosters running around out there."

I ran my finger over the handwritten lines. "Ladd was the descendant of Bonnie Prince Charlie, who tried to claim the throne of Britain as his own. Aileen said he told a story of being descended from Scottish royalty." I pulled out my phone and took a picture of both the handwritten letter and the typewritten page, as well as the book of poetry.

McCarthy took a couple of pictures as well, and then folded up the papers and slid them back into the envelope. He slipped it back into the book and put it down on Taffy's desk. "Your friend Julie would love to hear this story," he said to me.

I nodded, enjoying the thought of her enthusiasm over this fascinating mystery of history. "Morris Hart would be interested as well. He got the story all wrong in his novel."

"And you're going to call him up and set him straight?" McCarthy asked. Was that a hint of jealousy in his voice?

"Somebody's gotta do it." I searched through the contacts on my phone. "Here we go." I fired off a quick text under McCarthy's watchful eye. I didn't know why I was tormenting him like this, or why I was enjoying it so much. "Are you going to put this whole story in Ladd's obituary?" I asked the silent Taffy.

She shuffled the book aside on her cluttered desk. "I have to do some fact-checking first. Sure, it looks like an ancient document that tells a story that will forever change the fabric of history as we know it, but you never know, it could be a fake. It has to be authenticated. That's my job."

I hid a smile at her dramatic declaration and thanked her for sharing the book with me. I privately hoped Julie could swoop in as soon as possible to rescue this important relic of history from the chaos of Taffy's desk.

McCarthy led me out of the *Chronicle*'s offices. "Shall I spin you home?"

The *Chronicle* was in the heart of the downtown district, only a few blocks away from my downtown residential neighborhood. "We could just walk, if you want."

He grinned and accompanied me out the door and down the sidewalk. "I thought you might have work to do, or bestselling authors to contact."

"Already did that. I have to finish basting Corgi's kilt for a fitting tomorrow, and then I've got Breanna coming over to pick up her wedding gown. Her wedding is coming up next week, you know."

"I wasn't invited." He took my hand as we walked. "I don't do wedding photography, generally, so I don't get to go to many weddings. Who wants an obnoxious photographer hanging around when someone else is taking the wedding photos, right?"

I squeezed his hand. "Just what I was about to say!"

He smiled down at me, his eyes crinkling up at the corners the way they always did. For some reason, this time the sight took my breath away.

McCarthy walked me to the door, but I didn't invite him in. I really did have to finish basting Corgi's kilt. But we lingered on the porch for a few minutes, still holding hands. I didn't quite want to let him go.

"Thanks for sharing that book with me, Sean. It was fun to unwrap history like that."

He took my other hand as well. "Who else to share it with than my favorite historical seamstress?"

He leaned in close and kissed me gently. At that moment, a car screeched around the corner and roared up to the curb in front of my house. A red car with black flames painted on the hood. Aileen flung out of the driver's seat and bounded up the steps.

"I forgot the cord for my amp." She blasted into the house, leaving McCarthy and me laughing on the porch in her wake. He squeezed my hands and released me. "Happy basting, then. Goodnight."

A smile played on my lips as I watched him stride down the sidewalk, whistling. I was almost knocked over by Aileen on her way back out the door.

"Have a great gig," I called after her, but she was already gone.

Chapter 20

When I woke up the next morning, after spending the remainder of the evening setting the rest of the pleats in Corgi's kilt, I discovered that I'd missed a series of texts.

Julie expressed interest in my cryptic message that I had new and exciting information about Margaret Oliphant to share with her. She suggested I stop by the Tremington Museum at 4:45, just before closing, so I could get in and we could have time together uninterrupted by patrons or other staff. Morris Hart sent a dozen or more texts expressing delight that I'd contacted him and interest in my mysterious news as well. I decided to have him join me at the Tremington, so I could tell the two of them at once. Plus, Hart wanted to see Margaret's diary and wedding dress, which required Julie's participation. Perfect.

There were also a few texts from Corgi, saying he was glad the kilt was coming along, and could we meet at ten, and then another suggesting nine thirty instead, and finally a text saying he could come over first thing but was busy from ten onward. I called him to say he could come on over. I was pretty sure I woke him up.

I fixed a nice breakfast and a big cup of coffee, realizing Corgi was coming off the same gig with the Twisted Armpits that had kept Aileen up past midnight, at any rate. Well, if he wanted his kilt rushed, he was going to have to put in some time on the project as well.

It was ten minutes to ten before the doorbell rang. I let Corgi in and took him straight to my fitting room.

"Sorry I'm late, Daria. It was a late night last night, and then my alarm clock never went off." He grinned sheepishly. "It never does. I should get a new one." He glanced at his watch. "Thing is, I have to be on site at ten. Can we do this fast?"

I handed him the kilt. "Just slip off your pants and hold this around you so I can get a true fit on your waist." I motioned to the curtained-off area in the corner.

The vast majority of my clients were women, so it was just a little awkward to have Corgi standing there with his bare legs hanging out of the kilt I was fitting to his waist. I reminded myself that I was a professional and placed my pins as quickly as possible. "I should be able to get the waistband on and the lining set in by the end of the day, but I don't know if everything will be done by tomorrow." I steered him to the changing area again. "It would take a miracle."

Corgi popped his head out from behind the curtain. "That's what you're all about, isn't it?" He gave me a funny grin so full of hope that I hated to disappoint him.

"I'll do my best, but I can't promise anything."

He ducked out from behind the curtain and handed me the kilt. "How about if you forget about the inside until later? Just do whatever it takes to make it look good on the outside for me to wear it to Valley Forge tomorrow. Then you can add the lining or whatever later." He headed for the door as he spoke.

"I don't want you to wear it before it's stabilized if that might mess up all the pleats. I'll see how it looks throughout the day." I scooted him out the door and gathered up the kilt with both hands. I had my work cut out for me for today.

I took the kilt upstairs and spent the next two hours stitching down all the pleats, which were miraculously in the perfect spots so that none of them needed to be adjusted. Maybe I was a miracle worker after all. A finely made kilt would have all the pleats sewed by hand, but I was sure Corgi would prefer me to sew them discreetly by machine and get the thing done in a timely fashion.

I took a break for lunch, shaking out my hands and running them under warm water to work out the cramps. Then I plugged in the iron for an afternoon of pressing.

I started with Breanna's gown, which only needed a few touch-ups to bring it to perfection. I took it downstairs and hung it back up, ready for her final fitting at 3:30.

Then I set the iron for wool and carefully steamed and pressed the pleats into place. Everything I had read about kilt-making stressed the importance of this step, so I resolved not to take any shortcuts.

After a while, the quiet of the house started to wear on me, and I paused to put on some music. Without even thinking about it, I put on the Royal Pains' CD.

I wasn't a big fan of country music, but the blend of Ladd and Aileen's voices was a pleasant mix to give me something to focus on other than the endless ironing. But I was only up to the second song on the album when Aileen blasted out of her bedroom and into my workroom across the hall.

"What the hell are you listening to?"

She was casually dressed in a zebra-striped pair of leggings and a purple sequined tank top that exposed her midriff. Her hair was slicked back into an ordinary ponytail that contrasted with her habitual black makeup. I couldn't help marveling at how comfortable she was with her exotic style, so that she wasn't afraid to mix in some ordinary elements as well.

But I only had a moment to think about that.

Aileen stomped over to my CD player and popped the disc out of the machine. She lifted it high to smash it on my desk, but I snatched it out of her hands before it was reduced to shards.

"That's not mine," I gasped, holding the CD behind my back. "I have to give it back to Herman Tisdale." Not entirely true, but I didn't want her destroying the CD.

"Fine! Give it back. Just don't let me hear it playing in my house."

I bristled at her characterization of the house as hers but decided not to go there. "I didn't think you were listening. Sorry. You probably don't believe me, but the group is really good."

She snorted, and then sat down abruptly on my desk chair. "It makes me sick to hear the old songs. The sad thing is, we *were* good. If Ladd hadn't been so toxic, we could have hit the big time. I could have been on stage in Nashville, instead of playing in bars in the dinky town of Laurel Springs, Pennsylvania."

I slipped the CD into a desk drawer and picked up my iron again. "True. But even if he hadn't gotten caught up in gambling, he would have messed up something else. You would have been miserable sticking with him all these years. Plus, you wouldn't have met me or my brother, your favorite moron."

She raised her eyes to my face, for once neither sardonic nor caustic. "That's right. My life has been better without linking myself to that scumbag." She flashed me a grin. "Good for you too. If I was headlining in Nashville there would be no Twisted Armpits, and you wouldn't be ironing a kilt at this very moment."

"It's hard to imagine life without the Twisted Armpits." I said it with a smile, but in a deeper sense, it was really true. Life takes twists and turns, some of them planned, and some you have no control over. In my own life, if my fiancé hadn't left me before the wedding, I would have married him and probably been miserable the rest of my life. And I wouldn't have met McCarthy, who was by far the better man. I hadn't thought about the debt I owed to Randall for ditching me. Maybe one day I could bring myself to thank him.

I looked over at Aileen, sitting on my desk chair with both feet tucked up as if she planned to stay a while. "Speaking of Pete, what's the deal with you two?" I said. "All that romance business took me by surprise."

She hugged her knees to her chest. "For a woman who loves poking her nose into other people's business, you do show a lack of attention to what's going on at home."

"Well, you always call him Moron. What was I supposed to think?"

Her smile held a hint of tenderness that would warm Pete's heart if he saw it. "He didn't care, even the first time I called him that. How often do you meet someone like that?"

"So what, you like him because he doesn't mind that you call him a moron?"

She picked up a stray piece of fabric from my desk and threw it at me. "Don't be ridiculous! You know your brother pretty well. He's a great guy. He's kind, and funny, and he comes to my gigs and enjoys the music I play. He's worked so hard to stay out of jail, but he's not afraid to go there with me, even when he has no idea if I'm going to tear the place down. He makes me want to be a better person. Plus, he's damned attractive." She winked at me wickedly.

I threw the fabric back at her. "He's a sweetheart. Just don't break his heart, that's all I ask."

I expected an explosion, or a flippant "Whatever," but Aileen surprised me, like always. She picked up the piece of fabric and twisted it around her ring finger with a serious look on her face. "That's what I'm afraid of. I excel at breaking things. It's my strongest quality."

I bit back a smile because I knew she was serious. "Pete's pretty tough. I wouldn't worry about it."

She threw down the fabric and flashed me a grin. "I was hoping you wouldn't mind." She unfolded herself from the chair and ducked out of my room before I had a chance to respond.

I was touched. I hadn't expected her to seek my approval before dating my brother.

I hummed and ironed and hoped Pete and Aileen would be happy together. I closed my eyes, picturing my sensible, responsible brother with the volatile, passionate, take-no-prisoners Aileen. It wasn't a bad picture. A burn on my finger from the iron pulled me out of my reverie. I plowed through the last few pleats and shook out the fully pressed kilt. If I quickly attached the lining and sewed on some buckles, maybe Corgi really could wear the kilt tomorrow. I rousted out some heavy cotton duck cloth and cut the amount I needed for the lining.

I had just enough time to get it pinned in before Breanna arrived for her fitting.

She breezed in and tossed her purse down on the hall window bench with a flourish. Her lovely red hair was pinned up so that it cascaded down her back in a wave of curls. "I've just come from the hairdresser," she told me when I complimented her on it. "I told her I wanted to see how the curls looked while wearing the dress." She held out both hands in reverence to receive her dress, and then scooted behind the curtain to try it on. When she emerged, I almost applauded. She looked absolutely lovely. The crisp white satin shone under the ceiling lights, the princess bodice fit perfectly, and the tartan sash provided a splash of color that complemented her beautiful red hair. When I adjusted the headdress with its tiny tartan bows and sprig of heather, she could have been a Scottish bride straight from the Highlands.

She admired herself in the mirror, turning this way and that to take it all in. Everything was just right. "Thank you so much, Daria. This gown is just beautiful." She handed me her phone to take some pictures as she continued to gush over the gown. Finally, she turned around so I could unbutton the back. She slipped behind the curtain and emerged a few minutes later in her everyday clothes. The magical moment was over for now.

"You'll be coming to the ceremony, right?" Breanna sounded like a preschooler giving out birthday party invitations. "I hope everything goes all right. I'm a little worried about the dancers. Ryan King grounded Gillian for a whole week. I don't know if he'll forbid her from dancing or not. It doesn't seem right to punish me for Gillian's misdeeds."

"Of course I'll be there." I pulled the plastic covering over her gown. "I didn't know Gillian was grounded. What did she do?"

Breanna rolled her eyes. "She stayed out after curfew or talked back to her dad or something. There's always something with her. Sad thing is, with all her issues, she's far and away the best dancer I've got. I really want her to be there."

I handed her the gown and accepted the check she gave me. "Maybe you should talk to Ryan—ask for an exception for the ceremony or something. You could tell him he can take her home as soon as the dancing is finished without getting any cake, or something like that."

She laughed. "Maybe that would do the trick." She waved a cheery goodbye. "See you next week!"

I closed the door firmly behind her. I always felt a complex mixture of accomplishment and letdown when I sent a bride off with her gown. I loved to see the finished product, especially when it was as beautiful as Breanna's gown. But at the same time, I put my heart and soul into my work, so I knew I would miss the gown when it was gone. I always took photos to keep in my portfolio. Clients smiled when I showed them pictures of all the gowns I'd made because I always spoke of them as if they were old friends in a high-school yearbook.

I tidied up my fitting room and checked the time. I'd arranged to meet Morris Hart at the Tremington Museum, and it was almost time to head out for the bus. I ran upstairs to change. I picked out a swingy floral skirt I'd made and a blue cotton blouse to match. A few quick brushes reinforced my conviction that my thick hair had a will of its own. I popped in a couple of barrettes and called it good. It wasn't a date with Hart, I told myself, just a chance to share a fascinating historical mystery.

The bus was crowded with commuters on their way home from work, so I had to stand. I held on to the strap and swayed around the corners, thinking about Margaret Oliphant coming to the New Country knowing she was carrying the child of a royal Stuart. Surely she also knew she would never see him again. That was a lot to put on a seventeen-year-old. I thought about the fifteen-year-old Gillian, hoping she would never have to face an unmarried pregnancy like that. I knew she wasn't ready for the kind of responsibility and heartbreak Margaret had endured.

Hart was waiting for me when I got off the bus. He sat on a bench at the entrance of the Tremington, eating an ice cream cone. He waved as I walked over. "Hey, Catherine! So nice of you to get in touch with me."

I stood a bit awkwardly in front of him. "It's Daria. I knew you wanted to see Margaret Oliphant's diary and wedding gown, and there's something else I want to show you as well." I glanced at his cone. "We should go on in, before the museum closes."

He jumped up and tossed his cone in the trash. "Lead on!"

I led the way into the foyer, hoping we wouldn't be charged admission for the last ten minutes the museum was open. I said to the docent, "We're here to meet Julie Lombard."

She dialed the phone and spoke for a moment, then turned to me. "Julie will come out to collect you. You may wait for her here." She waved to a long row of bench seating and busied herself with her cash register.

I sat down next to Hart. "Have you had the chance to tour the Tremington while you've been in town?"

He shook his head. "I've been doing book signings, meeting with creative writing classes at the university, and spending all my free time promoting my book. I've barely had a chance to pursue my quest for Bonnie Prince Charlie's ring." He gave me a smoldering glance. "Have you had a crack at it?"

"The search for the ring?" It was my turn to shake my head. "I've been working on a wedding gown and a kilt for tomorrow, so I've been pretty busy."

He pulled out his phone and called up a website. He held it out for me to see. "I've got clues posted on my website." He grinned like a mischievous little boy. "I don't want to make it too easy for my fans."

I leaned in for a closer look, to see that the clues were written in another language. "Is that Gaelic?"

He laughed and nodded. "First, you have to translate the Gaelic, then you have to solve the riddle, and then go looking. So far, no one's found the ring."

I looked up from his phone. "Have you?"

He tucked the phone back into his pocket. "You ask many questions, my dear Catherine."

"It's Daria. McCarthy calls me 'nosy seamstress.' I guess he's on to something."

Hart folded his hands in his lap and focused his attention on me. "McCarthy. That's your photographer friend, isn't it? He's always on your mind, it seems."

I shrugged in some confusion. Luckily, Julie arrived at that moment, so I didn't have to go into detail about my relationship with McCarthy.

Julie wore a bib apron over her jeans and checkered shirt, and her hair wisped out of its ponytail to float gently around her face. Her oversize headphones dangled around her neck, as usual. She greeted me cheerfully and showed no awe when I introduced Morris Hart, the novelist. "Come on and take a look," she said, when I told her that Hart was interested in Margaret Oliphant's wedding gown and diary.

Julie led us through the delightfully chaotic rows of historical artifacts on her way to the back room. "How's the kilt-making coming?"

"It's great. Kilts have a lot of pleats in them." I paused at the end of an aisle and said to Hart, "You might be interested to see this kilt, which was worn by Jock Oliphant, Margaret's father, in the Battle of Culloden."

"I would indeed," Hart said, his eyes lighting up. I led him to where the kilt hung on the wall, surrounded by the other artifacts from the Clan Oliphant: the chipped sword that may have also been at the Battle of Culloden, the family Bible, and the silver ring with the big red stone.

Julie plucked the kilt down off the wall and displayed the bayonet tear to a fascinated Morris Hart. I heard their conversation as if from far away as I stared at that ornate silver ring. Margaret wrote of a gift from her lover, Bonnie Prince Charlie, who gave her a book of poetry and a ring. I had seen the book of poetry with my own eyes just yesterday and had pictures of it on my phone to show Hart and Julie. What about the ring? Could it be right here in front of me, on display for all to see in the gloriously disorganized basement of the Tremington Museum?

I felt like calling out Huckle Buckle Beanstalk, from the childhood game of hide and seek, but I held my tongue. I wanted to see what Hart thought about the diary and the letter about Eddy.

Hart's face was lit up with excitement as he examined the kilt and looked over the other items. I was almost sure he noticed the ring, but he made no comment. All he said was, "Show me this wedding dress and diary."

Julie unlocked the door marked "No Admittance" and motioned for us to follow her. She left the door slightly ajar. "Everyone's on their way home for the day, so we've got the place to ourselves." She put on her protective gloves and lifted Margaret's gown off the shelf and spread it out for Hart to see.

He gave it a cursory glance, apparently not blown away by the beauty of the faded embroidery. "I'd love to see the diary."

Julie turned back to the shelf and took down the brittle leather volume I recognized as Margaret's diary. She ran her fingers absentmindedly over the Oliphant crest embossed on the cover, and then laid it down on the table next to the gown. "Margaret started writing about her life at the age of eleven," she said to Hart. "Is there something in particular you're interested in, or do you just want to gaze at this historical document?"

He reached out to touch it, ignoring the instinctive movement of Julie's hands. "I'm interested in the Battle of Culloden, of course. Was Margaret still in Scotland during the Forty-Five? Did she write anything about that?"

Julie smiled, pleased that she didn't have to instruct him on the Forty-Five, no doubt. She told him about Margaret's flight to America after the disastrous battle, and how her father fought bravely at Bonnie Prince

Charlie's side. Through the slightly open door, I saw the lights go out in the basement exhibit area. As Julie had said, everyone was on their way home.

I chimed in when Julie got to the part about Margaret's ocean journey to America, and laid out my theory about her pregnancy and how she'd relinquished her son to the care of Mrs. Foster.

Julie's face perked up. "Where did you come up with the name Foster? I didn't find that in Margaret's diary at all."

I pulled out my phone and called up the pictures I'd taken last night in the *Daily Chronicle*'s offices. I held out my phone so they could both see. "And now, for the rest of the story."

Julie and Hart bent over the images on my phone. I showed them the book of poetry given to Margaret by her lover. "On the title page was the inscription, 'Remember me, my love,' signed C. E. S." I appealed to Julie. "Remember how she took care of that wounded soldier on the ship even when she didn't want to, but she did it for C. E.? He was her lover, and the father of her son." I scrolled to the next picture, a screenshot of Margaret's letter to Eddy. "She didn't put it in her diary, but here she writes to her son that his father was Bonnie Prince Charlie." I put down my phone in triumph, the better to see their reactions.

Julie stared in amazement from me to my phone and back again. "Where did you get this book?" she whispered.

"It came from Ladd Foster," I said, watching for the next reaction. "Right now, it's on a desk at the *Daily Chronicle*. You should grab it for the museum before it gets coffee stains on it or something."

I almost laughed out loud at her horrified gasp, but my attention was captured by Morris Hart's reaction.

He looked stunned. He leaned over my phone to try to read the letter on the screen. "Ladd Foster gave this to the newspaper?" he asked in a strained voice.

"Well, not exactly. Ladd gave it to a friend of his to get his opinion, and after he died, that friend gave it to the *Chronicle*." I pointed to Eddy's full name. "Ladd's name was Ladd Stuart Oliphant Foster, named for his ancestors, Charles Edward Stuart and Margaret Oliphant." I turned to Hart with a playful smile. "Bonnie Prince Charlie had a son with Margaret Oliphant, and Ladd Foster was his descendant. You got it all wrong in your novel."

In the split second those words crossed my lips, I knew. But by then, it was too late.

Chapter 21

Hart's face darkened with anger. "This story is a lie," he said, his voice ice-cold. "A malicious lie, intended to discredit my work." He stood stock-still for a moment, and then he moved with the lightning strike of a rattlesnake. He snatched up my phone and threw it across the room.

"Hey!" I ran across the room to grab up my phone, which was shattered. "You can't just break my things like that." I turned around to face him, shocked to see the veneer of civilization stripped away, revealing the murderer beneath.

Suddenly, several things happened all at once.

Hart reached out to grab up Margaret's diary, probably intending to heave it across the room as well. Julie threw herself across the table, covering the diary and the wedding gown with her body to protect them. "Don't touch them," she yelled.

Hart grabbed her instead. He jerked her off the table and spun her around until he had her pinned with one arm twisted behind her back. He shoved her up against the wall, released her arm, and hit her hard against the back of her head. She fell to the floor.

I screamed, for what good that would do. Everyone had left the museum for the night. There was only Morris Hart and me, with a long metal table holding irreplaceable historical documents in between us.

I snatched up Margaret's diary and clutched it to my chest with both arms. "You can't kill history," I yelled, edging around the table to avoid the jab he made at me.

"Give me that book," he said, feinting in another direction.

We circled around the table in a grotesque game of keep away. I could feel the fragile leather of Margaret's diary shredding under my sweaty grasp. I hoped the historians would appreciate the fact that I was trying to save it, not destroy it. I fought to control my panic, which was only intensified by the sight of Julie lying crumpled on the floor, unmoving. Maybe I could distract him. "You killed Ladd Foster after he told you that he was the descendant of Bonnie Prince Charlie." I continued to edge around the table, with my eye on the partially open door leading back into the exhibit areas of the basement. "What did he do, try to blackmail you?"

Hart picked up a long pair of scissors and hefted them like a spear aimed at my heart. "Yeah, he told me. He said he had proof that he was taking to the newspaper. He was looking for fame and recognition, trying to shift the spotlight away from me and leave me looking silly in the process. There are millions of dollars riding on the success of my novel. Ladd Foster's story put all of that at risk."

I could hardly believe my ears. "So you sneaked into the VIP tent and poured torch fuel into his whiskey flask, hoping his story would die with him. But you failed. Even if you destroy Margaret's diary and smash my phone, you can't suppress this story. Margaret's letter is at the *Chronicle*, and other people have pictures of it as well."

"Who, your photographer boyfriend? I can deal with him when I'm done with you." He threw the scissors straight at my head. I ducked and heard them clatter against the far wall.

I took the opportunity to make a dash for the door, but Hart was too quick for me. He bolted around the table and grabbed me from behind, tackling me to the floor. With my arms clutching the diary, I was unable to brace myself, so I fell heavily with him on top of me. My scream was cut off by the wind being knocked out of me.

Hart wrenched my shoulder to roll me over so he could rip the diary from my hands and throw it across the room. He straddled my body as I lay gasping, trying to get some air back into my lungs. I put up both hands to protect my face and neck. He raised his arm to hit me across the face, and then he stopped. A look of deep sadness distorted his features. "Catherine…" He pulled both my arms down to either side of my head and bent down, as if to kiss me.

I thrashed under his grasp and threw my elbow up to connect with his throat. He fell back, gasping and coughing. I shoved him off me and scrambled to my feet, shaking. I ran to the door, feeling Hart clutching at the swingy folds of my skirt from behind me. I grabbed the door and pulled it toward me with all my strength, slamming it into his shoulder as his hands seized me again. He staggered and lost his grip on me.

I darted out the door into the darkness of the Tremington basement. I could hear him blundering out the door behind me. I raced through the maze of aisles, not sure whether to hide or to make a break for the exit. I turned down a familiar aisle, only to find myself at the end of a cul-de-sac, stranded next to the Oliphant treasures. The only way out was the way I'd come, but Hart was too close behind me. There was no place for me to run.

I scanned the row frantically, looking for a place, anyplace, where I could hide. There was nothing.

Hart turned down the aisle, barreling toward me. His face was distorted with rage, and he hugged his left arm to his side. "You'll answer to a higher power for that!" he hollered, inadvertently quoting a line from his novel, when the would-be assassins were menacing Catherine and Stu.

But I didn't intend to answer to him or anyone else, nor did I plan to end up being tortured like Catherine. I breathed a quick prayer and wrenched Jock Oliphant's sword off the wall.

The blade clanged to the floor. It was far heavier than I'd expected. What good was a sword if you couldn't even heft it? I grunted out loud as I struggled to wield it.

My abrupt action in grabbing the sword had stopped Hart's headlong rush toward me. When he saw that I could hardly lift it, he advanced on me again, but slowly this time. "It's over, my dear Catherine. You're no match for me."

I pulled the sword up and balanced it with my left hand on the blade, ignoring the pain as it cut into my palm. Holding it with both hands, I managed to point it straight at Hart's heart. "Not one step closer," I shouted, jabbing the sword in front of me as if I meant business. "This is the Battle of Culloden and you're going to go down in defeat!"

Hart roared and ran toward me. I held out the sword, simultaneously hoping he didn't spear himself on it and wishing I had the strength to plunge it into his heart. At the last minute, I crouched down and swiped the sword at his legs as he rushed me. He cried out and fell to the floor, clutching at his shins. I sidestepped him and flew down the aisle to get away from him, dragging the sword behind me. I didn't let go of it until I got to the admissions desk and called the police on the museum's phone. "Hurry," I begged. "I don't know if he'll come after me again." I crouched down behind the docent's desk and prayed for the police to get there before Hart could find me, if he was looking.

It took the police less than three minutes to arrive. Four or five police officers swarmed into the museum, guns drawn. I stood up and called out to them, "I'm here!" I pointed them to the aisle where I'd left Hart on the floor and blurted out the fact that I'd hit him with a sword. "I don't know if I cut off his legs or if he's bleeding to death." I clutched my arms to my chest, trying to control the shakes that had seized my whole body.

A couple of teams of paramedics raced into the building. They split off in two directions, one team following the police down the aisle to the place where I'd left Hart and the other heading to the back room, presumably to take care of Julie. A tall police officer with the deepest voice I'd ever heard placed a blanket around my shoulders and asked to see my hand. I held it out to him, surprised to find it covered in blood from a cut running straight across my palm. The officer wrapped it in a bandage and said, "You'll need to get this looked at. Is there anyone you'd like to call to be with you?"

I clutched the blanket close, hoping it would stop my shivering. Who did I want to call to help me through the next few hours? Pete? Aileen? I looked up at the kindly officer. "Please call Sean McCarthy and ask him to come right away," I whispered. I started to give him the number, but I could see he had McCarthy's number in his phone already. I started to laugh with tears running down my face.

McCarthy arrived in less time than it had taken the police to get there. He strode into the room and folded me into a hug so tight, I almost lost my breath for the second time that evening. "Are you all right?" he whispered into my hair as I clung to him like I'd never let him go.

"I'm okay," I said, my voice as shaky as my knees. "I just hurt my hand, is all."

McCarthy held me off and looked me over, searching for other injuries, no doubt. He took my hand and cradled it gently, while snuggling my head so that it rested on his shoulder. He held me that way and watched as the police marched a handcuffed Morris Hart out of the depths of the Tremington basement.

I saw blood on Hart's pant legs, but his feet weren't cut off, nor had he bled to death. He did walk slowly, and he shot me a glare of pure hatred. The police hustled him out the door before he could say anything to me. I burrowed my head into McCarthy's shoulder.

"Did you take him down?" McCarthy asked me in a voice filled with admiration.

I nodded. "He's the one who killed Ladd Foster. He was trying to cover up that story about Margaret and Bonnie Prince Charlie because it would discredit his stupid novel."

McCarthy let out a long, low whistle and held me close.

"He smashed my phone," I went on, as if the two crimes were equal in their intensity. "He had me pinned to the floor. I didn't know if he was going to choke me or rape me or both. I slashed him with a sword." I started to cry. "He called me Catherine."

McCarthy's arms tightened around me. "You're Daria Dembrowski," he said, low into my ear. "You're the nosy seamstress who always seems to find the killer in the end. You're nobody's character, no matter how famous or successful they are. You're the one and only Daria. He should have known better than to tangle with you."

I took a shaky breath and lifted my face to look him in the eye. What I saw there left me breathless, as surely as if I'd had the wind knocked out of me again. "You..." I abandoned whatever half-formed thought I had and pulled his head down into a passionate kiss.

I've heard it said that you shouldn't get emotionally involved with someone right after a traumatic experience. That may be good advice at the beginning of a relationship, but McCarthy and I weren't at the beginning of ours. We were right where we needed to be.

Chapter 22

McCarthy stayed with me throughout the police questioning. I couldn't believe how many times I had to explain that Morris Hart killed Ladd Foster because he was descended in a direct line from Bonnie Prince Charlie, and his existence threatened the success of Hart's bestselling novel. The cops simply couldn't believe that the truth of something that happened over two hundred and fifty years ago could be enough to commit murder. "But the book is fiction," one cop kept repeating over and over, while scratching his head in disbelief.

Julie recovered consciousness with no ill effects beyond a splitting headache. The paramedics advised her to take it easy for the next forty-eight hours and watch for signs of a concussion. I sat down next to her on a museum bench while she waited for her roommate to pick her up. "I'm sorry about Margaret's diary," I said. "I tried to keep it from him, but I couldn't. Hart threw it across the room. It's probably ruined."

She gave me a brave smile. "When you restore historical documents, they come in all kinds of disrepair. We can probably fix it. Margaret's story won't be lost."

* * * *

McCarthy went with me to the emergency room and entertained me with some of his outrageous stories while the doctor cleaned my hand with half a dozen different solutions, set in three stitches, and gave me a tetanus shot for good measure. McCarthy squeezed my right hand when it was all over. "It must be intimidating as a doctor to be stitching up a seamstress. She's bound to be critical of the techniques used."

I returned the pressure gratefully. "That's probably why they put this dressing on, so I can't see what stitches they used."

He took my left hand gently and ran his thumb across my fingertips. "You'll probably end up with a scar. A badge of honor from the last battle of Culloden. I hope it doesn't interfere too much with your work."

My fingers tingled at his touch. "Poor Corgi. I won't be able to do any more work on his kilt, at least for a couple days. He'll have to use his old one at Valley Forge tomorrow." I sat up in the hospital bed and swung my legs over the side to stand up. My legs were a little wobbly, and I staggered into McCarthy's arms. He caught me and enfolded me into a warm hug.

"Need a ride home?" He kissed me gently and then offered me his arm to steady me on the way out.

My hand started hurting more and more on the way home, and so did my shoulder, where it had hit the floor under Morris Hart's weight. I gritted my teeth and tried not to cry in front of McCarthy. He glanced over at me a couple of times and moderated his speed to accommodate my injuries. That consideration almost made me cry in itself.

When we got home, I could hear the Twisted Armpits belting out their music before I even opened the car door. McCarthy walked with me to the door and accompanied me inside when I begged him to come in.

We found Pete in the kitchen finishing up his dinner while the Twisted Armpits shook the floorboards under his feet. He jumped up at the sight of my bandaged hand and bloodied skirt. "Are you all right? What happened?"

He fixed McCarthy and me each a plate of chicken and rice and listened in silence while I told him the whole story about Morris Hart being the murderer. At one point, he stopped me and popped downstairs to bring Aileen up so she could hear the tale as well. When I finished, they both sat back and stared at me as if in shock.

Aileen broke the silence. "Okay, so Ladd was a bastard, but he didn't deserve to die just so some author could keep up his frigging reputation. I hope Morris Hart sees his sales plummet while he wastes away in jail."

"Yeah." I poked her gently. "You could go visit him, just to rub it in."

"Not on your life!" She leaned back in her chair and cracked her knuckles, one at a time. "I'm not planning any trips back there any time soon."

Pete threw her a smile so full of love, I had to look away. I fumbled with my napkin and got up to deposit my plate in the sink. When I turned back around, I saw that the band had finished practicing. One by one, the members of the Twisted Armpits straggled up from the basement and made their way out the door. Corgi paused in the doorway of the kitchen to speak to me.

I held up my bandaged hand as exhibit A. "Sorry, Corgi, I won't be able to finish your kilt for tomorrow. But you can wear your old one to Valley Forge, right?"

He leaned against the doorjamb as if he had nothing in the world to do. "That's okay. I think I'm just going to skip Valley Forge. I'd have to get up at seven-thirty to make it to the registration on time."

I picked up a dish towel and threw it at him. It wasn't exactly professional, but it expressed my feelings better than anything else could.

McCarthy didn't linger much after that. He probably guessed I needed to unwind in a nice hot tub.

I walked him to the door. "Are you doing anything next Friday? I need a date for a wedding."

His eyes crinkled up at the corners as he smiled down at me. "Are you sure you want to be seen with an obnoxious photographer who never gets invited to weddings?"

I stood on my tiptoes to plant a kiss on his lips. "Always."

* * * *

I spent the next few days doing nothing—just sitting around the house having Pete and Aileen wait on me. A bandaged hand was particularly useful for getting out of doing the dishes. By Tuesday, I felt well enough to get back to my sewing, just in time for Gillian's sewing lesson.

Her dad dropped her off at precisely three o'clock. She bounced up the steps as if she were working on elevation in her Scottish dancing. "I heard they caught the murderer," she sang out before she even walked in the door. "It was that author, Hart."

"'They' nothing," I said, ushering her upstairs to my workroom. "*I* caught the murderer."

"You did not!"

I held out my hand, still covered with a bandage. "I took him out with a sword that was used at the Battle of Culloden."

Her jaw dropped and she stared at me in awe until I had to laugh. "That part was in the second paragraph in the article in the paper," I said.

"Yeah, well, I didn't read the paper. My dad told me."

Before I could say anything else, she pounced on the cut pieces for her blouse. "What do I do next?"

We spent the next half hour sewing the side seams of the blouse and setting in the sleeves. The lesson was going so well, I didn't want to spoil it by bringing up a delicate topic. It wasn't until we were sitting on the porch swing waiting for her dad to pick her up that I dared to broach the subject.

"Now that this murder is solved, you know your dad's not a murderer, right?" I took a deep breath, hoping I wouldn't mess this up. "Gillian, I found out something about your mother." I hurried on, before she could take offense and run off. "Your mother choked on some food. That's how she died. Your father tried to help her, but he was unsuccessful. Your dad didn't kill your mom. It was a horrible accident that was nobody's fault."

Gillian stared at me until I thought she'd gone into shock. Then she started to cry without making a sound. I handed her a tissue, and then another one. I longed to put my arms around her, but I knew she wouldn't let me. I settled for patting her on the shoulder until her sobs quieted. "How do you know?" she whispered.

"I've got an inside source at the newspaper." I told her about McCarthy's research. "If you don't believe me, you could ask your dad."

We looked up to see Ryan standing on the edge of the porch, watching us, his face reddening. He had obviously heard the whole thing.

Just for a second, I feared I might have precipitated an explosion. But Ryan came over and sat down next to Gillian on the swing. In a very quiet voice, he said, "You thought I killed your mom?"

Gillian shrank away from him, almost afraid to nod.

He took her hand, his eyes filling with tears. "I loved her," he said. "Sometimes we would fight, but I loved her. I would never hurt her." He bowed his head until his forehead touched hers. "My little girl. You've been living with this all this time, thinking I was a monster."

She threw her arms around him. "Oh, Daddy," she sobbed.

I left the two of them there on the porch swing, holding each other tight, as if they were making up for lost time.

* * * *

I spent the next few days making up for lost time myself. It took a few late nights and some very long days, but I finished Corgi's kilt the day before the promised delivery date. It was ready for him to wear at the opening of the Royal Exhibit at the Tremington.

Julie and her team had worked tirelessly to get the artifacts ready for display as the newest addition to the local history exhibit in the upstairs gallery. McCarthy took me to the gala opening, complete with speeches, hors d'oeuvres, and music from the Laurel Springs Pipe and Drum Corps. I wore a springy dress made of pale green moiré silk that broke just above the knee, and clipped my hair back with one of my Scottish bow ties. I chose the Oliphant tartan as a tribute to Margaret. McCarthy dressed up as well, with a gray suit coat over his customary white button-down shirt and black leather shoes on his feet. I noticed with amusement that he also wore the yellow bow tie I'd given him at the Highland Games.

I held his hand and watched the bagpipers marching in to the tune of "Scotland the Brave." Corgi was resplendent in his new kilt. Every pleat lay just the way it should, to create the proper swing in the back. The heavyweight wool in the Ancient Guthrie tartan gave the kilt a respectability that could have come from Scotland itself. If only Corgi had bothered to wear his new ghillie brogues with it...

Gillian led the dancers out to perform the sword dance. With a genuine smile on her face, she lifted both arms, rose to her tiptoes, and danced faster and faster, never once touching the sword or sheath beneath her. A flash of red glinted on her breast as she danced. It was a delicate silver chain strung with beads that looked like garnets.

I went to speak to Gillian when the dance was over. "That was beautiful. I love the sword dance." I indicated the chain around her neck. "That's a pretty necklace."

She touched it lightly. "My dad gave it to me. It belonged to my mom." She pointed to a display case in the middle of the room. "It kind of matches the ring."

We both wandered over to look at the ring under glass: the ornate silver ring with the big red stone that had lain for so many years in the delightfully chaotic basement of the Tremington. Now it occupied the place of honor in the Royal Exhibit upstairs, with a placard that proclaimed it to be from the "Crown Jewels of the House of Stuart, given to Margaret Oliphant by Charles Edward Stuart, otherwise known as Bonnie Prince Charlie, circa 1746."

McCarthy joined me as Gillian skipped off to hang out with her friends. He took my hand and twined his fingers through mine.

I kept my eyes fixed on the ring. "I always loved the story of Margaret Oliphant coming to America and falling in love with Judge Tremington. But that was fiction. The true story of her falling in love with Bonnie Prince Charlie in her Scottish homeland is much more romantic."

He squeezed my hand. "That's what comes of sewing wedding gowns all day long. You get carried away by the romance of it all."

I turned away from the ring. "Nothing wrong with that." I rose to my tiptoes and kissed him, right in the middle of the crowded exhibit. "We can all use a little romance and mystery in our lives."

* * * *

Breanna's wedding was at the Methodist church that evening. The church was a modern building on the edge of town that boasted a bowling alley in the basement and the biggest youth group in town. The sanctuary was filled with chairs rather than pews, arranged in three rows that angled toward one another to create a cozy feel. Bouquets of white roses combined with sprigs of purple heather and tied with red tartan bows filled the hall with their sweet scent.

The wedding was perfect. A lone bagpiper piped Breanna into the church, playing a sprightly tune the program identified as "Mairi's Wedding." Breanna looked stunning. Her gown fit perfectly, and the red tartan scarf was a beautiful touch. Best of all was the joy that shone through her face as she joined her groom at the altar. Her fairy-tale wedding had come true.

Four of the older Highland dancers filed out to dance the lilt, led by Gillian. The girls held out their full skirts with both hands and bowed to the congregation before rising to their toes and commencing the dance. I couldn't tear my eyes away from Gillian. She wore a minimum of makeup and her bright strawberry-blond hair was done up in French braids accented with a bit of heather. Her youth and beauty in the dance threatened to upstage the bride. I snuck a peek at Breanna, but she wasn't fretting. She watched her dancers with pride.

The reception was at the Scottish Rite Temple, in the spacious downstairs meeting room that had been decked out with the flowers and tartan bows from the church. Large round tables were covered with crisp white tablecloths topped with dozens of votive candles dropped into a bed of heather. The effect of all the twinkling lights was charming.

The Highland dancers made another appearance, led once again by Gillian. This time they wore their Highland kilts and vests and danced the Highland fling. As before, Gillian was the one to watch. When the dance finished and the crowd was applauding, I sought out Breanna.

"That was beautiful," I said. "Your whole wedding has been perfect in every way."

She hugged me. "It's sweet of you to say so. But that Morris Hart totally ruined my wedding."

I gaped at her, so she went on to explain. "I wanted to have the girls dance to 'The Skye Boat Song,' like they did at the ceilidh, while Isabelle sang. But I couldn't have her sing the words, 'over the sea to Skye'—not after I found out Hart was the murderer. I was counting on that dance. Now the whole thing is ruined."

I choked back a chuckle and assured her that the whole thing was just lovely.

McCarthy joined us and congratulated the happy couple. He took my hand and pointed to the dance floor, where numerous couples swirled around to the lilting music of a harp played by a beautiful young woman dressed in a pink silk ball gown. "Shall we dance?"

We sashayed out onto the dance floor. He clasped my good hand close to his chest as we swayed, and then he spun me out under his arm. Nobody else was twirling, but that was the way McCarthy danced, like he could fly, and me with him. I spun back into his embrace and said, "Sean. They'll all be watching us."

He laughed and spun me once more. "I just wish we had someone taking pictures for the Daria Photos."

I put both arms around his neck, before he could spin me again. "It's about time you showed up in that collection." I gazed into the depths of his pale blue eyes, suddenly overwhelmed. "I love you, Sean." I bent his head down for a kiss.

He held me like he'd never let me go. "I love you, Daria. I always have."

We spun and twirled across the dance floor, two people in love, on our way to completely upstaging Breanna's perfect wedding.

If you enjoyed *Royally Dead*, be sure not to miss the first Stitch in Time Mystery,

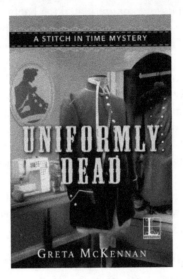

Historical seamstress Daria Dembrowski has her work cut out for her as she searches for a killer's pattern...

Daria has come up with a brilliant new plan to expand her seamstress business beyond stitching wedding gowns—historical sewing. And with Civil War reenactors setting up camp in her hometown of Laurel Springs, Pennsylvania, she has plenty of opportunities, including one client portraying a Confederate colonel who's a particular stickler for authenticity.

But soon the small-town peace starts coming apart at the seams as an antique doll is stolen from a Civil War exhibit and the cranky colonel is found impaled by his own bayonet. When Daria's brother is suspected of the theft and a bridal client's fiancé is accused of the murder, Daria is determined to untangle the clues to prove their innocence. She needs to get this case sewn up fast, though, before the murderer reenacts the crime and makes *her* history.

Keep reading for a special look!

A Lyrical Underground e-book on sale now.

Chapter One

My first meeting with Colonel Windstrom was a disaster. He marched into my fitting room—previously the formal dining room of my Federal-style house—as if it were a military headquarters. A hefty man, his tread shook the floorboards, jiggling the bolts of cloth leaning on the built-in shelf along the inside wall and toppling a rag doll on the mantel. He narrowly missed knocking into my antique spinning wheel. He took no notice of the books on the Civil War I'd carefully selected from the library, or the framed portrait of a Union soldier that I'd borrowed from an old lady at church. His bluster disrupted the cozy atmosphere I tried to create with my ruffled white organdy curtains and the hot cider simmering on the sideboard.

"I'll need coat and breeches from the gray wool," he instructed me, without even a *hello.* "The shirt of white cotton broadcloth. Mind the stitches now. Anything that shows has got to look authentic." He pulled on his long, "authentic" moustache and scowled. "General Eberhart won't tolerate any Farbs in his outfit."

"Yessir, no Farbs," I repeated, wondering if a Farb was some new kind of Velcro. "You can count on me." I brandished my measuring tape to reassure him of my competence.

Colonel Windstrom glared. "Ms. Dembrowski, you don't even know what a Farb is, do you?"

I drew myself up to my full five feet three inches. It was the first time I'd ever faced down a colonel, of any description. "Actually, no," I said. "But you can be sure I won't be using any Farbs on your uniform."

Colonel Windstrom's laugh startled me. His pudgy face turned bright red and he snorted through his nose. "Do you know a thing about reenacting?" he barked. "A Farb is someone who doesn't care about history or an accurate portrayal of the period. He just wants to go out on a sunny day and shoot off some cannons. He'll make his uniform out of polyester if he feels like it." Colonel Windstrom wiped his face with a grimy handkerchief. "You obviously need to learn a thing or two about Civil War reenacting," he admonished me, as if I were seventeen instead of twenty-nine. He strode out the door without a backward glance.

I rolled my eyes at my cherished silhouette of Betsy Ross that hung above the mantel. Betsy Ross had been my hero ever since I did a project on her life in the fifth grade. I sewed a miniature felt flag and a mobcap for my presentation and pretended to be the illustrious seamstress. Even if no one could prove that she designed the first flag of the United States, she continued to inspire me as I focused more on historical projects in my sewing business, A Stitch in Time. I wondered how many belligerent patrons Betsy had to put up with in her day.

I hated to admit it, but Colonel Windstrom was right when he said I should learn more about reenacting. I got my first lesson later that very evening.

* * * *

I didn't often do house calls, unless I was working on drapes or upholstery, but this time I made an exception. I'd never seen a Civil War reenactors' encampment before, and I wasn't going to miss this one. If I was lucky, I might get a few more uniform orders before the mock battle at the end of the week. I'd be well on my way to establishing myself as the premier historical seamstress of Laurel Springs, Pennsylvania.

I got off the bus on the outskirts of Turner Run Park. The reenactors had taken over. Normally the serene river valley, nestled between two wooded bluffs, hosted a few dog walkers or the Laurel High School cross-country team on a training run. Today rows of canvas tents filled the valley floor. Laid out in straight lines as if on a grid, they illustrated the kind of military discipline required from a commander who would not tolerate any Farbs in his outfit. Men squatted around campfires scattered among the tents. The smell of wood smoke mingled with the unmistakable odor of gunpowder. The scent reminded me of the Fourth of July—an ironic association for a camp filled with Confederate soldiers bent on dissolving the Union. The men all had beards and long moustaches, and wore homespun shirts or tattered uniform coats, with muskets and rifles propped carelessly by their sides. My heart beat a little faster as I approached these mock Civil War soldiers. I felt like I was taking a step back in time.

I glanced around the groups, wondering how I would find Colonel Windstrom, when all of a sudden I heard my name.

"Daria!"

I peered through the campfire smoke to see a beefy soldier waving at me.

"Hey, Chris." I knew Chris Porter through my work on his fiancée's wedding gown. With the wedding coming up next week, I needed all the time I could get.

Chris lumbered to his feet and came over to me. He held out his arms and pivoted slowly around. "What do you think—Confederate soldier extraordinaire?"

My lips twitched, but I didn't laugh. Obviously General Eberhart wasn't paying enough attention because Chris was a Farb if there ever was one. His coat looked more like a Halloween costume than a period piece. I didn't even need to feel the fabric—I could see the unmistakable sheen of polyester. His cheerful face was bare of beard or moustache—not because he was too young, but evidently he just chose not to grow one.

"This is such a rush, Daria! I get to march with rifles with real bayonets and everything. How cool is that?" Chris plopped down on a log. "You wanna come sit by the fire?"

"Just for a minute." I sat down carefully beside him. "I'm here to see Colonel Windstrom." I blinked smoke out of my eyes. "I didn't know you were a reenactor."

"A buddy told me about it—he said they needed more soldiers. People keep quitting or something. So I snagged a coat and here I am. I'm taking a whole week off work to get the full experience."

"A whole week, with a wedding just around the corner? What does Marsha have to say about that?"

He shrugged. "She's got all the wedding preparations in hand, between herself and her mom. There's nothing for me to do." He tossed another log on the fire, dodging a spray of sparks. "So you're making a coat for Colonel Windstrom, eh?" Chris didn't even try to suppress his smirk. "What do you think of our fearless leader?"

"Fear-inspiring, more like. I'm not sure I'd want to hang around here all day listening to him criticize everyone."

Chris nodded. "True, he can be kind of a downer. Yesterday he pulled all the infantry aside for a lecture. He told us that if we weren't shopping at YeOldeReenactors.com, then we were Farbs and not worthy to be in this outfit."

I laughed. "YeOldeReenactors.com? Sounds like a cross between a New England sweet shop and eBay for history buffs. So are you shopping there?"

Chris gave me a sidelong glance. "'Course I am—what do you think? Wouldn't want to stand out as a Farb, now would I?" He smoothed his shiny polyester coat with a wicked grin.

"Got it." I indicated the less-than-authentic coat. "Where did you get this, anyway?"

He leaned in close to whisper behind his hand. "There's a little costume shop on Baker Street, right next to the Keystone Playhouse. They sell leftover costumes from past shows. The Keystone did the musical *The Civil War* two years ago, and they wanted to get rid of the old costumes. I lucked out."

I mentally filed this information, ever on the lookout for leads for my sewing business. Maybe the Keystone would need a seamstress with historical expertise someday.

"There's a lot of interest in the Civil War these days," I said. "You know there's a Civil War movie filming in town right now. Do you guys have any interaction with them?"

"I dunno, they might want to film some of our skirmishes for background shots or something." He shrugged. "I just go with the flow."

A line of gray-clad soldiers marched past us, muskets held at the ready. I scanned their uniforms, looking for reassurance that I was on the right track with Colonel Windstrom's. Their coats came in a wide variety of colors: gray, butternut, and even some faded Union blue. "I don't get it, Chris. How come you guys are Confederate soldiers? There weren't any Southern troops in Laurel Springs, were there?"

"Nah, Laurel Springs was straight Union. But you can't have a battle with just one side, now, can you?" He lowered his voice to a dramatic whisper. "In actual fact, Daria, we're the bad guys."

Chris could never be the bad guy. He was one of the nicest people I had ever met. He worked in construction and remodeling—always a lucrative business in a town full of homes dating back to the early nineteen hundreds. The recession had slowed business a bit, Chris had told me, but he didn't think he'd get laid off. "I'm not worried," he'd said—three words that seemed to sum up his cheerful personality.

"So how come you're not wearing a hoop skirt?" Chris said. "I'll bet you could whip up a ball gown in no time."

I waved a persistent wisp of smoke away from my eyes. "I wouldn't need a ball dress to hang out with you soldiers, unless I just wanted to watch." I remembered a picture I'd come across in my research that showed women in long dresses and parasols standing on a hill watching the Civil War soldiers skirmishing down below. "If I wanted to fight for the glorious cause, I'd dress as a man, and you'd never know as long as I didn't get wounded or captured."

Chris slapped his knee in delight. "You got that right! In fact—"

Suddenly shouts and curses erupted from a tent about fifty yards away. I jumped and scooched a little closer to Chris.

"Who the hell has been messing with my stuff?" A stocky soldier stomped out of the tent, clutching a haversack in one hand and a small wooden box in the other. "You guys may think you're funny," he shouted, waving both arms for emphasis. "If I find out who did this, I'm taking him straight to the general!"

I leaned forward to look at the haversack dangling by its strap from the soldier's hand. A splash of red paint marred the flap of the small canvas bag. Dripping red letters spelled out the word *FARB*. The box bore the same message. I looked anxiously at Chris.

He shrugged. "Some guys want everyone to believe that they're really Civil War soldiers. I guess you could call them fanatics. They're messing with the guys who don't live up to their standard of perfection."

I reached out to touch Chris's polyester coat. "Are they messing with you?"

"Nah." He shrugged. "What can they do to me? I'm not worried."

I looked again at those red letters, paint dripping like blood, and shivered.

The commotion didn't faze Chris. He merely stood up, brushed some dirt off the seat of his pants, and led me to a cluster of larger, more imposing tents. "I think Colonel Windstrom's in a briefing with the general, but I'm not sure."

A smooth-faced sentry stood in front of the colonel's tent, musket held at the ready.

"Are these things loaded?" I said to Chris, waving a hand at the gleaming musket.

He looked me straight in the eye. "Of course, ma'am. You never know when the enemy might strike."

I shot him a sharp glance. "Are you trying to be funny?"

"We're supposed to stay in character at all times," he whispered with a grin. "I try to keep up appearances when the brass are looking."

I shook my head as Chris spoke to the sentry. The sentry was short, clearly a teenager. He wore a gray kepi pulled low over his eyes, so I couldn't see much of his face. No beard or moustache covered his strong jaw. Sandy curls peeked out from the back of his cap—he wore his hair long like boys did in the 1860s.

Chris turned to me. "Colonel Windstrom is busy, Daria. Private Rawlings is going to talk to the sergeant."

I was about to protest, when the sergeant stepped out of the tent. A tall man with a dark brown beard and moustache, he wore a tidy gray uniform coat over dark gray trousers and shiny black boots. He moved with a quiet military grace that came straight out of *Gone with the Wind*. When I held out my hand to introduce myself, he took it gently and bowed down to lightly kiss the back of my hand. No one had ever kissed my hand before, not even in jest. It didn't matter that I wasn't dressed in silk and petticoats—he saw me as a Southern belle. I could feel a sappy grin creep over my face as he lifted his eyes to mine. He had deep brown eyes, so dark you could barely see the pupils. They were eyes to get lost in.

The sergeant smiled, his whole face lighting up. "I'm Sergeant Jim Merrick," he said. "Pleased to make your acquaintance, ma'am."

"I'm Daria Dembrowski." I could feel the blush rising on my cheeks. "I'm making a uniform for Colonel Windstrom. I just needed to take a few more measurements."

"I won't hear another word!" a voice thundered from inside the tent. I jumped with a slight gasp. Sergeant Merrick smiled apologetically. "The colonel is busy at the moment. May I show you around until he's ready?" He held out his arm and tucked my hand into the crook of his elbow. I said goodbye to Chris, who headed back to his fireside with a cheery wave.

Jim Merrick walked me slowly through the tents, pointing out the cook tent, the infirmary, and even the photographer's quarters. "We have a camp photographer traveling with us for a few weeks," he said. "All the men want to have formal portraits taken to send to their loved ones back home."

It took me a minute to realize that I was talking to a Civil War soldier, not a twenty-first century man playing dress-up. This reenacting stuff would take a bit of getting used to. But I could play along. "So, it's the middle of the Civil War, huh? Where's back home to you?"

Jim flashed me a brilliant smile, obviously delighted by my willingness to get into the spirit of the game. "I hail from Tift County, down in Georgia," he drawled in a southern accent worthy of Clark Gable. "I'm a wheelwright, by trade. When this war is over, I hope to take up that useful pursuit once more."

I nodded slowly, chewing the inside of my cheek to keep from laughing. "A wheelwright? So what's that? You make wagon wheels or something?"

"Or something." Jim glanced down to see if I was really interested. "I work with wood, constructing the hub, spokes, and rim of the wheel, which is then reinforced with iron by the village blacksmith. Henry Fleisher and I work as a team, back home in Tifton."

"And the loved ones, back home in Tifton? Is there a Mrs. Merrick waiting at home for you?" I didn't usually ask such personal questions right off the bat, but the game seemed to allow it.

"Indeed yes," he replied. He reached into his pocket and pulled out a worn leather wallet. He fished through it to extract a tiny daguerreotype of a young woman, which he held out to me. "My dear Susannah, that is, Mrs. James Merrick."

I bent over the little picture, admiring the striking features under the modest ruffled bonnet. With her high cheekbones and dark, arching eyebrows, Mrs. James Merrick was a beautiful woman. A fitting partner for the attractive sergeant by my side. I caught myself feeling an absurd sense of disappointment, as if it mattered to me whether or not Jim Merrick had a gorgeous wife at home. I shook myself mentally. "She's very lovely." He tucked the picture back into his wallet. "Yes, she is." He extended his arm to me again with a half bow. "Shall we continue our tour?"

Jim steered me away from a smoky campfire on our way back to the officers' tents. I noticed a small tent off by itself under some trees. I didn't see a campfire near it, like with all the others.

"What's that tent over there?"

"Hmm? Oh, that? It's the isolation tent." He gave me that apologetic smile again. "You need discipline in any army, you know."

"You're kidding. What, it's like the box in movies, where you lock up the guy for…" My words faltered. I could tell by the look on his face that that's exactly what it was. "Wow," I said. "So is it pretend, or are you really disciplining guys in there?"

Jim gave just the hint of a small, mysterious smile.

We returned to Colonel Windstrom's tent, and Jim murmured to Private Rawlings, who nodded curtly.

"The Colonel will see you now," Jim said. He removed my hand from his arm and held it for a moment, his deep brown eyes fixed on mine. Then he bowed over my hand and once again kissed it ever so lightly.

My heart pounded. I dropped a little curtsy, wishing I had worn a ball gown, or at least a pretty sundress, instead of my faded blue jeans. Maybe another day…

Jim turned and walked away, leaving me to enter the colonel's tent alone.

It took a moment for my eyes to adjust to the dim light within. Colonel Windstrom's tent was crowded with a cot and chipped washstand in one corner, a trunk and traveling chest of drawers in another, and a large folding table surrounded by several camp chairs crammed into the middle. The stuffy smell of warm canvas intensified the claustrophobic feeling of the enclosed space.

Colonel Windstrom was in a foul mood. He stood in the center of the tent breathing heavily, his face a deep, unhealthy red.

"Ms. Dembrowski," he barked.

"Hello, Colonel Windstrom," I replied. "I, uh, I realized that I neglected to take your neck-to-waist measurement. If you'll permit me?" I pulled out my tape measure and squeezed behind him. "If you'll just stand up straight and hold your arms at your sides?" Of course, that was the way a military man *would* stand. I hastened to take the measurement and jot it down in the notepad I always carried in my sewing bag.

"Thanks. Sorry to bother you."

"How is the uniform coming?" Colonel Windstrom asked, a frown darkening his face. I wouldn't want to be disciplined by him, that was for sure.

"Great," I said with a big smile. He didn't need to know that I had yet to cut it out. "It'll be ready for your final fitting on Tuesday. I'll bring it here, if you like."

Private Rawlings poked his head into the tent. His face was white. "Excuse me, sir, there's been another disturbance."

"Not again!" Colonel Windstrom exploded. He snatched up his kepi and shoved it on his head, whirling for the tent opening. His eye fell on me. "Are we done?" he snapped.

"Yes, sir. I'll see you Tuesday at two."

And he was gone.

I folded up my measuring tape and ducked out of the tent. I was ready to get out of there. As I walked away, I could hear the colonel launching into Jim Merrick, berating him for a lack of leadership and failing to properly control the men. I covered my ears and walked faster. I didn't want to hear another word.

* * * *

The next morning, as I laid out the gray wool fabric on the floor to cut, a gentle breeze stirred the muslin curtains in my workroom. I did my cutting and sewing in a vacant bedroom on the second floor of the three-story house that was all I had left from the wreck of my last relationship. I loved the place, originally built in the mid-nineteenth century as a two-story Federal-style home. Over the decades, various owners had added a third floor with whimsical dormer windows and a deep front porch. The lacy Victorian gingerbread molding along the roofline clashed with the austere brick façade, but I didn't care. I loved poking around, looking for hidden passageways in nooks and crannies. My biggest find was a trapdoor in the basement leading to a cramped chamber below. Local lore held that it had been used as a station on the Underground Railroad.

I spent three happy years in the house, as my wedding shop flourished downtown and I started to reap the rewards of entrepreneurship. Then I met a charismatic law student and fell head over heels in love. I encouraged him to move in with me to save on the high cost of law school, and worked hard to support us while he passed the bar and began his legal career as a junior partner in his father's law firm. I envisioned marriage and a lifetime of happiness. What I didn't realize was that he was interested in me not as a fiancée, but as a means to finance his law school education.

When he cleaned out our joint bank account, left for New York on a weeklong business trip and never returned, I was left with a mountain of debt. I had to close the wedding shop and sell off my entire inventory to pay the bills. All I had left was my beautiful, quirky house and a lot of bitter memories.

Under the circumstances, I was happy to have a roof over my head, even though I had to share it with an impossible renter. Still, the lead guitarist in a metal band was a sight better than a domineering boyfriend best known for his disappearing acts. But I didn't want to think about loss and betrayal on this beautiful sunny morning. I pushed the dismal thoughts aside and surveyed my serene workroom.

A varnished wooden door stacked on two chests of drawers served as a desk to hold my new Bernina sewing machine. Grandma's antique Singer treadle machine occupied the place of honor between the two tall windows. My orange-striped cat, Mohair, lay curled on my worn easy chair, watching my every move. Everything seemed so normal and ordinary that it was hard to believe that I hadn't imagined the Civil War camp with its shouting and tension.

A loud knock on the front door interrupted my thoughts.

I hurried down the stairs yelling, "Just a sec!" Could it be Marsha? Her fitting wasn't until tomorrow morning. I'd heard of nervous brides, but that would be ridiculous!

I checked my hair in the mirror over the fireplace in the front hall, smoothing a few stray wisps into the bobby pins pulling my hair back from my face. I always wore my thick brown hair in a severe bun when I was working. It was hardly flattering, but how could I cut out a Civil War uniform with my hair falling into my eyes?

I peeked through the leaded glass of the front door. If it was Marsha, I would have to confess that I hadn't touched her wedding gown since her last fitting. With any luck, she wouldn't lose confidence in me.

Instead, standing on my doorstep, large as life, was my older brother Pete. I threw open the door.

"Daria!" Pete grabbed me into a big bear hug.

I pushed him away. He looked awful. He'd lost a lot of weight since I'd last seen him. His face was drawn and pale, with something weird about it that I couldn't quite put my finger on. He wore a plaid flannel shirt unbuttoned over a T-shirt, worn jeans, and an old Phillies cap.

"What are you doing back home?" I said. "I thought you and your movie camera were set up for life in Hollywood."

"Nice place you've got here." Pete eyed the rosy wallpaper and the sturdy hardwood floor. "Can I come in?"

I held the door open wide. "You can come up and chat, but I have to work. Want some tea? Something to eat?"

Pete shook his head and followed me up the stairs. "You always have to work. You're the workingest woman I know. What is it this time, a pregnant bride and her whole entourage?"

I gave him a sharp look. Did he know Marsha?

"So why aren't you in Hollywood?" I countered. "Did you finish filming, what was it, *Raiders of the Lost Park?*"

Pete laughed. "*Park Raiders.* It folded, and we all got fired. The producer decided he was bored with the whole thing, and the director was crazy. He was convinced we were all out to get him." He took off his hat and ran his hands through his wild brown hair. He needed a haircut, or maybe some of my bobby pins. "I'm so glad to be out of it. It's such a drag to work for a boss who's paranoid. But you know, Hollywood's not the only place to work in the movies. There's so much going on in Pennsylvania right now. I've got a union card that opens all kinds of doors. I just walked into an epic film on the Civil War."

His eyes flicked from the library books strewn on my desk to the gray fabric on the floor, and his face lit up. "Is that what you're working on—costumes for *God and Glory?*"

"I wish." When I had first heard the movie would be filmed in Laurel Springs, I thought it would be the perfect way to break into the historical sewing business. But the film came with its own union shop, and unlike Pete, I lacked that all-important union card. I was left with the Civil War reenactors and their tailoring needs.

Kneeling on the floor, I finished pinning on my makeshift pattern and held my breath as I made the first cut. So much of sewing was ripping out and starting over, but it was really hard to change what had already been cut.

"*God and Glory,*" I said. "Where do they come up with these titles?"

Pete straddled an old wooden chair that I'd picked up at a garage sale. Dark shadows smudged below his eyes. A memory shot through me, of Pete lying on the couch in the tenth grade, wiped out by mono. He didn't look much better now.

"When did your movie fold?" I demanded.

"Oh, it was the day after Halloween. Trick or treat!"

"But it's June fifth," I cried.

Pete cut me off. "Don't fuss, Daria. I've been out of work for seven months, okay? There's a recession on, in case you hadn't noticed. But I've landed on my feet here in Laurel Springs. Camera operator on *God and Glory* is good enough for me." He took a deep breath. "But there is one small detail." He grinned his crazy, pleading grin at me. "I need a place to stay. You've got this huge old house—got a spare room for your big brother?"

"Hmm." I pretended to consider him. "Can you provide any references?" It wasn't necessarily a stupid question. I hadn't seen him since he left to follow his Hollywood dream six years ago. We'd talked on birthdays and Christmas, but not much more. A lot could change in six years.

He dropped to his knees and clasped his hands in mock supplication. All of a sudden, I knew what was different about his face. His nose was crooked, bent along the bridge up between his eyes. He must have broken his nose in Hollywood—unless someone had broken it for him. It gave him a slightly desperate look that was intensified by the sharpness of his cheekbones. He looked like a panhandler down at Centennial Park.

As if he'd read my mind, he stretched out his arms. "Come on, Daria, give a guy a break. I don't want to have to stay with Dad."

That did it. "Okay, okay. You can have the third floor bedroom. But be forewarned, you'll have to deal with the renter from hell." A thump and a muffled groan came from the room next door. I looked up from my cutting and rolled my eyes. "There she is now."

Pete sat cross-legged on the floor. "What's the big deal?"

I bent over my fabric again. "Aileen's the lead singer in a metal band, the Twisted Armpits. They practice in the basement. Loudly." Slamming noises emanated from the next room. "She's recovering from a gig at the Hourglass Tavern last night. The band played till two a.m., evidently. She's just now getting up. Drives me crazy."

"So why put up with her?"

I heaved an overly dramatic sigh, and waved my naked left hand in his face. "Maybe you didn't notice, but there isn't anyone else lining up to share the house with me. I've got to make ends meet somehow, in the midst of this recession that you so kindly reminded me of."

Pete contemplated the fading tan lines on my ring finger. "What happened to what's-his-name, that lawyer guy you were with?"

"Good ol' what's-his-name. His name was Randall. It was Randall for the past four years." I took a breath, concentrating on the pattern pieces. It wasn't Pete's fault that he couldn't remember Randall's name. He'd never even met the guy. With any luck, I'd forget his name too. "But he's gone." I didn't feel like going into specifics at the moment. I didn't want to admit to Pete that Randall had conned me from start to finish. The hurt was still too raw, too new.

Pete didn't press for details. "So you never got to wear that white dress down the aisle, huh?"

The dress was gorgeous—rich white satin with an off-the-shoulder neckline and tight bodice flowing down to a flaring A-line skirt. I'd spent every evening for two whole months sewing lace and seed pearls on by hand. The dress was tucked away in a garment bag at the back of my closet. "Did you get an invitation? Or did you think I just skipped that part?"

"Obviously I didn't think much about it at all," Pete confessed with a grin. "I figured you'd get married someday, and I'd have to make a speech or something, after spending the night out on the town with your boyfriend." A teasing note crept into his voice. "At least it won't be old what's-his-name. He sounded like a loser—definitely not the guy for my little sister."

"I'll tell you about it sometime. You know all those lawyer jokes? They were thinking of Randall when they made them up."

Pete's laugh was drowned out by Aileen's dramatic entrance. Her door flew open with a crash that rattled the house, shaking my "Home, Sweet Home" cross-stitch right off the wall. She stomped out of her room and stopped in my doorway, glaring at Pete. He stared right back, his mouth dropping open.

Aileen always had this effect on people. Nearly six feet tall, with spiky black hair streaked with pink and black makeup that never really washed off, she was used to causing a stir. She thrived on attention, soaking it up like a dry plant drinks in water. If people didn't stare, she'd probably shrivel up and turn into an ordinary person like the rest of us. This morning she wore a black T-shirt with obscenities splashed across the front and a pair of lacy black panties.

Pete gulped and gave it his best try. "You must be the rock star," he said.

"You must be the moron," Aileen shot back. "I thought the men were going to stay downstairs," she said to me.

I pasted on a smile. "Aileen, this is my big brother, Pete. He's going to move into the third-floor bedroom."

"Like hell he is," Aileen snapped. "I'm gonna get some breakfast." She stomped off toward the stairs.

"Charming girl," Pete said lightly. "Has a real way with people, wouldn't you say?"

"Oh, stop. She pays her rent. Like I said, I can't afford to live here by myself." I scrambled to my feet and faced my brother. "If you can cover her share, six fifty a month, I'd gladly kick her out."

Pete picked up my pincushion and fiddled with the pins and needles. "Uh, yeah, I'm sure we'll get along great, once she gets to know me."

"That's what I thought." I crossed my arms and glared at him. "You will chip in for groceries, or you won't be staying here."

"Yes, ma'am. I'll clean the bathroom and take out the trash, and I make a killer lasagna." He stood up and folded his hands meekly in front of him like a good little boy. "You just say the word."

I laughed in spite of myself. "Come on, let's give it another try. Maybe some food will have mellowed her a bit."

We walked into my high-ceilinged kitchen. Aileen sat at the table, eating powdered sugar donuts straight from the bag.

I sat down across from her. Pete hovered in the doorway.

"How was the gig?" I asked.

"It was awesome," she mumbled through her mouthful of donut. "Three guys got into it and smashed a couple chairs and dumped a pitcher of beer on the waitress." Puffs of powdered sugar punctuated each sentence. "You like music?" she shot at Pete.

"Yeah, sure. I'm a big Springsteen fan."

Aileen snorted and stuffed another donut into her mouth.

"Pete's just moved back home." I ran my fingers along the vine pattern stenciled into the table edge. "He's been in Hollywood for almost six years."

She humphed and wiped her sugary hands on her shirt. "Big Hollywood dude, huh? What'd you come back to the boonies for?"

Pete shrugged. "Guess I didn't make it in Hollywood. Pennsylvania's the place to be in the movies right now."

"He's got a job as a camera operator on a movie here, *God and Glory*," I said. "It's about the Civil War."

Aileen grinned at me. "You're gonna get your fill of the Civil War." She scraped her chair against the floor and stood up as if she owned the place. "Alright, Moron, you can stay. For now."

"You can call me Pete. I don't answer to 'Moron,'" Pete said mildly.

Aileen clomped out of the room, waving her long black fingernails behind her. "Whatever."

About the Author

Greta McKennan is a wife, mother, and author, living her dream in the boreal rainforest of Juneau, Alaska. She enjoys a long walk in the woods on that rare sunny day, reading cozy mysteries when it rains, and sewing the Christmas jammies on her antique Singer sewing machine. She is hard at work on a new cozy mystery series set in Alaska. Visit her on the web at gretamckennan.com.

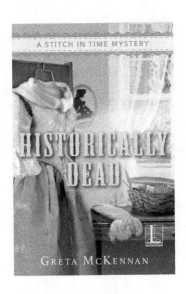

Seamstress Daria Dembrowski must find a historically-minded killer before the fabric of her peaceful town rips wide open...

When the reality show *My House in History* comes to Laurel Springs, Pennsylvania, savvy seamstress Daria Dembrowski sees a business opportunity. The show follows two elderly sisters' quest to restore their colonial mansion, and that means a heap of work for a seamstress who specializes in historical textiles. Although one of the old women is a bit of a grump, Daria loves the job—until she discovers one of the researchers dead, and the whole project threatens to unwind.

As a series of historical crimes pile up, from a stolen Paul Revere platter to a chilling incident of arson, Daria must find the killer quickly, for her life is hanging by a thread.

CPSIA information can be obtained
at www.ICGtesting.com
Printed in the USA
LVHW051051291020
670168LV00001B/161

9 781516 101733